I'd just bitten the hand that fed me when God called, again. Shaking her left hand, Claire picked up the receiver with her right. After asking who it was, she held it out to me, rolling her eyes. "It's God again." Her little joke. The Sultan's name was Mohammed, and he was more or less God to the million and a half citizens of the Republic of Saru, somewhere in the Persian Gulf.

The benevolent and visionary Sultan of Saru wants prizewinning architect Harry Radcliffe to build him a billion-dollar dog museum. Radcliffe is reluctant, to say the least, but he has been dancing dangerously close to the edge of insanity lately, and this project may be what he needs to call him back from the brink. In Saru, Radcliffe finds himself in a world even madder and more unreal than the one he left behind. The ordinary laws of reality don't seem to hold, and life, love, and death take on towering proportions as Radcliffe's magnificent building reaches for the heavens.

Jonathan Carroll is one of the most original voices in American fiction today. Imaginative and heartfelt, *Outside the Dog Museum* is a stunning addition to his work and, for those who have yet to experience Carroll, a dazzling introduction to his world.

OUTSIDE ~THE~ DOG MUSEUM

JONATHAN CARROLL

BANTAM BOOKS

New York Toronto London Sydney Auckland

All of the characters in this book are fictitious, and any resemblance to actual persons, living or dead, is purely coincidental.

This edition contains the complete text of the original hardcover edition.
NOT ONE WORD HAS BEEN OMITTED

OUTSIDE THE DOG MUSEUM
A Bantam Book / published in association with Doubleday

PUBLISHING HISTORY
Doubleday edition published February 1992
Bantam edition / March 1993

The Book of Imaginary Beings *by Jorge Luis Borges with Margarita Guerrero, translated by Norman Thomas di Giovani, translation copyright © 1969 by Jorge Luis Borges and Norman Thomas di Giovani. Used by permission of the publisher, Dutton, an imprint of New American Library, a division of Penguin Books USA Inc.;* "Batman Roams a Menacing, Absurd Gotham," *International Herald Tribune, June 23, 1989, "Weekend" section. Used by permission.;* Eccentric Spaces, *copyright © 1977 by Robert Harbison, published by Alfred A. Knopf, a division of Random House, Inc. Used by permission.*

ISBN 0-553-56164-2

Published simultaneously in the United States and Canada

Bantam Books are published by Bantam Books, a division of Bantam Doubleday Dell Publishing Group, Inc. Its trademark, consisting of the words "Bantam Books" and the portrayal of a rooster, is Registered in U.S. Patent and Trademark Office and in other countries. Marca Registrada. Bantam Books, 666 Fifth Avenue, New York, New York 10103.

PRINTED IN THE UNITED STATES OF AMERICA

RAD   0 9 8 7 6 5 4 3 2 1

To my brother
DAVID CARROLL
who from the very beginning,
has helped me to build my life

Instead of the standard "acknowledgments,"
these gifts, if it were at all possible:
An Ex Libris in stone and glass to my editor and friend
PETER LAVERY
for his constant enthusiasm and support over the years.
&
A lifetime's supply of Northern Lights to
SANDRA NEUFELDT
who was generous enough to tell me some of the stories
here.

"We cannot take a single step towards Heaven.
It is not in our power to travel in a vertical direction.
If however we look heavenward for a long time, God comes
and takes us up.
He raises us easily."

—SIMONE WEIL

PART ONE

"Present Tense"

"I would rather shape my soul than furnish it."

MONTAIGNE

I'D JUST BITTEN the hand that fed me when God called, again. Shaking her left hand, Claire picked up the receiver with her right. After asking who it was, she held it out to me, rolling her eyes. "It's God again." Her little joke. The Sultan's name was Mohammed, and he *was* more or less God to the million and a half citizens of the Republic of Saru, somewhere in the Persian Gulf.

"Hello, Harry?"

"Hello, sir. The answer is still no."

"Have you seen the Mercedes-Benz building on Sunset Boulevard? This is a building I like very much."

"Sure, Joe Fontanilla designed it. He's with the Nadel Partnership. Call *him* up."

"He was not in *Time* magazine."

"Your Highness, the only reason you want me to

work for you is because I was on the cover of that magazine. I don't think that's the best reason for choosing someone to do a billion-dollar project."

" 'It was announced last week that American Harry Radcliffe was awarded this year's Pritzker Prize, architecture's equivalent of the Nobel Prize.' "

"You're reading from the article again."

"I also liked the coffeepot you designed. Come over to my hotel, Harry, and I'll give you a car."

"You already gave me a car last week, sir. I can only drive one at a time. Anyway, the answer would still be no. I don't design museums."

"Your friend Fanny Neville is here."

My other friend, Claire Stansfield, stood with her long, naked back to me, looking out her glass doors down onto Los Angeles, way below.

Claire here, Fanny at the Sultan's. The salt and pepper on my life those days.

"How did that happen?" I tried to keep the word "that" noncommittal so Claire wouldn't get suspicious.

"I asked your friend Fanny if she would like to do an interview with me."

Fanny Neville likes two things: power and imagination. She prefers both, but will take one if the other's unavailable. I was the imagination in her life those days. We'd met in New York a couple of years before when she interviewed me for *Art in America*. I give good interviews, or *did* before I went off my rocker and had to drop out of life for a while.

I was back in it now, but wasn't doing much besides commuting between these two impressive women, who both said it was time I got off my ass and did something.

"Could I talk to him?"

"Him? You mean Fanny? With pleasure."

There was a pause and then she came on the line. "Hello. Are you at Claire's?"

"Yes."

"That always makes me feel cozy. Do you talk to her in this same voice when you call from *my* house?"

"Yes."

"You're an asshole, Harry. How come you didn't tell me the Sultan wants you to build his museum?"

"Because I already said I wouldn't."

"But you took the car he gave you?"

"Sure, why not? It was a gift."

"A forty-thousand-dollar gift?"

"He just offered me another."

"I heard." She "hmph'd" like a disgruntled old woman. "Are you coming to my house for dinner?"

"Yes."

Claire turned around, the sunshine from behind lighting her outline so brightly that I could barely make out her nakedness. Walking toward me, she did something with her foot, and the telephone line went dead. It took a moment to realize she'd pulled out the cord.

"Talk to her on your own fucking time, Harry."

Before going over to visit Fanny and the Sultan, I drove to my favorite car wash in West Hollywood. It's run by a bunch of fags who do everything beautifully and with style.

I've done some of my best thinking in car washes. Those few minutes under the mad flood and yellow brushes do things to some outlying but valuable part of my brain so that I usually emerge from those false storms wired and full of ideas. Are you familiar with the Andromeda Center in Birmingham, England? The one that brought me so much notoriety a decade ago? Born in a car wash. I remember "fixing" on the swishing arc of the windshield wiper blades on my car and, just before the hoses stopped, having the first inspiration for those juxtaposed arcs that are the heart of that justly famous building.

Sitting in the Hollywood car wash, watching my new Lotus get spritzed from all sides, I was a famous man with nothing to do. I was twice divorced; once even from an anorectic fashion victim whose sole creative act in life was to spell her name with two *d*'s. Anddrea. She liked to fuck in the morning and complain the rest of the day. We were married too long and then she left me for a much nicer man.

I am not a nice man. I expect others to be nice to me, but feel no compulsion to return the favor. Luckily enough, important people have called me a genius throughout my adult life so that I've been able to get away with an inordinate amount of rudeness, indifference, and plain bad manners. If you're ever given one wish, wish the world thinks you're a genius. Geniuses are allowed to do anything. Picasso was a big prick, Beethoven never emptied his chamber pot, and Frank Lloyd Wright stole as much money from his clients and sponsors as any good thief. But it was all okay finally because they were "geniuses." Maybe they were, and I am too, but I'll tell you something: Genius is a boat that sails itself. All you have to do is get in and it does the rest, i.e., I didn't spend months and years thinking up the shapes and forms of my most renowned buildings. They came out of nowhere and my only job was to funnel them onto pieces of paper. I'm not being modest. The ideas come like breezes through a window and all you do is capture them. Braque said this: "One's style—it is in a way one's inability to do otherwise. . . . Your physical constitution practically determines the shape of the brushmarks." He was right. Bullshit on all that artistic suffering, "agonizing" over the empty page, canvas. . . . Anyone who agonizes over their work isn't a genius. Anyone who agonizes for a living is an idiot.

Halfway through the second rinse (my favorite part came next—the dry off, when curtains of brown rags descended and slid sensuously across every surface of the car), everything stopped. My beautiful new blue Lotus (compliments of the Sultan) sat there dripping water, going nowhere. Checking the rearview mirror, I saw the car behind me was stopped too. The driver and I made eye contact. He shrugged.

Trapped in a gay car wash!

A few moments twiddling my fingers on the steering wheel, then I watched a couple of workers run by close on the right and out the other end. Another glance in the rearview mirror, the guy behind shrugging again. I got out of the car and, looking toward the exit, saw some kind of large commotion going on up there. I walked toward it.

"What kinda car is dat?"

"Fuck the car, Leslie, the guy's dead!"

A brown car (I remember thinking it was the same color as the drying rags) sat a few feet from the exit. Four or five people stood around, looking inside. The driver's door was open and the manager of the place was hunched down next to it. He looked at me and asked if I was a doctor—the guy inside had had a heart attack or something, and was dead. Immediately I said yes because I wanted to see. Going over, I knelt down next to the manager.

Despite having just been cleaned, the car still smelled of loaded ashtrays and wet old things. A middle-aged man sat slumped over the steering wheel. Remembering my television shows, I made like a doctor and put a hand on his throat to feel for a pulse. Nothing there under jowls and whiskery skin. "He's gone. Did you call an ambulance?"

The manager nodded and we stood up together.

"How do you think it happened, Doctor?"

"Heart attack, probably. But best to let the ambulance men figure it out."

"What a way to go, huh? Okay, Leslie and Kareem, give me a hand pushing this car out of here so we can let the rest of these people through. Thanks, Doctor. Sorry to inconvenience you."

"No problem." I turned to go back to my car.

"How embarrassing."

"Excuse me?" I looked at him.

"I mean I run this place and all, right? But I was thinking how humiliating it'd be to know that you'd die in a car wash—especially if you were famous! Imagine how your obituary would read: 'Graham Gibson, renowned actor, was found dead in The Eiffel Towel Car Wash, Thursday, after having apparently suffered a massive heart attack.' " He looked at me and grimaced. "*Washed* to death!"

"I know what you mean."

An *enormous* understatement. Some people fantasize their names on magazine covers, others on bronze plaques mounted on the sides of buildings. I did too, until some of those things happened to me. Then I started imagining what my obituary would say. I once read that the man who did the obituaries for the *New York Times* wrote them before people died (if they were well known) and only polished them with final details after the person croaked. That was understandable and I could see the logic to it, but the "polish" part was disturbing. Okay, you live a long and illustrious life, full of genuine accomplishments and praise. But then what happens? You finish, looking like a big dope if you're unfortunate enough to die choking on a bottle cap, or a tree branch hits you on the head and puts you down for the count. Tennessee Williams with the bottle cap, Odon Von Horvath with the tree. I know nothing about Odon except he was a writer and that's how he died—hit on the head by a branch while walking down a street in Paris. I could too easily imagine someone saying, "I know nothing about Harry Radcliffe except he was an architect who died of a heart attack in a car wash." The *Eiffel Towel* Car Wash, no less.

Walking back to the car, I reminded myself of the fact that I hadn't been doing anything with my days recently, so if it *had* been me keeled over in that brown car, my whole life would have looked pretty pointless.

"What happened up there?" The man in the car behind mine was out and standing now.

"A guy had a heart attack and died."

"Here?" He shook his head and smiled. I knew what he was thinking and it made me even more depressed: It *was* funny. People would grin if you said you were at the car wash today and someone died while on his final rinse. They'd smile the same way as

this man, and then there'd be one of those half-funny, half-fearful discussions at the dinner table about good and bad ways of dying.

Venasque used to say down deep we all know we're kind of silly and thus spend too much of our lives either trying to cover it up or disprove it— mostly to ourselves. "But then when it comes to dying," he would say, "you know you might end up looking more ridiculous than ever. Even though you're dead and won't be *around* to see people's reactions, you're still afraid to look bad. Why do you think people like expensive coffins and funerals so much? So we can try being impressive, right into the ground."

>>> Five minutes later, pulling up at a stoplight on Sunset Boulevard, I looked to my left, and who was sitting in the car next to mine? Markus Hebenstreit! Architecture critic for the *L.A. Eye*, Hebenstreit was my most vicious and long-standing enemy/critic. He'd probably written more bad things about my work than anyone else. The more famous I became, the more Hebenstreit frothed and spread his verbal rabies wherever he could.

"Markus!"

He turned slowly and looked at me with great Hoch Deutsch disdain. When I registered on him, his contempt turned into beady-eyed hatred. "Hello, Radcliffe. Coming back from your weekly shock treatment?"

"A new billion-dollar project, Markus! Man wants me to build him a *billion*-dollar museum. Do it however I want, just so long as it's an original Harry Radcliffe.

"Just think, Markus, no matter *what* you write, there'll always be someone who wants me to build them billion-dollar buildings!

"So suck on that a while, you Nazi fuck!"

Before he could say anything, I slapped the Lotus into gear and peeled out, feeling gloriously like an eighteen-year-old.

📌 Rumor had it the Sultan of Saru owned the Westwood Muse Hotel, which explained why he and his entourage invariably stayed there when they came to Los Angeles five or six times a year. It was designed and built in the 1930s by a student of Peter Behrens's and looked sort of like the jazzy factories Behrens designed for AEG in Germany. I liked the place because it was quirky, but couldn't understand why the Sultan would buy it when he could have so easily afforded *any* real estate within a ten-mile radius of the Beverly Hills Hotel.

When I pulled up in front, an extremely tall black woman dressed in a dove-gray shirt and slacks stepped forward and opened my door. As usual, I looked up at her in pure appreciation. She was exquisite.

"Hello, Lucia."

"Hello, Harry. Has he invited you again?"

"Summoned."

She nodded and took my place in the car. The two complemented each other perfectly; the machine should have been hers on the basis of looks and stature alone. But it wasn't. Lucia was only another beautiful failure in California, parking cars.

"He still wants you to build his museum?"

"Yup."

"And you don't want to do it?" Her long brown hands sat lightly on the steering wheel. She smiled up at me and that smile was a killer.

I thought about answering her, but asked instead, "What do you want to be when you grow up?"

Not sure whether I was being serious or not, she cocked her head to one side and said, " 'When I grow up'? An actress. Why?"

"You'd like that carved on your tombstone? 'Lucia Armstrong, actress'?"

"That would make me very happy. What about you, Harry? What do you want written, 'Harry Radcliffe, celebrated architect'?"

"Naah, that's too banal. Maybe 'The Man Who Built the Dog Museum.' " Said like that, the idea suddenly tickled the hell out of me. Walking up the gravel path, I turned to say something else to Lucia but she was already pulling away. I shouted to the back of my blue car, "That'd be a damned good epitaph!"

Was it because of the dead man in the car wash? Being able to throw the power of "a billion dollars" in Hebenstreit's face? Or simply envisioning (and liking) the words "The Man Who Built the Dog Museum" on my gravestone that did it? Whatever the reason, walking in the front door of the Westwood Muse Hotel, I knew I would design the Sultan's museum for him, although I had been saying no for months.

What I had to do next was get him to think he was not just lucky, but *blessed* to have me and, consequently, fork over the money I'd need both for myself and the project. A lot more money than even *he'd* imagined.

📌 "What are your earliest memories?"

Was the first question Fanny Neville asked me, the day we met and did our interview years before. I hadn't even had the chance to sit back down after letting her in.

Without thinking, I said, "Seeing Sputnik and Rocket Monroe at the Luxor Baths in New York."

"How old were you?"

"Three, I think."

"Who were Sputnik and Rocket Monroe?"

"Professional wrestlers."

📌 My father, DeSalles "Sonny" Radcliffe, came from Basile, Louisiana. He knew how to catch snapping turtles, charm women, and make money. He often said the three things had a lot in common and that was why he was so successful.

With his curveball Southern accent, he'd say, "The say-crit to catching a snapping turtle, Harry, is to stick your foot down into that soft mud and feel around really gently.

"Now, once in a while one of them monsters is in there and'll grab hold of that foot. Hold still den! This is where the patience comes in. He's thinking what to do with it. That turtle can't decide 'cause he's mud-dumb. So *you* just take a deep breath and wait. I know you're dying to pull it out and run like a motherfuck, but don't. Hold still, boy, and you'll be all right.

Women and money're the same: They clamp on ya
and want to pull you down, but just wait 'em out and
those jaws'll loosen up."

Pop liked someone watching TV with him at
night. That was usually me from the very earliest because my mother had no patience for the tube.

He liked wrestling because he said it relaxed him.
Channel Five from Uline Arena or Commack on Long
Island.

➤ "I remember sitting on my father's lap and he'd
say, 'That's Sweet Daddy Siki, Harry.' Or Bobo Brazil,
Johnny Valentine, Fuzzy Cupid. Because I was young,
and those names sounded so fairy taleish, I remembered them. Sputnik and Rocket Monroe were two
bad guys with long black hair and white streaks
painted down the middle of their manes so they both
looked like skunks."

Fanny sat forward and pointed her eyeglasses at
me. "That's where you got the names for your collection?"

"Exactly."

"You named furniture after professional wrestlers?"

"Yes, but then Philippe Starck stole the idea and
named *his* stuff after characters from some science fiction novel.

"Look, everyone takes design too seriously. I
thought by giving my work names, ridiculous names,
it'd put things in perspective. A person who pays five
thousand dollars for a chair doesn't have much perspective."

She slid the glasses back on for the fourth time.

Her face was oval and thin with large dark lips that sat in a fixed rosebud pout. The square black Clark Kent glasses made her look like she was trying too hard to appear serious.

"Then why do you *charge* five thousand dollars for a chair that you call 'Bobo Brazil,' Mr. Radcliffe?"

"Do your homework, *Ms.* Neville. *I* don't charge anything for the furniture I design—the company does. And they aren't charging for the chair or lamp, they're charging for my name. Anyway, I come cheap —Knoll charges ten grand for a Richard Meier chair."

"Don't you feel immoral being involved in that when you know so many people are suffering in the world?"

"Don't you feel immoral writing for a magazine that's only bought by pseudo-intellectuals and rich people who don't give a shit about the poor?"

"Touché. What were you doing at the Luxor Baths?"

"I was with my father, who was a Turkish bath nut. He believed you could do anything you wanted —drink a bottle of brandy or carouse all night, so long as you went to a Turkish bath the next day and sweated out your transgressions."

"Transgressions?" She smiled for the first time.

"I believe in words of more than one syllable."

"You like language?"

"I *believe* in it. It's the only glue that holds us together."

"What about your occupation? Doesn't the human community depend on its physical structures?"

"Yes, but it can't build them unless it can explain what kind it wants. Even when you're only making grass huts."

"What *do* you think of your work, Mr. Radcliffe?"

Without missing a beat or feeling the least bit guilty, I stole from Jean Cocteau once again. This time replacing only one word—"architect" for "writer." " 'I believe that each of my works is capable of making the reputation of a single architect.' "

"You don't believe in modesty."

It was my turn to sit forward. "Who do you think is better than me?"

"Aldo Rossi."

I waved him away. "He makes cemeteries."

"Coop Himmelblau?"

"They design airplanes, not buildings."

"Honestly, don't you think anyone is better than you?"

I thought for a moment. "No."

"Do you mind if I quote you?"

As obnoxiously as possible, I slid into my father's Basile, Louisiana, drawl. "Aww now, Fenny, do you really think that's going to hurt me? Every interview I give, they quote that. Know what happens? I get more commissions! People like hiring a man who's sure of himself. Most particularly when you're responsible for a few hundred million dollars!"

Which was true. While talking to Fanny Neville that first time years ago, I was also thinking about the three projects on my desk: the Aachen, Germany, airport, the Rutgers University Arts Center in New Jersey, and the house I was building in Santa Barbara for Bronze Sydney and me.

Footnote: Bronze Sydney was my second wife. Bronwyn Sydney Davis. Bronze Sydney. We started out as partners, then married, but quickly realized we functioned better together as professional colleagues.

A calm divorce followed. We are still partners and friends.

Both the Aachen and Rutgers projects came about because I'd assured specific people I was the best. That self-confidence, along with my plans and proposals, convinced them. I don't think the designs alone would have done it, although they were very significant and appropriate.

Ask anyone about the high point of their life. Odds are, whatever they say, it'll have something to do with being busy. I felt comfortable answering Fanny's question so bluntly because at that time I was a hurricane named H. Radcliffe, Important American Architect. I did feel like one of those tropical storms that builds in the Gulf of Mexico and scares everyone when the weather man says ominously, "Hurricane Harry is still biding its time out there, just growing bigger. But batten down those hatches, folks. This one is going to be a doozy!" I *was* a doozy, and getting bigger all the time because of the buildings we were putting up. There was fame, money by the pound, jobs designing anything I wanted. Bronze Sydney and I were working too hard, but loving the full-tilt feel of our lives. When we went to bed at night, we were still so wired that we'd often fuck for hours just to ground some of the electricity, angst, excitement, anticipation . . . that'd built up in both of us over the day.

Then the storm hit, all right, but *me*, not the mainland.

~ Months later, after I'd won the Pritzker Prize (the second-youngest recipient in its history, let me add), the real honor came when I was invited to participate in the seven hundred fiftieth anniversary of the City of Berlin. As part of the celebration, the city fathers had intelligently decided to ask prominent architects from around the world to design new buildings with which to give that fearful, nervous city a face-lift.

A late twentieth-century city perched like a crucial and formidable lighthouse on the edge of communism. I thought it was as noble and utopian as we were ever going to get.

They asked me to design a section of the Berlin Technical University. Within an hour of the request, I knew what to do: What could be more appropriate for a technical university than a robot, seven stories high? I kept a collection of toy robots on my desk, and friends knew if they ever saw an interesting one to pick it up for me.

After spending the better part of two days with the door closed, all calls held, and the desk lamp tipped to illuminate the various figures, I began sketching a building that looked like a mixture of Russian constructivist collage, the sexy robot girl in Fritz Lang's *Metropolis*, and a "Masters of the Universe" doll. It was brainy, but not exceptional. I needed more stimulus.

There's a store in Los Angeles on Melrose Avenue that sells nothing but rubber spiders, Japanese robots, horror movie masks. . . . Your typically overpriced, chic kitsch paradise where the pile of rubber dog shit you bought as a kid for forty-nine cents now costs seven dollars. Truth be told, I'd spent much time and money at that place when searching around for ideas for a new building. A thirty- or forty-dollar bagful of glow-in-the-dark werewolf fangs, little green-rubber-car pencil erasers, get-the-ball-in-the-hole puzzles . . . spread out together in front of me usually helped, for some unique reason. Mallarmé got his inspiration from looking at the ocean. Harry Radcliffe got his from a fake fly in a fake ice cube.

The owners of the store gave me the heartiest of hellos whenever I came in. I think they were nice people, but I'd spent so much money there in the past that I could never tell if they were really nice or only money-nice. Money-nice lasts as long as you're a good customer.

"What's new?"

"We just got something I think you'll like very much." The man went to the back of the store and waved me over to him. I walked back as he was reaching down into a box on the floor.

"Look at these." He held out two handfuls of vividly colored little buildings, each about four or five inches long. I picked one up and gave a tickled yelp. "It's the Sphinx!"

"Right. And here's the Empire State Building, Sydney Opera House, Buckingham Palace . . . all the famous buildings of the world as pencil sharpeners! Aren't they great? We just got them this week from Taiwan. Don't they look like pieces of bubble gum?"

I reached into the full box and rooted around for samples of each. A cobalt blue Leaning Tower of Pisa, vermilion Statue of Liberty (was that a building?), green Roman Colosseum. There were a surprising number of different ones. Taking a few to the front of the store where there was more light, I held them up and looked carefully at the detail. Superb.

I bought two hundred and fifty.

There was no screech of tires, screams, or thunderous crash when my mind went flying over the cliff into madness, as I gather is true in many cases. Besides, we've all seen too many bad movies where characters scratch their faces or make hyena sounds to indicate they've gone nuts.

Not me. One minute I was famous, successful, self-assured Harry Radcliffe in the trick store, looking for inspiration in a favorite spot. The next, I was quietly but very seriously mad, walking out of that shop with two hundred and fifty yellow pencil sharpeners. I don't know how other people go insane, but my way was at least novel.

Melrose Avenue is not a good place to lose your mind. The stores on the street are full of lunatic desires and are only too happy to let you have them if you can pay. I could.

Anyone want a gray African parrot named Noodle Koofty? I named him on the ride back to Santa Barbara. He sat silently in a giant black cage in the back of my Mercedes station wagon, surrounded by objects I can only cringe at when I think of them now: three colorful garden dwarves about three feet high, each holding a gold hitching ring; five Conway Twitty albums that cost twenty dollars each because they were "classics"; three identical Sam the Sham and the Pharaohs albums, "classics" as well, twenty-five dollars a piece; a box of bathroom tiles with a revolting peach motif; a wall-size poster of a chacma baboon in the same pose as Rodin's *The Thinker* . . . other things too, but you get the drift.

My car was so loaded down in back that one might have thought I was transporting bags of cement. But all I was carrying was the alarming evidence of my dementia.

Why did it happen? How did I end up driving a station wagon full of plastic garden dwarves and Conway Twitty albums when I was at the height of my success? Believe me, I've thought about it since I recovered, and that's a long time. The standard explanations could be used to good effect—I was overworked, there was too much pressure to succeed, my marriage with Sydney was beginning to hiss and spit ominously at its seams. . . .

Or none of the above.

After Venasque introduced me to the journals of Cocteau, I came across a passage which touched me deeply.

"Then I realized that my dream life was as full of memories as my real life, that it *was* a real life, denser, richer in episodes and in details of all kinds, more precise, in fact, and that it was difficult for me to locate my memories in one world or the other, that they were superimposed, combined, and creating a double life for me, twice as huge and twice as long as my own."

When I showed that to Venasque, he patted my shoulder.

"Exactly. That should answer your questions, Harry. You *needed* to go nuts! Most people do it either to hide, or because they can't cope. But you did it because no matter how much you thought you were doing things right, you weren't. And something inside knew it.

"Look at it this way: Your dream side decided you and it needed a vacation from your awake side, so it bought the tickets and packed bags for both of you. And off you guys went, leaving your awake side at home."

It was nice of the old man to call them my "dream" and "awake" sides when we both knew he meant Crazy Harry/Sane Harry. Yet what he said makes more and more sense the further removed I am from that turbulent time of my life. Some people *do* need to go crazy. To live fully in your "dream life" a while is like putting all the weight on your left foot when your right is exhausted. I wasn't crazy very long, but in certain specific ways those months adrift in "Lu-Lu Land" gave me two of the most important things in my life: a fuller, more balanced vision, and the indispensable Venasque.

I'm moving too fast. Rerun the tape to where Noodle Koofty and I and our inanimate friends in the back of my Mercedes station wagon are tooling up the Pacific Coast Highway, some of us mad and some of us still, all of us enjoying the sunset over my first day in bedlam.

Suddenly the thought of all the magnificent things I'd bought overcame me. I had to share my enthusiasm with someone, so I pulled off the road at a phone booth to call Bronze Sydney.

Later, she said I sounded like a public-address system announcing departing trains. What I took to be wild enthusiasm, according to her, came out sounding half-dead: "Just described what you'd done in this dead monotone," she said. "I-went-to-the-trick-store. I-bought-yellow-pencil-sharpeners. I-am-very-happy . . . like that."

"I sounded *that* creepy?"

"Yes. I thought you were doing one of your funny voices."

"What was I like when I got home?"

"Very pleasant and friendly. Back to your old self.

Remember, the really bad things didn't start immediately."

Sydney liked the parrot and thought the other *objets* were a part of some labyrinthine plan I was cooking up. She was used to me arriving with whoopie cushions, joybuzzers, or boxes of toy soldiers which I'd take into my study and play with or stare at until the message I needed from them arrived. To her full credit, the woman didn't even bat an eye the time I spent a quiet evening at home gluing animal crackers together.

One image that's remained is of my wife's back as she carried two of the garden dwarves under her arms into our house. She was wearing a black dress and bright orange stockings. The colors reminded me of Halloween.

After we ferried all of the new goodies into my room, Sydney went back to her book. While I, hands on hips like a pirate-ship captain, surveyed the lay of the land.

My "desk" is a round Danhauser dining table, perpetually overloaded with stuff. That night for the first time in recent history, I removed this stuff from the table. After placing it in careful piles on the floor, I set to work building the world.

In no time I had all two hundred and fifty pencil sharpeners arranged across the mahogany table. But that was uninteresting, so I took one of the dwarves and plunked him down in the middle, a giant alien-invader centerpiece.

Some hours later I reemerged into the light and land of the sane to ask if there was anything to eat. Both of us hated to cook. As a result, meals at the Radcliffe home were either vile, bizarre, or not at all. I was informed there was a bucket of fried chicken in the kitchen.

Mrs. Radcliffe later said she started suspecting something strange was up when, minutes later, she saw me come out of the kitchen wearing a full-length apron and carrying a long barbecue fork in each hand.

"How do you want your chicken? Well-done?"

"What do you mean?"

"How do you want it cooked?"

"Harry, that's Kentucky Fried Chicken. It already *is* cooked."

I smiled enigmatically and returned to the kitchen.

Ten minutes later the smoky tang of barbecue drifted into the room. She found me out on the patio, flipping chicken pieces on the grill.

"What are you doing?"

"How do you want yours cooked?"

She looked carefully at me. I remember that. She looked for so long that I finally got embarrassed and went back to my chicken flipping.

"How're you feeling, Harry?"

"Good. A little tired. I haven't eaten much today."

"Then why don't you go lie down awhile? I'll finish here and bring it to you when it's ready. Okay?"

"You don't have to do that, Syd. They're almost done." I pointed to what was once a chicken wing but was now only a smoking lump of black.

"Okay." She went to the nearest phone and called our doctor/friend/neighbor, Bill Rosenberg.

I was all right for a while after that. Bill said I was overworked and suggested that I take these pills and go up to San Francisco for a few days' rest, which we did. We stayed at the Mark Hopkins, ate red pasta at Ghirardelli Square, stood outside the old Fillmore West and talked about Janis Joplin . . . a nice trip—romantic and restful.

There are several American cities to choose from if, in secret, you really wish you were living in Europe: San Francisco, New Orleans, Seattle. Their buildings are quirky and original, bakeries make things like baguettes and *Dinkelbrot*, and there are long harbor views from the smallest windows.

And bridges. How I love bridges. There is a stern precision and authority to them that you see almost nowhere else in architecture. Unlike buildings, they are there to serve only one purpose. Form limited to function in the most succinct way. Design it wrong, you're headlines.

After we'd made three trips to the Golden Gate Bridge, where I stared at it like Moses at the burning bush, my wife reasonably asked what was going on.

"I need toothpicks!"

Sydney's mistake was not having me committed *then*. Or outside the supermarket where I bought thirty boxes of toothpicks and seven tubes of glue. Or back at the hotel where, tongue outside my mouth, I began the toothpick bridge.

Enough was enough! Sure, she was used to me buying plaster lawn dwarves and Sam the Sham records, but hadn't I already cooked the cooked chicken? Covered a table with yellow pencil sharpeners?

Know what Cocteau says about situations like this? "It is easy to behave well in disaster. That is when a good education shows. The hard thing is to behave well in good fortune, that is the proof of real spirit."

Now look, you know by now I already had my head up like a panicky spaniel, sniffing the ripe air madly. But the madness was my problem. Sydney's was to see that cocked head of mine, gleaming eyes, robot voice back on my tongue . . .

Later, she said there was nothing uncommon about what I was doing, but I disagree. Do you know where your children are tonight? Do you know where your mate's sanity is tonight? I am sure if Bronwyn Sydney had gone as demonstrably mad as I did those days, *I* would not have sat there and watched television while she crawled on the floor, making something that looked like a spiderweb spun by an arachnid on LSD.

The ex–Mrs. Radcliffe disagrees. That is one of the reasons why we share an office now but no longer a life.

Anyway, back home in Santa Barbara it became all too apparent that I was hanging-ten way out over the edge of the real world and something had to be done.

If you're rich or famous, they don't come with butterfly nets or giant syringes full of sedatives to subdue you till they can get you to a padded cell. In my case, during the infrequent moments of clarity that whizzed through my mind like hummingbirds, I remember being asked by serious types if I felt "all right." But hell, I felt great—the view from *my* window was interesting!

At this point Sydney did something truly inspired and for which I will be forever indebted. Every doctor I saw said something different about what was wrong with me. Overwork and stress were the preferred villains, although my favorite came from one German with porcupine hair who said I was suffering a *kreislauf* collapse.

But the only thing I sincerely regret about that time was that no one photographed what I created with teapots, yellow pencil sharpeners, a Chinese wok, a black bird cage (and bird), rubber bands . . . in the space of about a week on our living room floor.

I have visions of it being a cross between the 1939 New York World's Fair, one of the lost cities of the Incas, and most disturbing of all, perhaps the most visionary work I have ever done. The pisser is, I remember nothing about it except how much fun it was to do. Sydney says it was only a drooler's maze of nonsense, bad Gaudí, and our largest kitchen utensils. I'm not so sure. When I asked why she didn't at least take pictures, she said, "Harry, dear, it was bad enough living with you. You looked like the guy in a science fiction movie who sees the monster first. That was enough for me. I wasn't in the mood to get out a camera. We *weren't* on vacation!"

I certainly was. While in Pakistan a few years ago on a project, I twice saw naked men walking down the street in Islamabad. Nobody paid any attention. It was explained that the insane there are considered "touched by God," so they are left alone.

I wish they'd left *me* alone. On the other side of the world, Sydney was told the best thing would be for me to spend a few months in an exclusive home with a bunch of other "exhausted and confused" souls who could afford the thousands of dollars a week it cost to reside there. Personally, I was happy as a clam at home building my city on our living room floor.

But my good and open-minded wife didn't do what the "experts" suggested, bless her.

At that time there was a notorious show on the radio in Los Angeles that both of us loved. It was called "Off the Wall," and the title puts it all in a nutshell.

Five nights a week the host interviewed various screwballs, zealots, and 100 percent looney tunes from the area. My favorite segment was the one where a group from Pasadena was on, claiming to be *the* lost tribe of Israel.

Once, after we'd made love and were in the midst of that slow parachuting to earth that follows, I turned on the radio in time for "Off the Wall." The host, Ingram York, was interviewing a man who spoke with a European accent.

"Have you actually taught people to *fly*, Mr. Venasque? Or are we speaking metaphorically now?"

"You ever thought about how many times you've heard 'Chopsticks' played wrong? Probably the world's simplest piece to plunk out on a piano, but people get it wrong every other time. Then they laugh, like, who cares if I played this dumb thing wrong? It's the same with what we know about ourselves, Ingram. 'We shelter an angel within us. We must be the guardian of that angel.'

"Sure, I've taught people to fly. But that's only because they had it in them already. They'd just been playing their own personal 'Chopsticks' wrong all along and accepting it."

"Could you teach me?"

"No." There was a pause before Venasque continued. "Because you don't have it in you."

"What would you do if I came to you for help?"

"Cook you lunch and watch how you ate it."

Sydney and I looked at each other and both slid closer to the radio so we could hear this guy better.

"How would eating my lunch tell you anything?"

"What you like tells me something. How you want it cooked tells me something. The *way* you eat it.

"People look for wonder and for *themselves* in the wrong places, Ingram. In church, or when you're dying, when a child's being born . . . But those things are too strong. When life expands like that, when we're overpowered by a moment or an event, the small things go away. Whether you believe me or not, I'm saying the most important facts are in those small things."

This "Venasque" went on talking like that, and more than anything else, Sydney and I were charmed by him. He mentioned being the child of a circus family in France, his pets, and how much he enjoyed watching television and cooking. Yet very little about his "magical powers," although he clearly came across as both a learned and canny man. We liked him. He sounded like the perfect next-door neighbor.

So, after I'd seen all the doctors, and their unanimous verdict was to pack the celebrated architect off to a madhouse, Sydney contacted the producer of "Off the Wall" and asked for Venasque's telephone number.

The first time I saw my savior, I was playing with my toys. Imagine a very large living room with an ocean view that leaves you breathless. Imagine me on the floor of that room with my Heavenly City set up and ever-expanding. By then I'd assembled a bunch of scale models of famous buildings—Richard Rogers's Lloyd's of London, the Secession Museum in

Vienna, the Brandenburger Tor, and set them down among the other chaos there.

Suddenly light fell across the room. The front door had opened and there were hellos. When I looked up, this big hairy gray pig came oinking and trotting into the room. Right past me, crushing and scattering buildings, pencil sharpeners, the wok . . . right over to the sandwich I'd been eating. It was on a table exactly level with the pig's mouth. One "shloooop!" and my lunch was gone.

"What was it, Connie, a peanut butter?" Were the first words I heard Venasque say.

"Hey, what's going on here?" he said next, walking into the room, hands on hips. "You got enough buildings, Harry. We gotta get you a clarinet."

He and the pig (a "Vietnamese pig") and a dog moved into our guest house out back. Poor Bronze Sydney: a mad husband, a shaman, a pig and a bull terrier named Big Top all under her roof.

Big Top and Connie the pig were inseparable. They spent much of their time in the kitchen hoping something edible would happen. Which often did because Venasque took over all the cooking—one of the few pluses for my wife. The meals he created! Even in my wonkoed condition I realized what he was serving us was Mozart to the tongue. It came out later that he and his wife (long gone) had for years owned a very successful diner in L.A.

That first afternoon after talking to me for a few minutes, he wrote out a grocery list and asked Sydney to go to the store immediately for those things. When she returned, he made us "a real lunch" and then went out to the car for his bags. The animals naturally followed close behind. I asked Sydney if he was going to stay with us. She said she guessed so.

For the next two days, he sat with me on the floor and together we slowly took my city apart. Once in a while he would ask me what something was. I'd say "a fork" or "ballpoint pen" and he'd nod as if just learning the word for the first time.

"You were crazy then, Harry. I held up an orange once and you said it was a book. I almost kissed you. What you knew about the world and how you saw it was unique and specific. Never in a million years would I have seen a book in that orange, but you did. I kept an orange on my dresser for a while to see if I'd ever be lucky enough to see the book in it."

"You sound like R. D. Laing in *The Politics of Experience*, Venasque: Only the nuts are sane. Very 1960s stuff."

"Wonder doesn't fit in a book, Harry. It's too big."

I haven't described him yet, have I? I always assume the people I know well are just as familiar in strangers' minds as they are in my own.

He was a round old man. Short white hair, a large, always smoothly shaven face that looked its most comfortable listening or considering. He had green eyes but once told me the color had changed as he grew older. He wore overalls a lot because he didn't like belts or suspenders. Overalls and running shoes. He loved running shoes and must have owned twenty pairs.

When the Heavenly City was dismantled and put back in its rightful drawers (or garbage can), and the

living room floor was visible again, the old man took
me outside.

We sat by the swimming pool and ate M&M's
chocolate candies, which were the animals' favorite
snack. Venasque said nothing; only spilled M&M's
into his hand from the jumbo-size bag and doled
them out to the three of us. I was content to sit there,
look at the still blue water and enjoy the sun on my
legs. The only noise was the snuffling of the pig and
dog as they ate their shares.

The old man got up and walked two steps to the
water. Once there, he turned the bag upside down
and shook it over the pool. The candy flew out like
buckshot across the surface, *plink-plopping* into the
water like the beginning of a rain shower. Since I'd
taken a Valium just before leaving the house, this
strange act didn't bother me a bit.

"Come on, Harry, get up. We're going for a
swim."

We were already in our bathing suits, so Venasque
took my arm and led me to the shallow end of the
pool. The animals preceded us and, fearlessly walking
down the steps into the water, floated out together. A
white head, a hairy gray one.

I felt the first cold stab of water on my left foot.
The pig was in the middle of the pool, shoveling up
M&M's with an open mouth.

"Connie, leave those candies alone!"

He kept hold of my arm and moved us out. We
kept bumping into candy buttons, which were already beginning to lose their color, in bright, unrav-
eling swirls, to the pool's chlorine.

"Okay, here." Venasque stopped us and put his
hand over my face. Through the heavy velvet curtain

of Valium and madness, I felt something extraordinarily vital and new open inside me.

"We're going down now, Harry, and we'll stay down awhile. Don't get scared, 'cause you'll be able to breathe. Let's go."

We settled like stones at the bottom of the pool. He pointed to the surface. Besides the wavering shimmer of the bright world on the other side of the water, I could see the many dark dots of M&M's that had survived Connie's mouth.

"Look at those candies, Harry. Arrange them in your head. Look for a connection and tell me what you see." His words were clear and distinct, as if we were sitting *by* the pool and not *in* it.

What I saw was music. Music I could instantly read although I didn't know how to read music then. The dark brown M&M's were notes on the wavering "note paper" of the surface and it was all instantly, completely recognizable. Sublime music that made the greatest sense. Venasque later said it wasn't music, it was me, "written properly."

"That *really* sounds 1960s! Who arranged it like that, while we were at the bottom of that pool?"

"Don't *always* be a wiseguy, Harry. It's like a plaid jacket that goes good with some outfits, but with others it looks like shit. You want to ask an important question, ask it. Don't always hide behind a plaid jacket."

"Sorry. Who wrote the music on the water?"

"God."

"I'm sorry, Venasque, but I don't believe in God."

"Then who do you think spread them over the water like that, Mantovani?"

"You, Venasque. You're the closest to a God I've

ever gotten, although I used to think a great building was God. You know, stand near the Treasury in Petra, or Mendelsohn's Einstein Tower, and that's as immortal or in touch with the Almighty as we will ever get."

He shook his head as if I was a slow fool. "Someone said, 'It is easier for an imagination to conjure architecture than human beings.' Know why that is, Harry? Because buildings only go up so high. No matter how big they are, they stop somewhere. God doesn't stop. Neither do human beings, given the right direction. Immortality doesn't mean a hundred or two hundred floors. It means forever."

Once Venasque determined I wasn't seriously insane, he drove me into Santa Barbara to buy a clarinet. "*Serious* crazies are very industrious, Harry. They cut their own roads and then drive up and down them, alone, all day long. You only took a detour to see what the countryside was like off the main turnpike."

Never in my life had I had any desire to play a musical instrument. In college I dreamt of being in a rock group, but that was only because of the girls that came with the occupation. Other than that, I was content to listen to music as background while working or for a mood boost when I was feeling sexy or depressed.

Venasque said the twentieth century generally doesn't like quiet, and that's why there is so much annoying or useless noise (and music) surrounding us constantly.

"Some centuries are happy being quiet and looking at the sky. Ours spends all its time trying like crazy to fill that sky up!

"There's no silence left: a minute when you can think or be still awhile. How about places like elevators or the 'hold' line on a telephone: Elevators used to give you those few precious moments when you could stop in between floors and think about what you were going to say or about what'd just happened in your life. Now you walk into a little box full of 'Strangers in the Night.'

"It also ruins the whole idea of music, which is something you should pay attention to, not resent or ignore while you're waiting for your call to go through!

"I'm going to teach you to read and play music, Harry, both so you'll learn more about yourself, and as something to focus on when you start losing it again."

"Will I lose it again?"

"Only if you want. Other people can't help it. You have the luxury of choosing if you want to be crazy or not."

A few months later Venasque and I saw the film *The Karate Kid* on television. What ant shit. The sagacious old man from the mysterious East who can both chop a board in half and guide a teenager down the Yellow Brick Road of enlightenment via aphorisms and apothegms that sound pretty good, until you realize ten minutes later you could have thought them up yourself.

However, Venasque liked it, as he did most things on TV. I have never met a person who liked television more, which certainly wasn't in keeping with what I'd learned about the man in the time we'd been together.

"What's the matter with a movie about a kid finding his center, Harry? So what if it's a little 'Hollywood'? That's what we watch movies for."

"But you, of all people, know how that process *really* works. Doesn't it piss you off to see enlightenment served like fast food? Pull up to the drive-in window and order some nirvana, with fries, to go?"

"Close your eyes, Harry. It's time to travel again. I want to show you something."

"Traveling" was Venasque's term for the way he made one return to their past. He'd tell me to close my eyes and moments later, I'd be back in some obscure moment or corner of my life, experiencing things I hadn't thought about in twenty years.

"There is an art to falling down, you know."

I continued looking at the camera, afraid to let my eyes click over to him as he got up off the floor. His assistant stood nearby, but obviously knew he wanted to get up alone; to achieve the small victory of rising after the large defeat of falling down for the third time since I'd entered his studio with my father.

Robert Layne-Dyer was the first homosexual I had ever recognized, if that is the correct word. Since I was only eight, I had no idea what was "with" him, other than his gestures were more theatrical than what I was accustomed to in other men, and his speech was overly precise, his voice too sweet. I knew my father's Southern accent and elbows on the dinner table. I was used to my dad's friends, who talked about money and women, politics and other things, with the same appreciative deep-chested chuckles and rumbling growls of indignation or anger.

Layne-Dyer was a flit. That is not a nice word to use these days because it's like calling a woman a "bimbo," but let's face it, there *are* flits and bimbos in this world. However, the flit who had me posing for him was one of the most famous photographers in the world. Thus he was allowed, back in those dark Republican days of the 1950s, to wave his homosexuality like a mile-long banner at the world. When I think now how much courage it must have taken for a man to behave like that in 1957, it's awe-inspiring.

My father, who even then was rich and influential, had decided it was time I had my picture taken. A devoted and voracious reader of magazines, he leafed through Mother's *Vogue* and *Harper's Bazaar* almost as carefully as she did. On the basis of photographs he'd seen there, he chose Layne-Dyer to immortalize me.

After due inquiry and negotiation, Dad and I arrived one July morning at the door of an attractive brownstone house in Gramercy Park. On the cab ride over, I was told the photographer was probably a "fag," but that I shouldn't let it bother me.

"What's a fag, Dad?"

"A guy, backward."

" 'Guy' backward is 'yug.' 'Fag' is 'gaf.' "

"You'll see what I mean when we get there."

What I saw was a very sick man. He answered the door and, smiling, shook hands with both of us. But there was so little light left in him. He reminded me of a lantern with only a very small flame inside.

He was about thirty-five, middle height and build, with a blond wave of hair sweeping down over his forehead like a comma. His eyes were green and large but rather sunken in his face, diminishing their size until you looked carefully. Which of course I did because I kept looking for the "fag" in him. He was also the first person who ever called me "Mr. Harry."

"So, the Radcliffes have arrived. How are you, Mr. Harry?"

"Fine, Mr. Layne. I mean Mr. Dyer."

"You can call me either. Or Bob, if that's more comfortable."

Then he fell down.

Just boom! No warning, no tripping or flailing of arms—one moment up with us, the next down on the floor in a heap. Naturally I laughed. I thought he was doing it for me—a crazy kid's joke. Maybe that's what Dad meant when he said fags were guys backwards.

My father gave me a jab in the ribs that hurt so much I cried out.

Layne-Dyer looked up from the floor at him. "It's okay. He doesn't understand. I fall a lot. It's a brain tumor and it makes me do some strange things."

I looked at my father for explanations. We were pals and he was usually straight with me, but this time he gave a small head shake that meant "wait till later." So I turned back to the photographer and waited for what he'd do next.

"Let's go in and get you set up." He pushed himself slowly off the floor and led the way into the house.

To this day I remember the way his place was furnished: Dark "Mission" furniture, pieces of ornamental glass everywhere—Steuben, Lalique, Tiffany—that caught and turned light into beautiful, intricate performances for anyone interested.

Some of his more famous photographs were on

the walls: Fellini and Giulietta Masina eating picnic lunch together on the set of *La Strada;* Tour de France bicycle racers steaming in a tight pack together down a Paris street with the Eiffel Tower looming behind them like a monstrous metal Golem.

"Did you take that picture?"

"Yes."

"It's President Eisenhower!"

"Right. He let me come to the White House to do it."

"You were in the *White House?*"

"Yes. A couple of times."

I didn't know who Fellini was, and anyone could race a bicycle, but to be invited to President Eisenhower's house to take a picture meant you were big stuff, in my book. I followed Bob closely to his studio.

Later I read in Layne-Dyer's autobiography that he hated being called anything other than "Robert." But "Bob" is a pair of soft familiar jeans to an eight-year-old boy, rather than "Robert," which is the black wool suit you're forced to wear on Sunday to church, or the name of a distant cousin you instantly hate on meeting for the first time.

"What kind of picture are you going to take of me?"

"Come on in and I'll show you."

The studio was unremarkable. There were lights and reflectors around, but nothing challenging, nothing promising besides many cameras that said only matters were more formal in here, watch your step a little more. But I was eight, and having my picture taken by someone famous seemed only right: a combination of what was due me because I was Harry Radcliffe, third-grader, and because my father, a rich

and nice man, wanted it. At eight you're dead serious
about what the world owes you: Civilization starts in
your own room and moves out from there.

"Sit here, Harry."

A pretty assistant named Karla started moving
around the room, setting up cameras and tripods. She
smiled at me sometimes.

"What do you want to be when you grow up,
Harry?"

Looking to see if Karla was watching, I said confi-
dently, "Mayor of New York."

Layne-Dyer ran both hands through his hair and
said to no one in particular, "Humble fellow, isn't
he?"

Which made my father laugh. I didn't know what
the word meant, but if Dad laughed then it must be
okay.

"Look at me, Harry. Good. Now look over there,
at the picture of the dog on the wall."

"What kind of dog is that?"

"Don't talk for a minute, Boss. Let me get this
right and then we'll chat."

I tried to watch what he was doing out of the corner of my eye, but couldn't make my eyeball go back
that far. I started to turn.

"Don't move! Don't move!" FLASH. FLASH.
FLASH. "Great, Harry. Now you can turn. It's a Great
Vendean Griffon." FLASH. FLASH.

"What is?"

"The dog on the wall."

"Oh. Are you finished taking my picture now?"

"Not yet. A little while longer."

Halfway through the session he collapsed again.

"There's an art to falling down, you know. When

you go like I do, with no warning, just *plotz*, you learn after a few times to watch and take as much with you as you can before you hit. The design on the drapes, whatever you can grab with your eye, a hand. . . . Don't go empty-handed, don't just go down scared. Do you understand what I'm talking about, Harry?"

"No, sir. Not really."

"That's okay. Look at me."

The dying have a quality that even a child senses. Not because they are already removed, but because even young hearts sense their inability to stay longer. Behind the looks of sickness or fear is also the look of the long-distance traveler, bags on the floor, eyes tired but nervous for any change that may come. They are the ones going on the twenty-hour flights, and although we don't envy their coming discomfort or time-zone skips, tomorrow they will be *there*—a place that both terrifies and thrills us. We peek at the ticket they hold, the inconceivably far destination written there, impossible yet monstrously alluring. What will it smell like for them tomorrow? What is it like to sleep there?

"Are you sick?"

Karla stopped walking across the room and looked away. My father started to say something, but Bob cut him off.

"Yes, Harry. That's what makes me fall down."

"Something's wrong with your feet?"

"No, my head. It's called a brain tumor. Like a bump inside there that makes you do odd things. And ends up killing you."

I am convinced he didn't say it to spook or scare me. Only because it was the truth. Now I was entirely impressed by him.

"You're going to *die?*"

"Yes."

"That's weird. What does it feel like?"

The camera flashgun in his hand went off, making us all jump. "Like that."

When we'd shivered back to earth, he put the flashgun on a table and gestured with his head. "Come with me a minute, Harry. I want to show you something."

All three of us would have followed at that moment if he'd asked. I looked at my father to see if it was okay to go, but couldn't catch his eye because he was watching Layne-Dyer so intently.

"Come on, Harry, we'll be back soon."

He took my hand and led me farther back into the studio, through a large woody kitchen with silver pots of different sizes hanging from the walls like drops of frozen mercury, a big bunch of red onions and one of ivory garlic.

"Does your wife like to cook?"

"*I* like to cook, Harry. What's your favorite food?"

"Spare ribs, I guess," I said disapprovingly. Men weren't supposed to cook. I was not happy with his disclosure, but he *was* dying and that was thrilling. At my age I'd heard a lot about death and even seen my grandfather in his coffin looking rested. But being near a death actually taking place was something else. Years later in a biology class, I watched a snake devour a live mouse bit by wriggling bit. That is what it was like to be with Layne-Dyer that single day, knowing something was killing him even as we stood there looking at his red onions.

"Come on." We left the kitchen and came to one last room that was quite dark and empty but for

"Yecch!" I spit and spit to get it all out. Bob smiled and continued to chew and then swallow his piece.

"Listen to me, Harry. You can't eat it because it's not your house. Sooner or later in everyone's life a moment comes when their house appears like this. Sometimes it's when you're young, sometimes when you're sick like me. But most peoples' problem is they can't see the house, so they die confused. They *say* they want to understand what it's all about, but given the chance, given the *house*, they either look away or get scared and blind. Because when the house is there and you know it, you don't have any more excuses, Boss."

Once again I was baffled by what he was saying, but the tone of his voice was so intense that it seemed imperative I at least try to understand what he was so passionate about.

"I'm scared at what you're saying. I don't get what you mean."

He nodded, stopped, nodded again. "I'm telling you this now, Harry, so maybe you'll remember it later on. No one ever told *me*.

"Everyone has a house inside them. It defines who they are. A specific style and form, a certain number of rooms. You think about it all your life—what does mine really look like? How many floors are there? What is the view from the different windows. . . . But only once do you get a chance to actually see it. If you miss that chance, or avoid it 'cause it scares you, then it goes away and you'll never see it again."

"*Where* is this house?"

He pointed to his head and mine. "In here. If you recognize it when it comes, then it'll stay. But accepting it and making it stay is only the first part.

Then you've got to try understanding it. You've got to take it apart and understand every piece. Why it's there, why it's made like that . . . most of all, how each piece fits in the whole."

I sort of got it. I asked the right question. "What happens when you understand?"

He held up a finger, as if I'd made a good point. "It lets you eat it."

"Like you just did?"

"Exactly. It lets you take it back inside. Here, look where the roof is gone. It's the only section of the house I've been able to understand so far. The only part I've been allowed to eat." He broke off another piece and popped it into his mouth. "The fuck of the thing is, I don't have enough time now to do it. You can't imagine how long it takes. How many hours you sit there and look or try to work it out . . . but nothing happens. It's so exciting and frustrating at the same time."

Whatever he'd said after "fuck" didn't go anywhere in my head because he'd said *that word!* Even my father didn't say it and he was a pretty big curser. I'd said it once and gotten the biggest smack of my life. Whenever I'd heard it since, it was like someone flashing an illegal weapon at me or a pack of dirty playing cards. You were dying to look, but knew it'd get you in a hell of a lot of trouble if you did.

"Fuck." You don't hear that much when you're an eight-year-old. It's an adult's word, forbidden and dirty and owning a dangerous gleam of its own. You don't really know what it means, but use it, and you sure get fast results.

The whole wonder and awe of Layne-Dyer's model house—what it was, what he *said* it was—fell

from the horizon the moment this big orange
"FUCK" roared up. The magic of death, the magic of
great mysteries, lost to the magic of one dirty word.

A short time later both Karla and my father began
calling us from the other room. Bob put his arm
around my shoulder and asked again if I understood
everything he had said. Lying, I nodded in a way I
thought was intelligent and mature, but my mind was
on other things.

The photo session ended soon after, which was
just as well because I couldn't wait to get home.

When I was safely in my room and had locked the
door, I ran for the bathroom. Locked in there too, I
turned on the overhead light and said the word to
myself over and over again. Loud, soft, as a plea, an
order. I made faces around the word, gestures, I did
everything. Hearing it from Layne-Dyer had set
something loose in me and I couldn't let that thing go
until I had exhausted its every possibility. Fuck.

When I opened my eyes, I saw Big Top lying on
my foot. Venasque was looking at me and eating from
a bag of sour cream and onion potato chips.

"That was a dream I had twenty years ago,
Venasque. The only thing true about it was I went to
Layne-Dyer as a kid to have my picture taken and he
fell down once."

"How old were you when you had the dream?"

"I don't know, graduate school, as I remember."

"Why do you think you had it then?"

"Cause I was thinking a lot about houses then. I
was studying to be an architect!"

"Harry, don't be a dope. Before, you were saying

things like *Karate Kid* are bad because they water down important issues. That's true, but here you were having a . . .

"Listen to me carefully. Sometimes dreams turn into soldiers. They'll fight your battles and defend your land, but you've got to take good care of them. Feed and protect them, give them the attention they deserve. Forget or ignore a dream that size and the soldier dies. That one especially. You've got to write that thing down as much as you remember and study it till you realize how important it is. And for God's sake, keep it protected. You're going to need it again, believe me.

"*Karate Kid is* nonsense, but you were given a gift of real enlightenment, Harry, and you forgot it, till now. Wrote it off like it happened because you were eating hot peppers before you went to bed."

Besides the "traveling" and clarinet lessons, Venasque had me do autogenic training to drag my flapping kite of a heartbeat back to earth, as well as create a new quiet room in the house of my life. It would be both easy and false to lie and say our time together was full of miraculous events, profound aphorisms, and enlightenment every step of the way. But being healed and helped by Venasque didn't work like that. There *was* magic, times when my jaw dropped open and troops of cold-footed lizards ran up my spine. But the norm was quiet talk and laughter, always. I am convinced the great teachers do two things that outweigh everything else—they explain clearly, and they exude an almost palpable feeling of benevolence.

A shaman, teacher . . . must be fundamentally and at all times benevolent. None of this half-devil, half-angel stuff, which is a very modern, convenient conceit that misses the point. The point is that while the teaching methods these men sometimes employ are odd and unorthodox and even horrifying, ultimately they know something about us that we ourselves don't know—they have faculties functioning in their brains that don't function in ours. And most important, behind all their strange behavior is the benevolent intent to bring us to our spiritual senses.

Since my time with Venasque I have met or read books about other so-called shamans. But these characters aren't the real thing. They are simply mischievous, intuitive, supersmart little opportunists who pass for spiritual teachers because they have psychic abilities. But psychic powers are a dime a dozen. Someone made the point somewhere that we must learn to distinguish between the occult and the religious, between magic and true spirituality. The two do sometimes come together—saints do have magical powers, sure. But they don't exploit these powers, and more important, they consider them only by-products of their real concern, which is spiritual development.

Let me tell you one last Venasque story. When I was well again and he was preparing to return to his home in Los Angeles, he still hadn't mentioned his fee. So I asked. He told me the normal charge was five thousand dollars, but because I was a famous architect, he'd rather I design a new kitchen for his house. The one he had was both old and too full of sad memories of the happy days he'd spent there together with his wife.

"Now it's your turn to figure me out, Harry. Decide what kind of environment I should have."

"Is this part of my therapy?"

"No. I need a new kitchen and it'll be a good way for you to get started again. Something small and tasty!"

I went down to L.A. with him to look at his house, but wasn't impressed by what I saw. The place itself was postwar, pseudo-Spanish, but the greater cause for concern was the interior: ghetto-chic, shag-rug hell. Too many colors, too many patterns, too many different textures of furniture that didn't go together at all. It looked like a schizophrenic from Tahiti lived there, or someone wildly enthusiastic for variety, but color blind down to the difference between blue and yellow.

Worse, with great pride Venasque said his wife had decorated the house and he hadn't changed a thing since she died.

The kitchen was no different. The touching thing was it looked and felt like the favorite, most lived-in room of his whole house. It was easy to envision the two old people in there, one leaning up against the fridge while the other bustled around, getting their meal ready. I could understand why he wanted me to change its too-familiar face.

"How do you want it, Venasque? Sexy? Mediterranean?"

"What's a sexy kitchen?"

"White. Silver. Sleek."

"Sounds like an operating room. I don't take out tonsils here, Harry. Make me something nice and alive."

I'd designed buildings that, even on paper,

shamed every other structure in the neighborhood
both in look and stature. Houses, skyscrapers, factories . . . the gamut. But coming up with a dumb
twelve-foot kitchen for the old man was a real pisser. I
wanted to give him my very best in return for all he'd
done. When I told him that, he patted my face and
said, "Just make sure to leave room for the microwave."

First I thought Adolf Loos. Venasque would like
the Loos style, wouldn't he? Clean simplicity that
went right to the heart of the matter. I showed him
pictures but he shook his head. "I'd get cold in a
house like that, Harry. The man forgot to use his
heart." Out went the king of twentieth-century Viennese architecture. Ditto Gaudí was "too crooked,"
and Frank Gehry's work looked like "the fence
around the schoolyard."

And what did the shaman think of Harry Radcliffe's work?

"Some of the buildings are beautiful, but others
look like a light bulb that's been left on during the
day, or a telephone ringing in an empty apartment."

Besides being hurt, I had no idea what he was
talking about—light bulb? empty apartment? Later I
discovered the line came from Cocteau's journals, literally word for word. But that was no help in deci-
phering what he meant. Only later, when I was in
Saru and looking at the proposed site for the dog museum, did it come clear: You can always fill space
with form, but it's like filling an empty room with
light, i.e., what good does it do if the light has no real
purpose? Or there's no one to hear the phone's message? He never said it, but I'm sure Venasque thought
I'd clevered my way to prominence while, along the

way, forgetting (or consciously neglecting) to use what I was best at, rather than what I was capable of.

Naturally that was an even greater incentive to design a kitchen that would knock his eyes out. I showed him the work of architects as diverse as Bruce Goff, Richard Meier, and even Daniel Liebeskind. I showed him buildings, furniture, kitchen utensils. Anything to get even the smallest feeling for what he wanted, but he was of little help.

"I don't know what I want, Harry. I want a kitchen where I can cook a good meal and where the animals and me'll feel comfortable just sitting around, relaxing."

So I sat down with my pens and paper and designed a kitchen. Black and white tiles, bird's-eye maple, German stainless appliances. A few original bits and a few surprises. I liked it. Venasque did not.

"This is nothing, Harry. This is for anyone. I want a kitchen that's *mine*. Venasque cooks here—not Betty Crocker or Julia Child. This drawing is Harry Radcliffe, Mr. Famous Architect's kitchen. But this isn't your place, remember, it's mine!"

He rarely became angry, but this time he glared at the drawing. I was ashamed although I honestly believed the plans had been done with him foremost in my mind.

"Give me a thousand dollars, Harry. I want you to write me a check right now."

Without a thought, I wrote the check and handed it over. He looked at it, shook his head, put it in his pocket. "Every time you draw something that's not mine, I want another thousand dollars. Do you understand? Maybe that's the only way to get you to learn."

"Venasque, I'm telling you, I did that design—"

"Shut up! Shut up and go back to work! You're not crazy anymore. You don't have any excuses. Just remember, a thousand dollars each time you design for yourself and not for me!"

I worked like a paranoid student preparing for the final examination. I thought kitchens most of the day and did more drawings than I had for the forty-floor Andromeda Center in Birmingham. Only when I was sure I had it *this* time did I dare go to the old man and nervously hand over what I thought was surely *it* this time.

I gave him seven drawings, which immediately resulted in handing him seven checks for a thousand dollars. Once, when writing the sixth, I thought to myself not only was he getting a free kitchen, but two thousand bucks more than his previously stated fee. As I wrote my name on the check, Venasque said, "Lucky I have such a rich and famous architect to sponge off, huh, Harry?" Which was the first time I realized he could read my mind. I was embarrassed, but not surprised.

His reaction to my seventh idea was novel. We were out on his patio, the pig and dog sitting at our feet. He took the drawing, looked at it for perhaps a second, then put it down on the ground between the animals.

"What do you think of this one, guys?"

The pig sniffed the paper loudly and put her head down again. The bull terrier got up, moved a bit over, and calmly pissed on my drawing. Pissed and pissed until urine ran off the expensive paper onto the concrete.

"What the fuck do you *want* from me, Venasque? I'm giving you a hundred percent! I can't help it if

you don't like them! Can I help it if you don't understand architecture?"

"You can go crazy again, Harry, but stop being an
asshole so much. You make me tired."

I got up and started away on angry feet. "I'm not
wrong about this, Venasque. I'm giving you a hundred percent. I don't care *how* much you know. You're
just not seeing that."

"Go make me another thousand-dollar drawing."
He flicked a dismissive hand at me, leaned down and
petted the pig.

We didn't speak for two days, although I didn't
come out of my room much, doing drawing after
drawing in a rage of "I'll show *that* fucker!" But what
came of my creative fury? Very little. What I realized
later was he probably goaded me into that anger to
see if I could get mad without going mad.

He set meals out on the dining table—always
sandwiches, always delicious—and stayed away, except for the occasional meeting in the hall where he'd
either wink or ignore me completely—both of which
were infuriating.

How I struggled to get it right; how I yearned for
his approval. Our real fathers are not always the ones
who give us the final, necessary approval. If we're
lucky, we're able to recognize and work toward the
right one. If not, confusion and dissatisfaction sit like
dust on the rooms of our lives.

I was lucky, but that didn't make it easier. The
calmer and more normal Venasque acted, the more
paranoid I got. What did he know that he wasn't telling me? What was so wrong with my drawings that
he put them down to be pissed on?

Nothing. Nothing was wrong with them.

I could spend a lot of time describing how I came
to that correct conclusion, but there's so much more of
this story to tell that it's time to move on, even if it's
in the middle of a long and rich Venasque story. He
would forgive me the abridgement. In another con-
text, he once said, "The future is hungry, Harry. It's
waiting with its big tongue out and a knife and fork
like the giant in 'Jack and the Beanstalk.' Fe Fi Fo
Fum! I smell the life of Harry Radcliffe! Then *spoink!*
He spears and eats you."

"What am I supposed to do about that? Talk him
out of it?"

"No. Learn to be eaten. Then learn to see in the
dark as you go down his big throat. Some parts in
there are boring and you can skip 'em, but most are
interesting."

So I'll cut to halfway down the giant's throat and
tell about how I stood up from the desk, took the first
drawing I'd done (seven thousand dollars ago), and
walked into the living room where the old man and
his animals were watching "Miami Vice." I went up
next to the couch and shoved the picture at him.

"This is it, Venasque. You were wrong before. This
is the one."

Without looking, he put out a hand and casually
took the paper from me. He glanced at it and handed
it back.

"Good. Tell me what materials you need and I'll
order them."

"Wait a minute! Did you look at this? It's the first
drawing I did. The one you said was shit."

"Right. Now it's good. I like it."

"Why now and not then?"

He looked at me for the first time. "Because when

you first showed it to me, you wanted my approval. This time you thought it through and know for *sure* it's the right one. You have your own approval and that's enough. I accept it now. I like it. Let me see the end of this show and then we'll talk."

"And what about my seven thousand bucks?"

"I bought a new Mitsubishi entertainment center with it. Big wide screen TV, beautiful wood cabinets . . . top of the line. You should see it."

So we built his kitchen and I returned to sanity.

In the months that followed, Venasque died of a stroke, Bronze Sydney and I divorced, then I got involved almost simultaneously with Claire Stansfield *and* Fanny Neville.

Claire was tall and fragile-looking. A living breeze. Air with brown hair. Like a figure in a Pre-Raphaelite painting, she often appeared on the verge of either levitating or drowning in the complexities of life.

Fanny was pure Antaeus—bound to the earth—short and intense, a chain-smoking, eat-with-her-fingers realist who'd fooled (or frightened) a lot of people into thinking she was very tough.

But I don't really want to talk about either woman now because although they are a large part of my story, it's not *this* part. So excuse me, girls, if I only make introductions here, then open a trapdoor and disappear you both until the next act.

Zip. Gone!

Suffice it to say I met them and was intrigued enough to end up commuting back and forth from one to the other like a crosstown bus.

The most profound effect this semi-demi-madness (and the subsequent events) had on me was a yawning indifference to my job. Our firm was in the midst of several important projects when I went on my self-imposed vacation to deep left field. And although my recovery was quick, on returning to the office I looked at these projects as if they were advertisements for lawn furniture with a seahorse motif.

I just wanted to hang around. Shrug. Drink beer, watch lots of daytime television, watch my divorce happen. . . . Shrug.

Before, I had been driven both by a hundred-megaton ego and a will to succeed that knew no limit. Now . . . shrug.

Look at it this way: Have you ever noticed how difficult it is for fat people to put on their coats? One first assumes that's because the person is so damned big they simply can't find or maneuver themselves into the arm holes.

But seen from another angle, maybe it's because the coat can't handle *their* demands. Until I needed Venasque, life had been a too-small coat I was always stretching to fit myself into.

After he'd helped me, I realized one day how easy it had become for me to put on this same "coat." That in itself was okay, but as I grew increasingly more apathetic, the thing grew (or I shrunk) until it was almost too big and heavy for me to even carry, much less put on and wear. Does that mean I was suicidal? No, because potential suicides strike me as being full of desperation, and that emotion took far too much effort.

When Venasque died, I inherited Big Top the bull terrier and the two of us lived alone for a while in the

Santa Barbara house. But that was too beautiful and lonely, so I moved us down to L.A., where I met a few times a week with Bronze Sydney, who was holding the fort of our business until I either returned or drifted away, never to be heard from again. The rest of the time I spent with Fanny or Claire, walked the dog, saw few people, and one day came across a little poem by Emily Dickinson which stuck in my mind.

> *My life had stood a loaded gun*
> *In corners, till a day*
> *The owner passed-identified*
> *and carried me away.*

➤ The Sultan was wearing skis.

I always wanted to begin my memoirs with some unbearably pompous line like "My mother told me the night I was born, there was an eclipse (tornado, red scarf of cloud across the moon . . .) which meant fate was up to no good." Or "There was a time in my life when I only loved beautiful women with bad teeth." Memoirs written in a gloomy Swiss hotel by an old fart who's the only one in town amused or interested by his memories.

Now, whether *this* constitutes a memoir or not, I must begin with "The Sultan was wearing skis" because that's really where I began, notwithstanding a four-decade history, a family, a shaman, various experiences and fame that had already marked me.

The Sultan of Saru was standing in front of a full-length mirror wearing a kaffiyeh on his head, a yellow, purple and black ski suit like you see on the slopes of St. Moritz, and fire engine red boots and skis on his feet. We're talking about a hotel room in Los Angeles in the middle of eighty-degree weather, mind you. Out of the corner of my eye I saw sweet little Fanny Neville sitting on one of the many couches in the room.

I crossed to her and sitting down, purposely bumped her with my ass to let her know who was boss.

"I didn't know you were a skier, sir."

"I am a very good skier, Harry. There are very wonderful mountains in Saru." He turned to some of the other men in the room who were sitting around with nervous smiles. Professional smilers. "The only problem with our mountains is they are inhabited by our enemy these days."

The smilers didn't know how to react to that— their uncertain lips flapped up and down like wash on a line in the wind until the Boss opened *his* mouth and laughed loudly. He was quite a sight, guffawing in that ski get-up. I looked around the room like I'd landed on another planet. Fanny pinched my leg.

"Ah, Harry, I'm a funny man. A funny, funny man. We have our enemies, of course. Led by a madman named Cthulu who's sure he should rule. But he is a speck of dust on my pants. What is unfortunate, however, is that our people can no longer ski in their own mountains because this Cthulu and his men have interrupted our ski trade for the time being. A terrible shame. However, after this trouble is cleared up, I envision Saru one day as the Kitzbühl of the Mideast.

"In the meantime, we spend part of each winter in the beautiful mountain town of Zell am See, Austria. Superb skiing and a very lovely lake. Do you know it? About an hour from Salzburg? You must come and visit when we're there. Last year we bought some land."

Knowing the Sultan's vocabulary, I envisioned "some land" as being two or three thousand acres, if not an entire mountain.

"I'm not a skier, Your Highness."

"What do you do for exercise, Harry?"

"Stumble and fall into a coma."

Fanny creased with laughter, but the Sultan and his smilers didn't move a lip for about ten seconds. Then out of courtesy, he smiled a millimeter. Thus cued, the boys gave me a millimeter too.

Good old Fanny laughed so hard she started coughing. I decided not to tell her the line was Oscar Levant's and not my own. With wit, I'm always happy to take credit where it's not due.

"Harry, what can we do to convince you to design this museum? You are my only choice for architect."

"Sir, since you originally asked, I've been doing a little research. According to Muslim law, aren't dogs 'haram'?"

The temperature in the room dropped several hundred degrees.

"Yes, Harry. That's true."

Fanny knelt over and pretending to cough some more, whispered, "What's *haram*?"

"Forbidden."

"According to the Prophet, there is something in their spittle and breath that is detrimental to man's spirit."

"Then how can you even *consider* building a dog museum in your country?"

"I believe it is my responsibility." He smiled. "Because my life has been saved by dogs on three separate occasions. One time perhaps is coincidental, but when you are shielded from death three times by something as small and unimportant as a dog, Harry, then there must be very large forces working. Do you understand?"

"Can you tell us about the three times?"

"No, because I must give it to the people of Saru first. My story will be told in one part of the museum. Afterwards the world can know, if it is interested. That is a major reason why I want this place built."

"But won't you get in trouble with the fundamentalists over there?"

"Yes. That is a difficulty."

Ski outfit notwithstanding, the Sultan of Saru was one of the most dignified people I had ever encountered. He said this last small sentence with so much cool and grace that it sent a shiver of admiration through my heart.

To rule today in the Mideast is tantamount to a lifelong sentence. Cynicism toward politicians aside, it astounds me how these people withstand years of bullet-proof cars, bodyguards, no moment when you can swim in the open sea or eat pizza without someone nearby holding a gun or carefully watching your every move.

"I'm not a political man, Your Highness. Plus, the idea of designing a building that could be the death of us all *isn't* great incentive."

Fanny piped in, "Oh come on, Harry. You built the Jarrold Theatre in Belfast. Said every night you heard something blow up there. What's the difference?"

"The difference, dollink, is that too many people don't like dogs in Saru. Remember *haram*. They *do* like theater in Northern Ireland. The chances of survival there were greater."

"Chicken."

"*What* did you call me?"

"A chicken!"

Then the earthquake hit.

Around an 8.3 on the Richter scale, I first noticed it when Fanny's head started bobbing up and down like one of those dolls on springs on the back deck of a car. It took a moment to realize *she* wasn't fooling around.

I looked from her to the Sultan, but the room was moving in big bobs and waves and everyone was in funny motion. Later I learned Saru is famous for earthquakes, so these men knew what was happening much sooner than Fanny and I. The Sultan bent over and pulled his feet from the boots. Then he fell down when the hotel literally leaned to one side.

Fanny and I were knocked off the couch. I'd just enough time to grab her before we started rolling again. The sound of screeching, twisting metal and exploding glass was the world.

I barely heard the others shouting in Arabic. Someone grabbed the back of my shirt. The Sultan.

"Out to the hall, Harry! Get away from the windows!" He dragged me backward by the shirt. I held Fanny in a headlock. I saw he was barefoot. The barefoot Sultan in a ski suit in a California earthquake. I started laughing. He wasn't laughing. The door was open and we staggered out.

In the hall one of his men lay crushed under a gigantic fallen support beam. He must have died seconds before because his teeth were still chattering. That small fatal clicking sound was alone for a moment, then the roar of the outside world fell on us again.

How long does a big earthquake last? Thirty seconds? But it ain't over when you think it's over. Like a cow, the skin of the earth may stop twitching a moment against us flies, but not for long.

On the floor in the hall, all our arms entwined in a pathetic attempt at protection, we looked up as one when things stopped. Looking suspiciously at each other with hope and dread, as if one of us were about to start the whole thing again, our heads raised more and more as the cease-fire held.

"I don't think we're in Kansas anymore, Toto."

"Are you all right, Fan?"

"I think you broke my neck, but besides that, I'm just ducky." She started to get up but the Sultan grabbed her arm and jerked her back down.

"Don't move! This is not over."

It wasn't. The aftershocks came fast and just as viciously. We rode that floor like Ahab clinging to the side of Moby Dick.

"When does it fucking *stop*?" Fanny moaned as things shook and rolled on from bad to worse.

"Go to the doorway! We must be in a doorway. The floor's too dangerous!"

His voice sounded sure and scared; perfect in that instant to convince me to move. Also he was right— doorways do offer the most protection in a quake because that's where the supports of a building are centered.

Scuttering over on our knees, I saw the bottoms of the royal bare feet were sliced and bleeding. Turning around as another aftershock rose and rolled, I went to the dead servant and jerked off his shoes.

"Take these!" I stuck out my left hand, loafers dangling.

At the other end of the hall a window crashed and something blew in. I saw a dark blur at tremendous speed coming my way. Dropping the shoes, I knew, *knew*, it would hit me.

Before I could move, the Sultan shouted something like "Koucarry!" or "Kou-karies!" and a black telephone insulator fell dead out of the air at my feet.

The earth screamed, but the Sultan of Saru and I looked across a million miles and a million years of silence:

You just did magic.

That's right—and saved *your* ass.

That was all that passed between us then in lieu of the fact our world was still doing the cha cha cha. Did Fanny see his miracle? No. Did anyone else see him save me? No, because his other smilers were running around, trying to find us a way out of there before the Westwood Muse Hotel decided to give up the ghost and collapse.

A smiler I later knew as Djebeli came staggering toward us, waving. He said something loud in Arabic. The Sultan got to his feet and pulled Fanny with him. "There is a staircase that's still all right!"

By the time we reached the stairwell, the tremors had stopped again.

"Hurry. It still might not be over."

In retrospect, running down a hotel staircase in the middle of an earthquake isn't the world's dandiest idea, but you're *doing* something then and that's worth everything. Moving, not lying on the floor scared shitless and hoping to God it'll stop.

The stairwell looked okay—a few broken concrete

stairs, a steel banister bowed and gracefully bent like a silver swan's neck—but all essentially navigable. We took the plunge without a second's pause.

Fanny Neville has a magnificent head. Now *that's* love, huh? Racing down the cracked steps of hell into guaranteed more hell at ground level, I marveled even then at her terrific head in front of me. It's a big one for someone so small, but you don't really notice that at first. First you see the seal black hair combed and sprayed tight to the head, natural plum lips, the big little-girl eyes—

"Stop! Don't move!"

Fanny, Djebeli, and I all froze on command. I was still thinking about her head, so it took a moment to realize we'd halted.

"Come on, let's go!"

Leading our pack, the Sultan turned and looked at me. "Something bad's in here, Harry. Earthquakes come from the anger of the dead. They bring dangerous things out of the earth with them. I can feel—" He put up a hand as if to silence himself.

But not me. "Screw the dead! Let's go while we can." I moved down the steps and reached for Fanny.

"Wait!"

A floor below the door opened and a couple came slowly out onto the landing. The man looked up at us.

"Can we use these stairs?"

Pulling Fanny along, I started down. "I don't know, man, but I ain't stopping to think about it!"

"Harry, please don't move. There are jinn!"

In my state I thought he was talking about the people on the stairs—the fact they were both wearing jeans. "It's okay, sir, they're very popular. Let's just get the fuck out of here!"

The man was still holding the door open and a
dog came out. A dog I knew well, having fed him that
morning before leaving my apartment: Big Top.

He looked at me with his normal expressionless
stare, then gestured with his head to follow him. The
kind of casual, flick-of-the-chin-toward-one-shoulder,
Humphrey Bogart head toss, real cool.

"Can you get us out of here, Big?"

He looked at me stonily, turned around and went
back through the door. I started after him.

Fanny squeezed my hand. "What're you doing,
Harry? You're not going back *in*?"

"It is a verz! Follow it, Harry, it's a verz."

The man on the landing and his girlfriend started
down the stairs. "I'm not following no dog. C'mon,
Gail."

I was already moving, but had to ask over my
shoulder. "What's a verz?"

The Sultan and Djebeli were close behind. "A
guardian. A guide."

"How can you tell?"

"It speaks with its eyes. Hurry!"

Whether Big Top was a verz or not, I knew he was
full of magic. I'd seen it before. That's why I asked for
his help. He was the shaman's dog. I'll tell you about
it later.

As the door swung shut, there was a thunderous
boom from somewhere immediately above. Big Top
trotted blithely down the hall followed by four not-
blithe people.

Everything was chaos—a sofa lay split almost in
half out in the corridor, a chandelier scattered in hundreds of diamonds and glittery slivers over the brown

couch and floor. The Sultan yelped. I remembered his bare feet.

Big Top took a left. Incredibly, rock music started playing nearby. A song called "Sundays in the Sky" that was too familiar—a hit I'd heard so often that I wanted to wring its neck. But here in the middle of disaster, it sounded wonderful and reassuring—an angel's voice singing, hold on, you *will* get through this.

Then there was another body—a child's. Black and green and pink sweatshirt. United Colors of Benetton. Water sprayed down one of the halls, steam shot furiously from behind a door on another. Big Top went fast, then slow, never looking one way or the other. No uncertainty. There was also no time to think if we should be doing this: We needed a verz to get us out of there and onto the street.

Like being slapped very hard and in shocked, frozen silence taking moments to realize what's happened, the world outside finally began to howl its disbelief and pain. First the sound of what must have been an air-raid siren calling its all clear. Then the smaller, insect-shrill cries of moving sirens: ambulances, fire trucks, police cars. Even six stories up in the hotel, their wavering wails came from every direction.

On the fourth floor Big Top led us into a room with its door ajar. Inside, everything was in perfect order except the doors to the balcony, which were both open. Curtains flapped wildly in and out of the room.

The dog went to these doors and stood by them, tail wagging. Why there? Why had he stopped?

The Sultan went over and hesitantly walked out onto the balcony.

"There is a tree here! We can climb down on it. It is very big!"

"Why? Why not use the stairs?"

Djebeli pointed at Big Top. "The verz. He knows something we don't. Come."

Outside, the branches of our lifesaver tree waved cheerfully. A moment later they were gone with a crash. The Sultan jumped back, shouting in Arabic. The dog started barking.

"Fuck it—I think we just lost our way out of here." Fanny turned and started for the door.

Big Top, who was normally sweet on Fanny Neville, ran from the balcony and, blocking the door, started snarling and snapping at her. He looked vicious, prehistoric.

"Big, get out of here!"

"A helicopter!"

The whack-whack of a rotor came up louder and louder, drowning out even the dog. What *more* could happen?

Djebeli ran to the balcony, saw whatever it was, and yelled, "It's Khaled! We're saved!"

You forget titles and who you're suffering with in the middle of an earthquake. Luckily in our case it was a Sultan—and Sultans have money and power and loving subjects. They also have devoted minions who go looking for them in helicopters when they're in trouble.

Khaled swooped down the side of the Westwood Muse Hotel in a gold-and-black chopper that looked like a high-tech bug from heaven. I later learned the Sultan himself was a professional helicopter pilot and always had one on call wherever he went. The first thing I saw of this one was the garish seal of Saru on its weaving tail.

The cockpit dipped into view and a pilot with sunglasses and a million-dollar smile waved gayly at us.

"How come he's so happy?"

The Sultan waved back. "He is always happy when there's trouble. Stand back—he is going to shoot."

I looked out the door and the guy was aiming some kind of bizarre-looking rifle at us. Over the "wopping" of the blades there was a bang and something shot through the balcony doors: a beautiful thick rope. His Majesty, the Sultan of Saru, grabbed it and insisted Fanny and I go out first. I didn't argue.

When I was fifteen and about as full of shit as one could be, my father shipped me off to an Outward Bound survival school for a few weeks one summer to humble me a little. We climbed mountains, fought forest fires, once even rescued a woman who'd fallen into a glacial crevasse. It was a tough, interesting experience that gave me some important perspective. But what's remained most has been the banal realization you can never really say you know another until you've seen them under fire. One fat guy there was everyone's friend in base camp, but poisoned down into a cowardly, selfish, *dangerous* SOB when we were hanging off the side of an obsidian cliff or walking through a forest of burning treetops.

The converse of that is how remarkably the Sultan behaved the day of the earthquake. On the ground again, he sent Khaled off in the helicopter to help wherever he could. And after finding a pair of shoes, the ruler of one and a half million people joined diggers outside the hotel trying to save those trapped beneath rubble. We did this too, of course, but he not only jumped right in, he *jumped-right-in:* When a hole of any size was opened, he was the first to go in burrowing for life below. Time and again I'd hear a shout and, looking up, see only the bright pants of his ski suit leaping into a pile of smoking rock as if it were something soft.

Hours later, when we had a chance to sit down and eat some Red Cross sandwiches, I noticed that his borrowed shoes—a pair of white canvas sneakers— were blood red almost to their tops. I nudged Fanny and pointed at them. She nodded and said in a quiet, loving murmur, "He's been working the whole time with those cut-up feet. The man is my hero." Which summed it up perfectly.

He saw us looking at those poor feet and, grinning sheepishly, held one up for our inspection. "Next time I will wear some shoes to the earthquake, huh?"

"We were just saying how impressed we are by what you did today."

He shrugged and slowly unwrapped a piece of chewing gum I offered him.

"The only thing we can do is try to give life back some of the justice it loses sometimes. Is trying to save people's lives right? I don't know. All I *can* say is our intentions are good. I read about a man who said, 'God's memory is failing and that's why there are so many tragedies and terrible things like this today happening in life: God doesn't remember the justice or goodness He gave the world in the beginning. So it's Man's job to try and put it back.'" He put the gum in his mouth, but took it out again and pointed it at us. "I do not agree with this. It's a fool's line. But I liked the idea about putting justice back into life. It's like our lives are dolls that have gotten rips in them and have lost some of their . . ." He snapped his fingers, looking for the right word. ". . . their . . ."

"Stuffing?"

"Yes, 'stuffing.' God gave us these dolls in the beginning, but if they begin to lose their stuffing, *we* must find the right materials to fill them again. Is this Juicy Fruit? Aah! I like Juicy Fruit gum—it's so sweet."

"But we didn't make earthquakes! Auschwitz, okay, but what did man have to do with what happened today?"

"Now you're talking with a monkey's tongue, Fanny. Man is responsible for *everything*. Why do you think we control the planet? Why do all the other animals worship us? Everything in life is our work—Auschwitz, earthquakes. Good things too! We just do not want to recognize and accept the fact it is all our doing.

"Listen, I will tell you a funny story. A woman I know went into a restaurant here where you get the food yourself. She got her meal and put it down on the table but forgot to buy a drink, so she took some coins and left her tray to get one. When she returned, a very fat black man was sitting at her table eating her meal! Sitting there with a smile on his face, eating *her* food!

"Now she sits down very angry, pulls her tray back across the table and starts eating her food. But this crazy man will not stop. Still smiling, he reaches over and takes her soup. Then he takes the salad! She is driven so crazy by this, she must suddenly go to the bathroom badly.

"When she comes back from the bathroom thank God the man is gone, but so is her tray of food and handbag too! Now he's stolen her *money!* She runs to the cashier and says, 'Did you see the big black man go? He ate my lunch and stole my bag!' The cashier says, 'We'll call the police. Where were you sitting?' 'Right over there!' the woman responds. She turns around and points to her table. Only what she sees makes her scream: *One* table in front of where she was sitting with this bad black man is a tray full of food and her handbag on the seat."

"Huh?"

Hooting with laughter, Fanny turned to me and said, "The woman sat at the wrong table! She ate the *black* guy's lunch, not vice versa."

"And he let her! He was very friendly and smiled the whole time she was stealing his food.

"This woman acts like Mankind, Fanny: He always wants to blame himself on others. That's why there is a devil. We created him because he is convenient. And then sometimes when we really have no one else, we put the fault on God. But God is like this black man—He smiles at us when we eat His lunch, but doesn't stop us from doing it."

How Claire Stansfield could eat! Hard to believe looking at her in the hospital, barely able to take a straw in her swollen, ripped mouth.

Since this is my story, I get to digress one last time and bring in this last major cast member. It won't take long—I'll just tell about the first time we met, six months before the earthquake.

She was the friend of a friend who gave me her

number and said we'd like each other. Over the phone she sounded strong and calm. She had a high reedy voice; sometimes she lisped a word. It was Sunday afternoon. When I asked what she was doing, she said, "Only watching the rain on the window." Rainy days made her feel like a little girl again.

"How come? Listen, Claire, what are you doing? I mean right now? Would you like to go out?"

"Of course."

Of course! Not "Wellll, I don't know" or "Let me check my Filofax" or some other coy syrup you'd have to stir and stir until it dissolved into "all right." Of course. Superb.

We met at Café Bunny because rain was still blitzing down and the place was halfway between our apartments. We'd recognize each other because I'd been told she had a great head and looked like a Burne-Jones painting. As you can tell, I love women's heads. Fanny has a great one, even in an earthquake. Claire too. But she said if I missed her head, she was wearing a sweatshirt that said "Big Stuff" on it—the name of her design store. Before hanging up, she also said she was nervous about meeting Harry Radcliffe. I said I was nervous about meeting a great head.

"Hi, Harry? Will you think I'm awful if I order lunch right away? I haven't eaten all day." Hers *was* a great head but rather than being beautiful, what I liked most was she had a true face: square chin, long straight mouth, green eyes as direct and no-nonsense as a bridge.

We started off talking about our mutual friend, Claire's store, my buildings. She ordered Wiener schnitzel and a stein of beer. She cut giant golden pieces that looked like breaded continents. Despite chewing each one slowly, the whole thing was gone before I'd finished my coffee and cheesecake.

"I'm still hungry. What else should I eat?"

"Stay with the frieds—fried mushrooms?"

She ordered a plate of mushrooms, a large radicchio salad, another beer, a slice of chocolate cake heavy enough to sink a ship.

I wasn't feeling particularly sexy in those days right after my divorce, but watching Claire Stansfield eat, the question wandered my mind, if she was this voracious about food, what was she like in bed?

"What are you thinking about?" Her voice crept slowly out through the hive of bandages.

Holding her hand, I squeezed it gently. "About the first time we met—how much food you ate. I wondered if you'd be as good in bed as you were at the table."

"But I wouldn't let you touch me for a long time."

"That's right."

The room held the silence only a hospital room knows; the silence in waiting for things to return to normal, the silence of the body's betrayal versus secret hope.

"I was afraid you'd grow tired of me and my fears and leave." She shifted slightly under the covers, groaning once when turning her head toward me. "But you only sort-of left, didn't you, Harry? With Fanny."

"Let's not talk about it now."

"All right. Tell me more about the first day we met. I want to hear your side of it. Keep holding my hand too, please."

"You were wearing those big clunky shoes and

that black coat you bought in Budapest. You know how much I love women in clunky shoes."

Her hand was cool and dry in mine. Normally they were warm, often the slightest bit sweaty. She had only one hand now. What was left of the other lay hidden in a swirl of bandages and pain across the bed. When the earthquake came, Claire was riding her motorcycle down Sunset Boulevard and was thrown off, straight into the back of a truck. At the last moment she put up a hand to protect her face. It worked. But the hand caught on something.

"Harry, what do you think are the sexual fantasies of the blind?"

"Smells. Different kinds of touch. Didn't you ever make love blindfolded?"

"No. Is it exciting?"

"Funny. Strange. We'll do it some time." I wondered when we would make love again. How she would feel about doing it without the hand? *Without* the hand.

"Why'd you ask?"

"I was looking at your nose and thinking how big and nice it is. I wondered what it'd be like to know only through touch or if you could know something as completely with only touch *or* sight *or* smell. Now my right hand'll have to do all the touching for me."

"What are you going to do now, Harry? What's been going on? You never tell me anything, especially since I've been in here. Sometimes you're as slippery as a pack of new playing cards."

"I'm going to wait till you get out of here, for one thing."

"That'll be a while. And don't use me as an excuse not to be doing something."

I smiled like a fool caught. Talking to Claire was often like sliding my cold feet into a warm place. She was trusting but perceptive. I *had* been using her misfortune, in part, as a further excuse not to make a decision I'd been avoiding: The Sultan had asked me to come to Saru and at least look at the site where he wanted to build his dog museum—no strings attached. He'd pay a handsome fee but far more important, after our earthquake together, it was nigh onto impossible to say no.

So I told Claire the whole story for the first time. I'd not done it before because she'd had enough to suffer through and I couldn't imagine that hearing my tale of glorious escape was good for her in those first days without her left hand. As usual when I'd finished spouting, what she said surprised me.

"I was in Saru once."

"*What?* Why didn't you ever tell me?"

"I was saving it as a surprise. I stopped off there on my way to visit my sister Slammy in Jordan a couple of years ago."

"What's it like?"

"The cities are very modern. A lot of Palestinians fled there after the 1967 war with Israel and built them up. I stayed in Bazz'af, the capital. The rest of the country is desert."

"Buzz Off? The capital of Saru is really named 'Buzz Off'?"

She chuckled. "No, it's pronounced *bats-hof.* Sort of rhymes with *hats off.*

"You know what I liked most about it? There are these desert castles in Saru that date back to the Crusades and before. You take a bus a couple of hours out of Bazz'af and in the middle of nowhere are these

ruins that aren't so ruined because the dry desert air
has preserved them so well."

"Are you all right, Claire? You don't have to talk if
it makes you tired."

"I've been quiet for days and I like talking about
that trip. Let me tell some more. There's a major road
that runs literally across all of Europe through Turkey
and into the Middle East. Trucks start in Sweden or
Northern Germany and drive right across the whole
continent in just a few days. On Monday they're in
Rotterdam and by the end of the week they're on the
Saudi border! Isn't that romantic? It's like the old
pony express.

"Anyway, one of these castles was right off that
road, just before the Jordanian border. We were there
on New Year's Eve and decided to stay because part
of the place had been converted into a rest house.
Nothing ritzy, but some rooms to sleep in and a restaurant. Ours looked out onto the road about half a
mile away across the flat desert. We watched the sun
go down and those trailer trucks, barreling on toward
the border in big flying puffs of smoke and sand.
Where were they going? Jordan? Saudi Arabia? Iraq?
Every one of those countries was nearby. Someone at
the castle told us that when the Iran-Iraq war was on,
a truck a minute passed down the road carrying sup-
plies to Iraq. One a *minute*, Harry!

"About seven o'clock that night, we began to
smell these delicious waves of lamb grilling out behind the restaurant. Both my sister and I had our boy-
friends with us out there in the Saruvian *desert*. . . .
We felt so adventurous and sexy. The rest house was
comfortable, we'd seen some real wonders that day
. . . God, we were happy.

"Things smelled so good, we went right down to eat. There was no one else in the restaurant but us, but the interesting thing was this one big table over in the corner of the room. It was set for about twenty people, but set so that all the chairs and settings were on the same side of the table—no one would face anyone else. Odd, huh? But even odder was that at every place there was an unopened quart bottle of Johnnie Walker scotch. A whole bottle!"

"But Saru's Muslim. Where'd the booze come from?"

She gave my hand a small squeeze. "I'll tell you. Could I have another drink of water, please?"

I took the plastic bottle with the integrated straw off the bedside table and held it to her mouth. Her swollen, cut lips sucked hard. Pimps punish whores by slicing their lips with a knife because lips don't heal in a smooth line; mouths are ruined by the cut. Claire's mouth was ruined. She pulled her head back to signal she'd had enough water.

"The guy who ran the restaurant came over to our table to see if everything was okay. I asked about the bottles and he looked at his watch. 'The drivers will be here soon. Tonight they celebrate. The whiskey is theirs.'

"That's all he'd say, but fifteen minutes later, we heard the first truck coming. What a sound! Slammy went to the window and called us over. They were rendezvousing for their New Year's party out there in the middle of the desert!

"The four of us stood at the window letting our dinner get cold watching them pull into the big lot in front of the place. There were real Nordic blonds, redheads, Arabs wearing kaffiyehs and thick black moustaches. But you know what they all had in common, Harry? They were the fiercest-looking bunch of men I have ever seen in my life. No matter what they were wearing or what color they were, they all looked like gladiators."

"Wait a minute." I started up from my seat, undoing my hand from Claire's before she could say anything. I had to get out of the room as fast as I could. I was afraid I'd throw up. I was scared shitless.

"Harry, what's the matter?"

Her question raced me to the door.

Outside, a startled nurse glared accusingly as I ran for the drinking fountain down the hall. The water was so cold it stung my lips. I slurped it down as fast as I could. Then I put my hand in and smeared it across my face, neck, the back of my neck.

I was *there*. I climbed out of one of those trucks. I saw this woman looking at me out of a window and wondered if I'd get to fuck her that night. Why not? New Year's Eve everybody got loose.

We'd been on the road forty hours. There'd been trouble and delays the whole trip. We were running a half day late. I remembered everything: the acid stale smell of the cigarette the Bulgarian border guard was smoking as he looked over our papers; the ratcheting of bugs by the side of the road in Turkey when we stopped to piss; the warm sun on the back of my neck there after the cool in the truck.

I was this man. I remembered everything. His name was Heinrich Mis. I'd never seen him before in my life.

This . . . immersion happened once before with Venasque when the shaman was still alive. We were sitting in a diner in Silver Lake having breakfast when a man came in and sat down a few stools from us at the counter. Just a guy in overalls. Venasque and I were talking about something. When I looked up and saw the man, I . . . went away. Went away into his life and in an instant, knew everything that he was. Completely. His name was Randy. He was a union metal worker. He was a son of a bitch.

"Come. Come on. Come back!" Venasque, a hand on my arm, was calling me like he would a naughty puppy on the other side of the room. I looked at him flat stoned. He got me up and out of there and into the parking lot. Leaning on a white car. All the energy I had in the world was gone. When I came around, I looked at the old man. He was smiling.

"What the *fuck* was that?"

"Sometimes you meet up with your future, Harry. Usually it's a person, but sometimes it's a place or a thing. What you gotta do now is figure out where that guy fits into yours. It could be very important."

"But I *was* him, Venasque! I was him!"

"You are your future, Harry. It's in you every minute you're alive. You just saw part of it for the first time. Now figure out where that guy belongs in it."

But I didn't get a chance to do that because three days later Randy was dead: the first man ever killed on a Harry Radcliffe project. Fell off the top floor of the almost-completed Gröbchen Building in Pasadena.

Poor sweet Claire was very concerned when I returned to her room a few minutes later, looking ill. I said it must have been something I ate for lunch but she wasn't fooled.

"Don't lie, Harry. Is it because of how I look?"

"No, honey, I saw a lot worse in Vietnam. No, it

was . . . How much energy do you have? Tell the truth."

Her smile, what there was of it, calmed me. "It doesn't take energy to listen. Are you finally going to reveal one of the Radcliffe secrets?"

"Sort of. Remember what you were talking about before, that rest house in Saru? I have to tell you this. It's disturbing, but I must tell you."

Her good hand lay palm down at her side. She turned it over and wiggled the fingers. "Hold my hand and tell me. But I want to say something first: I talk to you all the time when you're not here. We have long conversations. I know you better than you think, Harry. We can have a happy ending if you want. I just don't know if you *want* happy endings. Artists are kids—they only want to eat junk food. Candy bars of muddle and unhappiness. They give you a charge, but only for a few minutes.

"I don't know if you love your silly confused life now or what. I haven't been able to figure that part out yet." She winked. "But I will—in our next conversation when you aren't here. Now, what were you going to say?"

"Do you love me?" I asked, trying to sound naughty and cute. But our eyes locked and her answer came out serious as religion.

"More than you know. More than you deserve."

"I *don't* know what I'm doing these days. You're right, but I can't imagine you and I undone."

"Well, then what about you and Fanny?"

"When I was a kid, my mother and I were walking down the street one day and saw two dogs screwing. They were really going at it. I knew what was up, but naturally asked Mom what they were doing, just to hear her answer. She said, 'The dog underneath is hurt. The one on top is pushing it to the hospital.' "

"What does that have to do with my question?"

" 'Cause I don't know whether you're asking or telling me: You want the truth, or an answer to that?"

Claire was silent. "I don't know. I keep wondering whether I love you for what you are, or what I think you could be with a little tinkering on my part. Maybe you're simply not a monogamous person anymore. I am. What do I do then? I don't want to hear that. Maybe you'll want Fanny and me both for the rest of your life. Would *she* put up with that?"

"I think so, yes."

"Not me. Let's change the subject. My heart's beginning to get a stomachache. Tell me what you were going to before. No wait a minute, there's one last thing. I just remembered it. 'The evil of another person can be averted: There is no escape from one's own.' Go on."

"What do you mean? How does that apply? Are you saying I'm evil?"

"No. Take out the word 'evil' and put in 'confusion.' But maybe there *is* some evil in there too." She closed her eyes.

🔜 Claire's reaction to my story about being at the Saru rest house with her was disconcerting, to say the least: She smiled and patted her good hand on the bed as if applauding, because she'd experienced the same precognition or voodoo empathy or whatever-youwanttocallit throughout her life!

"Doesn't it scare you?"

"It used to. Now it helps me see better. Like those

people who die and come back. The one thing they have in common is, afterwards, none of them is afraid to die anymore because they've experienced what's coming and it's wonderful. When I've traveled out and seen myself from different perspectives, it makes me less afraid. And makes me feel better about myself generally. Compared to most people, I'm better. More thoughtful, kinder . . . things like that.

"I'm glad you were there, that you know what it was like. I remember that truck driver. He was so young. I could tell he was interested because he kept looking at me. But he'd never have done anything— he was so shy and unsure of himself. He sat with the drivers and drank his scotch, then put his head down on the table and passed out! He was still there when we went up to bed."

🔖 Bananas are the only democratic food: Everyone looks ridiculous eating them.

Bronze Sydney, Big Top, Dr. Bill Rosenberg from next door, and I were all standing around the ruin of our Santa Barbara house, eating bananas. I'd peeled Big Top's for him.

"Bill, is that cologne you're wearing or an insult?"

"You're just pissed off because your house looks like a miniature golf course."

"We've got insurance."

Sydney looked at me surprised. "You're not going to rebuild, are you?"

"Naah. You don't want to live here anymore and neither do I."

Bill ate the rest of his banana and threw the peel into what was once my garden. "But your apartment in L.A.'s screwed up too. Where are you going to live?" He wiggled his eyebrows suggestively. "Are you two going to start living together again?"

As one, both Sydney and I said, "No!"

"Harry's going to the Mideast for a few weeks."

"I'll decide what to do when I get back. I may not take a place at all if I accept the job. It's a big project. They'll need me on-site for a while."

"What's the deal?"

I finished my banana and threw the peel after the other. "A dog museum in Saru."

Big Top wagged his tail slowly.

"A *dog* museum? You going to take the dog with you as technical advisor?" Bill snorted.

"Actually, he is going with me. They're going to make a statue of him for the front gates."

"How come?"

"Because he's a verz."

"That says a lot, Harry."

Sydney looked at me. "Are you really going to take him?"

"Absolutely. He's already had the necessary shots."

"Who wants a dog museum in Saru? Isn't that where they're having all that trouble with the Muslim fundamentalists? There was a thing on TV the other night. I'd steer clear of *that* Casbah, Harry. Unless you want a rhino-horn scimitar up your ass." Adventurous Bill took another banana from the bunch Sydney was holding and unpeeled it. We watched with interest.

It was going to be another beautiful day in Santa Barbara. The only thing marring it was the landscape immediately in front of us: the ex–Radcliffe homestead, which looked like ground zero after a slight nuclear attack.

Rosenberg called immediately after the earthquake to tell us there wasn't much left of our house. This was the first time we'd been able to come up and survey the damage. Yet it wasn't damage so much as total destruction and disappearance. In fact, I was shocked more by what wasn't there than what was. Okay, sure, the earth opened its big mouth and swallowed up this and that, crunched other things in its teeth down to nothing. I could accept those rationalizations, but almost nothing was left on the sight of what had once been a large and detailed house. Not that Harry Radcliffe designs were all meant to survive the full volume of God's wrath, but this whole motherfucker was gone!

"It's like a flying saucer came, vacuumed it up, and took it back to Saturn."

"How do you feel, Harry?"

I looked at Sydney and squinted because the morning sun was directly over her shoulder. "Raped. It was a beautiful house. Fit perfectly on this hill and added nice human color to the landscape. I feel raped." I wanted to say something more but my voice lost all of its appetite to talk.

"Why do you think my house wasn't touched, Syd?"

"Luck of the draw, Bill."

I grabbed Sydney's arm and pulled her close, like a lifesaver on the vast sea that was suddenly roiling all around me. "They're the only real I know, Syd. The only ones I knew how to do well."

She nodded. Kept nodding.

"What do I do when they disappear like this?"

"You can build it again, Harry."

"But it's not the same! It's like cloning someone from one of their hairs. We can use the old plans, sure, build it exactly the same. But it's *not* the same! This one's dead. It's gone. Put up a stone over it."

I started down the hill to the car. At the point where the ocean shows again after a thick stand of pine trees that perfume the dry California air with crisp northern smells, I turned and shouted back, "You know what the difference between tragedy and comedy is? Tragedy keeps reminding us how limited life is. Comedy says there are no limits."

"Put on the Sex Pistols."

I turned around and scowled back at her on the bed, naked, leering at me. She had on a black baseball cap with the word "Fritos" in yellow across the front. She tipped it at me.

"Fanny, my idea of good sex is not fucking to a Sex Pistols album."

"No, *you'd* fuck to *Hotel California* if I gave you the chance."

"Those are Bronze Sydney's albums."

"Which you've kept." She accused.

"Why do we have a fight about this every time we go to bed?"

"Because we like music when we do it but hate each other's taste."

"That's true." I took out a Simply Red album and put it on the turntable. When it came on, it hissed and sputtered terribly. "How come all my albums lisp?"

"Because you don't take care of them. I keep telling you to buy a CD machine."

I walked back to the bed, sat down on the end, and took her right foot in my hand. "CD machines and microwave ovens are too late twentieth century for me. I still need a record player where you load records on the spindle and they drop down on top of each other."

"How come you're such a jazzy architect but conservative about things like that?"

I started massaging her foot. "I'm not conservative. I simply believe soup should be heated on a flame and not shot full of radiation. Records should be black and full of scratches. You go to the record store and ask the guy for a diamond needle." I put down her foot and picked up the other. She rubbed the free one up my back.

"How come you've been such a pain in the ass lately?"

The massage stopped. I didn't turn around. "How have I been such a pain in the ass lately?"

"Look at me. You survived the earthquake, you're going to crazy Saru for one of the great projects of your career, women love you—"

"Ah ha, is *that* what we're talking about, Fan? All these women who love me? Is that why I'm such a pain in the ass? I just had this same damn conversation with Claire."

"Well I'm not Claire! She's the tall one, remember?" She whipped off the hat and threw it at me. It hit my chin.

I reached down to the floor for my pants. "She wanted to know what's going on between you and me. She has that right."

"And do I have that right? What *is* going on between you and me?"

"You have a really original way of getting on my nerves, Fanny: accuse and cringe. Point a stiff finger and then whine. Sometimes you have the backbone of a stick of butter.

"Yes, you have the right to know what's going on between us. I've always told you. But now it sounds like you want a life commitment, and *that* you can't have."

"I didn't say that. I wouldn't want to live with you, Harry. Your car only has room for one person."

"I didn't *ask* you to live with me. Where's my fucking shirt? You know something? Life just dries up sometimes. Dries up and turns into a brown withered pod."

She grabbed my hair from behind but I wouldn't turn. Seeing that, she came around and squatted in front of me.

"You're so full of shit, Harry. Your life didn't 'dry up.' If anything, you *grew* up a little and saw that what you were doing was a bunch of baloney.

"You designed all those exquisite buildings, ignoring the fact, beyond some calculations for space, that real live human beings lived inside them! That's why you went nuts—for once you clicked out of the Ptolemaic universe of Harry Radcliffe and realized there were some brighter, more important suns than even you. Know what a couple of those suns are? Responsibility and love. That's right!

"I'll tell you what's making you so nervous these days: You've got the love of two damned good women but you don't know what to do with us. You can't just draw us as a couple of lines and make some estimates. Love is hard work! It breaks your bones. Stop getting dressed. I'm talking to you!"

"Keep talking, Fanny. I'm sure the walls would love to hear your next soliliquy. Come on, dog. Time for a walk."

➤ The Spider Club meets every Wednesday for dinner at Rachel's Restaurant in Santa Monica. Club membership varies between ten and twenty people depending on who's in town, who's feuding with whom, who's still alive. The only requirement is invitation by another club member who's willing to vouch for the fact you can tell a good story. Over the years there've been celebrities at the "conclaves," but stars don't like sharing a stage so they've had a hard time listening to the others. And generally, it is those others who tell the better stories.

My last night in America was also Claire's first out of the hospital. She insisted we go to the Spider Club meeting, which was a real surprise because she'd only been one other time. But when it was her turn, she'd told a long, very eerie story about the funeral of a close friend some years before.

We were late getting there because she moved slowly and I didn't want her going over any unnecessary bumps. When we walked into the restaurant, the whole club table stood up and gave her a loud round of applause. She sat down next to Wyatt Leonard, alias Finky Linky, infamous kid's TV show hero. I liked Wyatt, but thought his "Finky Linky Show" one of the most overrated programs I'd ever seen. Unlike everyone else, I didn't cry when it went off the air.

When he was in town, Finky was the unofficial president of the club because he'd originally thought it up. After everyone had disgustingly stuffed their faces full of Rachel's Chinese/Hebrew cuisine, he stood up and tapped his glass for silence.

"Fellow Spiders, there are three things tonight that give me immense pleasure—seeing you all again and knowing you've survived the earthquake, eating Rachel's food, and hearing that Harry Radcliffe is leaving town for an indefinite period. Just joking, Harry.

"I'm also glad to see that Claire Stansfield is here and has asked to be the first up. Ready, Claire?"

"When I was a girl, I knew only two things for sure: Love was pinkish yellow, and Romaric Jupien was the handsomest boy in the world. I grew up in Winnipeg. Winters there are so cold that the water on the lake freezes in perfect waves. Policemen wear buffalo-skin coats, and the place looks like a town of bandits because so many people go around wearing full face masks to keep the cold off.

"We lived next door to a French family named Jupien who had three children: twin girls, Ninon and Prisca, and a boy, Romaric. He hated his name because he wanted to be as American as possible, so he expected you to call him Mark.

"When this happened, I was eight and he was thirteen. I was at that age where you're discovering love is not just your father's lap or Mom's pulling your jacket tighter before you go out. This love was eight years of innocence and energy and desire that's finally decided to step out of the family and go looking for new ground. It just happened a marvelous older boy lived next door who didn't have the slightest idea I existed, which made it all the more torturous and necessary.

"I watched him from behind curtains, standing in our driveway holding the hose for my father while he washed the car, and like a secret agent of the heart, sitting in Mark's own living room while he watched television and I pretended to play with his sisters. I was so much in love that every time he was out of my sight I forgot what he looked like.

"I was crazy for the Greek myths then and had read them many times. My secret name for Mark was Achilles because he was my Achilles' heel. I was a tomboy, but when it came to him, there was no fist in my glove: I would've gladly put on a dress and given a tea party if it would have pleased him. A thing I remember so well was writing 'Achilles' heel' on my school notebook twenty times in different scripts and colors. I came in from recess one day and found someone had added the letter W in front of every one of them so they all read 'Achilles' Wheel.' I honestly think I would've killed the person if I knew who'd done it. It was as if they'd put that W on Mark's face.

"The strangest thing about my obsession was it seemed every time I looked at him, I saw this pinkish yellow aura emanating from his whole body. He was very masculine and I'm sure if I'd told him he would've had my head, but I couldn't help it—if there was Mark, there was the aura.

"My mother loved doing things with the family. She also liked the Jupiens, both because they were nice people and because they were French, which gave them an exotic twist. So we often had cookouts together or went swimming in the summer. . . . All of which was fine by me as long as Mark came.

"It's so cold in Winnipeg in the dead of winter that it often doesn't snow much, but one January we had a real Manitoba blizzard that stopped the whole town in its tracks. There was nothing anyone could do but

wait for it to end or have snowball fights. My mother
decided we should go tobogganing and sent me over
to the Jupiens to ask if they wanted to go. I walked
across the front yards as slowly as I could, for what if
I fell down and he happened to be looking out the
window at that very moment? And if he wasn't at the
window, what if he opened the door and saw me covered with snow? You have to walk carefully in the
beginning of love. The running across fields into your
lover's arms can only come later when you're sure
they won't laugh if you trip.

"I didn't fall on the way over, which was just as
well because Mark opened the door. And he was
smiling! I thought, 'Oh God, Oh God, it's for me. He's
smiling because it's me.' But as I was about to say
something, I saw he had a comic book in his hand and
obviously wanted to get back to it.

" 'Hi, Claire. Waddya want?'

"His mother called from somewhere asking who it
was and he said three words that almost cut me in
half 'It's only Claire, Ma.'

"Luckily Mrs. Jupien came bustling to the door
and pulled me into the house. She said something in
French to Mark that sounded like a scolding, which
only made things worse. What saved my visit from
total catastrophe was that he stayed there and didn't
leave. He'd probably been cooped up inside the house
all day and was glad in his own way to see someone
new, even if it was 'only Claire.'

"In a blurt I said my mother wanted to know if
they'd like to go tobogganing with us. The two girls
came downstairs and instantly took to the idea. So
did Mrs. Jupien, but Mark rolled his eyes as if tobo-
ganning was the dumbest idea he'd heard. I wanted

to protest and say it wasn't *my* idea, but by then his mother was ordering them all around, saying bundle up and where's the sled and Mark go tell your father we're going. With a big fake yawn he turned and went off to find Mr. Jupien while I stood there feeling love and failure in equal amounts.

"Outside the snow was still coming down. Part of me wanted to crawl down into it and hibernate until I was older and beautiful and he would have to love me. The other part was excited—like it or not, he was going with us and I would get to be around him for the next few hours, no matter what happened.

"Running back to our house, I kept wondering what I could do to impress him once we got there. Should I show off and try something dangerous? Be adoring and impressed when he did anything? I wanted to be older. I knew when you were older you'd understand how to act around people you loved. The boys I knew who loved me at school did things like punch me in the arm or call me names because they didn't know anything else to do. But I was smart enough to know there was more to it than that. What *was* it though? How did you show a person you loved them without looking stupid? How did you do it so well that they started to love you back?

"Half an hour later our two families met out on the street and started walking to the sledding hill. It was only midafternoon but already getting dark and the snow somehow made things darker. It was nice but too much, you walked with your head down and your face tight.

"I walked with Prisca and Ninon, who bubbled on about things and people we knew. Mark walked with 'the men' in front and our mothers a few steps behind them. Everyone was loud and there was a lot of laughter. My father told Mr. Jupien a story about a storm he'd once experienced. I'd heard the story many times because it was a favorite of mine, but listening now, it sounded so long and boring and I was embarrassed.

"Normally the walk to the hill took about ten minutes, but the snow and their leisurely pace kept us at it for a half hour. When we got there, I couldn't stand it anymore and strode ahead for the hill with our toboggan. Why not? Everything else had gone wrong. Even more than Mark, all I wanted then was some speed around me and wind splitting across my face and that great safe fear in the heart that's there when you're doing something like sledding or jumping off the high board into a swimming pool.

"The new snow was light and slippery under my feet and I slipped twice as I began to climb. But by then I almost didn't care because he never liked me and never *would* like me and to him I was 'only Claire' anyway, so what difference did it make if I looked dumb climbing a hill? I just wanted to get away from them and him and be by myself in the wind and snow and falling dark. Maybe if I was lucky something magical would happen—I'd sled off into that dark and never be seen again. Everyone would be broken-hearted and they'd have to bury an empty coffin. Mark would stand by my grave and weep. . . .

" 'Claire, wait! Wait up!'

"I heard his voice, but couldn't believe he was calling me. So in the first mature move of my life, I kept walking and didn't turn around.

" 'Claire! Willya wait up!'

"I heard him coming and stopped where I was, out of breath and my heart pounding like a gong.

" 'Jeez, didn't you hear me calling? Come on, let's go down together.'

"How the hell I ever managed to climb the rest of the way to the top of that hill I don't know. I got up there a little after Mark but that was because I was still pulling the toboggan. He might've wanted to go down with me, but he hadn't offered to pull.

"There were a few other people on the hill. Down below we could see our families working their way slowly up and having a good laugh when one of them fell down.

"Mark and I stood there for a few moments watching them come. Then he turned to me and said, 'You know that girl Alayne in the seventh grade? Long blond hair?'

"I didn't know Alayne, but was smart enough to know he was telling me a kind-of secret: that he was interested in the girl and wanted to know more about her without showing his hand. I also knew his interest didn't help *my* cause any. But he'd not only recognized me for really the first time. He'd also taken me into his confidence in a way, and I was thrilled.

"I told him I could ask around if he wanted, but he said no, that was okay.

"Almost as if it had been cued, the snow suddenly stopped. Ding—just like that. Both of us looked around, as if it were somewhere else. But no, it really had stopped.

"Because there was nothing else to do, I put the toboggan down and asked if he was ready to go.

" 'Sure. I'll get on behind you.'

"I sat down and then felt Mark Jupien's arms and

legs around me. I died and went to heaven. What did I care about Alayne? She wasn't here now, *I* was, and that was enough. Mark gave a push and off we went.

"That hill, if you went a certain route, was very long and bumpy. We'd gone down it hundreds of times and knew it well, but once in a while if you weren't paying attention or were being silly, you'd hit something and fly off. There was even one of those apocryphal stories we'd all heard again and again each winter, about the boy who, years ago, fell off and cracked his skull open on a rock. Nobody paid much attention to that, but at the same time you were usually careful when you went down this hill.

"I can remember everything about the ride. I could probably tell you where every bump we went over was situated. About halfway through the ride, Mark started singing 'Somewhere Over the Rainbow' very loudly, and even though I didn't know many of the words, I sang along with him.

"Voom! we soared. Past our families, past trees full of snow, dogs jumping around, kids trying to make a snowman . . . I remember everything.

"We curved and twisted and then . . . BANG!

"Whatever it was we hit must have been sizable because one minute we were singing and the next flying through the air.

"Until we hit.

"God, how we hit! I came down on my bottom and although I was full of padding down there, I must've landed smack on my spine because for a time I was utterly paralyzed with pain. So much pain I couldn't breathe.

"When I began to come around again, I kept hearing Mark ask, 'Are you okay? Claire, are you okay?'

"I wanted to nod and tell him I was, but it hurt too much to do anything but lie there and feel it stabbing through my whole body. I couldn't even open my eyes.

"Claire, are you okay? Claire? Huh?

"Finally, finally I got some of my breath back and felt I would live. I opened my eyes to tell him okay.

"But when I looked up, Mark Jupien was hovering over me, more beautiful than ever, absolutely surrounded by brilliant, shimmering, angelic light.

"At first I thought I'd gotten knocked out and was a little cuckoo. When his 'lights' didn't go away, I thought, It's his aura. Even here, he glows! Wrong again. Seen more clearly, there was no yellowish pink here, his normal colors. These were all blues and reds and silvers moving across the whole sky behind him like some great cosmic light show.

"Was I going crazy? Was Mark Jupien a saint? Or God? Was *this* how God came to men on earth? Was *that* why I'd always been able to see an aura around him? I was so in love and in so much pain. . . .

"Only when some of both started to subside did I realize that what I was seeing behind him were the northern lights doing their frantic magical dance across the sky. Something we were rather used to, living so far north.

"But if you have never seen them, the only way I can describe them to you is to say, Imagine what I *thought* those lights were when I opened my eyes and saw them for the first time that day. When I woke from my shock of pain, and for a moment looked up into the face of the boy I adored. I lived a miracle of possibility then that has lifted and will reassure me for the rest of my life."

PART TWO

"The Very Talented Back of My Head"

"As yet the new city seemed forbidden to me,
and the strange unpersuadable landscape darkened as though
I didn't exist. Even the nearest Things
didn't care whether I understood them."

RAINER MARIA RILKE,
"The Vast Night"

I WAS DANCING with the cleaning woman when the doorbell rang.

"I'll get it, Harry. You look like heart-attack city."

Frances Place moved across my living room floor like a panther on ball bearings. She didn't walk so much as glide, and when she glided, you didn't seem to see any moving parts—she just was here and then she was there and you had to think about how she did it.

Like Lucia, the beautiful parking attendant at the Westwood Muse Hotel, Frances came to Hollywood to become famous but ended up cleaning apartments to tide her over between jobs as a dancer. She was only a so-so cleaner, but in the months she'd worked for me, she'd taught me dances like The Razorblade and The Horse's Neck, which I thought was fair trade for some dust mice under the bed or mysterious crust

on a kitchen shelf. Both Fanny and Claire were convinced Frances and I were doing the horizontal
rhumba as well as our other dances, but they were
wrong. I think I vaguely feared what it'd be like to go
to bed with her, judging from the way she moved
both on and off the dance floor; I'd already been
screwed by one earthquake.

"Oh hello, Frances. Is Harry here?"

"Hi, Fanny. Nice haircut. Yes, he's in the living
room."

Fanny came staggering in with a Tin-Tin haircut
and a suitcase as big as her.

"Jesus, Harry, what've you been doing? You look
completely fucked out." She shot a lethal look at
Frances.

"Hiya, Tin-Tin. We've been dancing. Frances was
showing me how to do The Funky Chicken."

"I'll bet. Are you packed? We've got to be at the
airport in two hours."

I pointed to the corner where my little black bag
stood alert and ready to go.

"What's in there, three bottles of cologne? Are you
planning on buying all new clothes in Saru?"

"Fanny, there are two essential differences between men and women: Most women would rather
shop than fuck, and women always pack everything,
no matter how long the trip or where they're going."

"That's the most obnoxious thing I've heard all
week."

Frances did a slow, deep knee bend. "Sometimes
I'd rather shop than fuck."

"See! Now look at the size of your suitcase, Fanny.
I rest my case."

"Harry, first we're going to Austria, where it's

cold. Then to Saru, where it's hot. Doesn't it make sense to take some clothes?"

"Yes, but all *my* clothes are freeze-dried. They fit into small envelopes. When I need them, I put a drop of water on them and they open up.

"I'm taking a shower, then we can go."

Big Top was lying on the floor in the bathroom, one of his normal stations. I always assumed it was because he liked the feeling of cold tiles on his stomach. He was also the only animal I'd ever known who liked to bathe. Depending on his mood, he would often walk into the shower with you, then stand with his eyes closed and not move while the water soaked him.

"Is *your* bag packed, dog?" I turned on the water and stood looking at the spray, thinking about something Claire had once said after making love. I'd asked her what it'd been like. Without a second's pause she said, "Like a waterfall at night."

"What the hell am I doing, Big Top? Thinking about how sweet she is, but I'm about to fly off with Fanny to Cuckooville. Does any of this make sense to you?"

His tail thumped on the floor but the eyes stayed closed. I took off my clothes looking at a crack on the wall the earthquake had made. "Why do we always want to be someplace else? Venasque used to say that. And where is *he*, now that I need him? Being dead is no excuse.

"You know what I'd tell Venasque if he were around? Hey, I just realized this! I'd tell him I don't want to design buildings anymore because I can't see any people in them. I see these big beautiful buildings but not one person inside. Like San Francisco in *On the Beach*, or an abandoned movie set." The realization so excited me that I flung a towel around my middle and, leaving the shower on, went back to the living room.

Music was blasting. Fanny and Frances were standing next to each other, doing a dance step to Frances's lead.

"Fanny, I just had an epiphany in the bathroom!"

"I hope you have Kaopectate for it."

"No, seriously."

"Wait a minute, willya, Harry? Frances is showing me something."

Besides the step, both of them were smoking and had cigarettes stuck in the same corner of their mouths. Nicotine choreography.

"The hell with you both. My epiphany is more important than The Stroll." I turned around and headed back to the shower.

"Harrrry . . ."

"Forget it!"

I was hurt by her indifference. This was something important, although I could only catch the first vague scent of it in the immediate air.

Architecture is either creating space, or whittling it down: The glass is half-empty or half-full. In my heyday I liked to think we were creating new space, consequently better and more fulfilling ways by which one could both experience and view life. But I'd recently read somewhere, "Perhaps in all cities the past so overbalances the present that they are more dead than alive; certainly the ones which inspire pilgrimages and far-fetched love are the deadest, where one goes for the remains not the activity." This led me to think architecture has always been the death of space—like big-game hunting, we kill it and then mount its massive head looking permanently startled and glassy-eyed on our wall.

"Hey, Big Top! Look out, huh?"

All these deep thoughts kept me from seeing the dog, sitting stolidly in the middle of the shower stall. Stumbling over him, I snatched the soap off its metal perch and went to work on my last United States wash.

Halfway through washing my hair I saw the building. Hands on my head and a foot against the dog, I opened my eyes and saw, as if projected against the shower door, what looked at first like a cross between a steel birthday cake and an old-time railroad steam engine standing on its nose. My first thought was, Fanny's pulling another prank. Once, when I was taking a shower, she'd scared the shit out of me by attacking me à la *Psycho* with a rubber knife. But this wasn't that. This was a three-foot-high projection of a building on the inside of a wet, translucent glass door. Only water, steam, the dog, and I were inside, so how the thing even *got* there I didn't know. Baffled but fascinated, I reached out and tried to touch it. Nothing to touch. Only a picture as distinct and three-dimensional as a hologram and looking like a building by Takamatsu. All I could think of was a lavish, eccentric cathedral to some steel-cold deity: a nightmare prayer to God as inscrutable machine.

Big Top started to bark. He stood there yakking away at the thing like he'd gone mad.

"Harry, what're you doing? Why's the dog in there?"

I saw someone on the other side of the door and

just as Fanny pulled the door open, the picture disappeared.

"What's going on?"

"Fanny, go to my library and get down the book about Takamatsu!"

"Why—"

"Just get me the fucking book!"

I leapt out of the shower and dried off in two seconds. Big Top got a quick rub with the same towel. I left him there three-quarters damp, wagging his tail.

Frances was vacuuming the couch and gave me only a glance as I scooted by her in a pair of rumpled pants and nothing else.

Fanny was standing with her back to the door, hands on hips, looking at the shelves of books in the room I used as a study.

"You've got every Japanese architect here but naturally I can't find him."

"Right here." I took the book down and opened to his ingenious Ark Dental Clinic in Nishina, Japan. Shin Takamatsu is the only real star of what I've always called Robot Love architecture. Buildings for a time in the future when machines have long ruled and Mankind's around only to oil their wheels, stand in awe, and feel pointless. Everything Takamatsu designs, wrote one critic, is 'unbelievably heavy, forbidding, frightening, but sculpturally brilliant, a sort of locomotive architecture with nuts and bolts and steel plates, great circles and huge diagonals.'

What I'd seen in the shower was something I was sure he'd created. Only now, looking at photographs and drawings of his work, did I realize there were other things about the building Takamatsu's work didn't have. Humor, for one. Simply put, there was something innately *funny* about the building on the shower door. As if whoever drew it was telling the kind of joke that didn't make you smile until ten minutes later—when you howled.

"What's going on, Harry?"

"I think Venasque's trying to tell me something." I had my eyes closed. When I opened them again, Big Top was coming into the room, his tail still wagging.

〰 "What's the word in Saru for airport?"

"I don't know. Aeroporto?"

We'd been met at my place by a smiling chauffeur driving a limo that looked like it belonged in a cartoon. Judging from the outside, I wouldn't have been at all surprised if there'd been a small swimming pool inside.

For some peculiar reason, many people today think riding in a limousine is just this side of nirvana. But I have never ridden in one without being acutely embarrassed. People look in (or try to look in through those smoked windows) with expressions of hope or disgust. Mostly disgust. But those who are interested gape until you emerge and they see you're only another Nobody with some money to waste. Ho Hum.

Anyway, this prairie schooner had the requisite telephone, television, bar . . . and it made me feel like throwing up. Plus the chauffeur spoke no English and looked like a terrorist on speed.

"Does this man know where he's going?"

"I'm not sure. You can take La Cienega to the airport but it's the long way."

"Maybe he wants us to enjoy the ride."

"I feel like a black record producer in this car."

"Harry, now you're a racist?"

"I'm not a racist—I'm a 'tastist': Anyone who thinks these cars are classy have living rooms full of crushed velvet furniture." I got out a pad of paper and pen from my briefcase and pulled down one of the nifty little tables big enough to hold a martini glass. I went to work sketching from memory the building I'd seen in the shower. Fanny took out a Walkman and plugged herself in.

As I worked, the building became clearer and clearer in my mind. I had no doubt Venasque had had something to do with its appearance. Before he died he'd made a number of allusions to the fact he would be gone soon but would leave Big Top behind to keep an eye on things till I was really ready to go again. That is why I wasn't surprised on the day of the earthquake to see the dog in the hotel. And why I was more delighted than surprised to see this building an hour ago.

"Magic is just what you don't know, Harry," Venasque would say. "More often than not, it's God bored trying to tell us something and using other means.

"So don't jump back when it happens, or is given to you. There's a reason, a specific reason for it when it does. But people are usually so shocked by it that they either run away screaming, or think there are wires attached—someone somewhere's tricking them. Wrong, Harry—it's a gift. Unless you're a jerk, you don't ask why a gift's given or what it cost—you appreciate and use it."

"Hey, hallo?"

I looked up from my drawing and saw the chauffeur's smile in the rearview mirror. He was holding something in his hand, offering it to me.

"Saru! Saru!"

It was a heavy coffee-table book that he could barely support with one hand. I took it and smiled my thanks to him.

Fanny unplugged one ear and said much too loud (the disease of the Walkman listener) "WHAT'S THAT?"

"A book on Saru."

"Let me see it when you're done." She put the earphone back in.

I am obnoxious, but sometimes Fanny outdid me in that department, if only by the way she phrased things or the timbre of her voice. There was almost never a "Please" or "May I?". It all came out sounding like a cop telling you to pull over. We'd talked about it before, but she had the additional bad habit of getting aggressively defensive about things when she realized she was wrong. I wasn't on her side that day anyway because of her indifference to my epiphany, so that infuriating tone of voice encouraged me to throw the book out the window rather than hand it over.

I took a deep breath, opened to the first page. And started smiling right away because there, in the daft, hilariously bad English of a hack translated by an even worse translator, was the standard orgasmic introduction to a book of this sort.

"Saru has launched itself into the late twentieth century with a speed that touches on transgression. It has always been a maverick amongst its Middle East brethren states, but since the midseventies, when the Sultan launched his first Six-Year Plan, there has been no stopping this country from taking distinct advantage of its glorious natural resources, oil and natural gas, and using them to place itself even further on top of the world map."

That oatmeal went on for twenty painful pages, but I read it all, in between glances out the window to see if we really were going toward the airport and not Disneyland.

The contrast between the Los Angeles out my window and the photographs in the book was appalling. Like the other Arab countries I'd visited, the real Saru appeared to be a beautiful sand land full of emptiness and unearthly quiet: a place for religious zealots who had their choice of deserts to disappear into to find God; a country where people built fires three thousand years ago and you could stand on a windy mountain and see camel caravans or black bedouin tents off in the distance. It reminded me of driving across Jordan and seeing, a hundred miles from Amman and then again deep in the sand hills of Wadi Rum, men standing motionlessly by the side of the road, doing nothing. Looking serene as dead saints, they didn't appear to be going or coming from anywhere. Just *there*, maybe for all time. It struck me as both spooky and marvelous; it hinted that if I only knew a little of how things worked here, I'd discover some new and very important facts of life. There was none of the fatal despair or angry madness on their faces that is seen on the motionless ones dying slowly on the street corners in Los Angeles or other American cities.

Unfortunately the book also had too many pictures of the graceless, ultramodern buildings that didn't fit into the natural landscape at all but had been thrown up presto chango as soon as the bottom-less pits of oil had been discovered in Saru forty years before.

For example, one Sultan had had vague socialist leanings, so someone in his cabinet had commissioned Felix Förcher, Walter Ulbricht's favorite architect, to build a university complex that looked as if it belonged in the middle of Volvograd rather than a desert. What made me even angrier, looking at the other shameless abortions in the book (by some pretty damned famous people!), was that I knew exactly what a number of these architects had done: either pulled something out of a drawer that'd been around for years because no one wanted to build it, or rubbed their hands together thinking, Oh boy, now I get to try out every wacky notion I've ever dreamed of because no matter what I come up with, they'll build it and pay me a fortune. Screw the needs of people, the geography of the site, the demands the building would have to fulfill over the years. Wotton, rewriting Vitruvius, said "Well-building hath three conditions: Commodity, Firmness, and Delight." What cynics or scoundrels like Förcher had done in places like Saru was delight their bank accounts, or whims, and fucked the rest with no further ado.

Closing the book on a finger, I swore to myself that whatever I designed for this Sultan of Saru, it would incorporate everything I could find out about his country, the people, the culture. Sure, it would have Radcliffe's signature on it, but unlike other work I'd done, that signature would be very small and at the bottom of the picture. In fact, one might even need a magnifying glass to find it. I thought about those mysterious men on the desert road. Make something for them. Make something they could stand in forever and be content.

📌 The flight to Vienna was funny and uneventful. Big Top had to be pushed into his cage/prison by three handlers who were not a bit happy about the fact he farted continually while they pushed. Ah, stinky revenge.

From Vienna the Sultan wanted us to fly in his private jet to Salzburg and then drive on to Zell am See, but both Fanny and I agreed we'd rather spend a couple of nights in Vienna and take the train to his mountain town.

Fanny didn't know it, but there was another reason why I wanted to stop off there. The man who had been with Venasque when he died, Walker Easterling, lived in Vienna, and I wanted to talk to him about the old man's last day. Easterling had called me from the Santa Barbara hospital to say Venasque had had a stroke and was in a coma. But when Sydney and I got there in the middle of the night, I was much too upset to have any kind of logical, calm discussion about details.

📌 If you've never been to a place, you naturally create an image beforehand of what it will be like. Although my images have rarely been correct, I am always slightly resentful of how "off" I am in my conjuring, i.e., Radcliffe's Vienna was going to be a "Guidebook City"; a combination of living museum and quaint wine gardens.

There are "Guidebook Cities" and there are "Living Cities." You can visit a "Living City" with nothing more than your wallet and a map, but after a few days of walking, eating, and sleeping there you begin to "get it"; to feel and understand its idiosyncrasies and greatness without guides or tours or visits to the place's famous spots: London, Venice, Athens.

"Guidebook Cities" are stern and demanding—no slackers allowed. To know this town you *must* experience certain things: walk this street, smell this garden, visit this cathedral (page 82 in your books). See the Michelangelo, Mozart's house, Napoleon's sword. Words like "essential," "extravagant," and "tragic" are commonplace. There will be a final examination before you're permitted to leave. Any questions?

The first Viennese surprise was passing through customs and seeing who was there to meet us: our smiling chauffeur from Los Angeles. Was it déjà vu or did he have a twin brother?

He took our baggage, struggled it out onto the street and while setting it down, gestured for us to stay put while he went for the car. After a particularly big smile, he raced off for the parking lot a few hundred feet away.

"Do you think they make those guys en masse in Saru?"

Fanny was sniffing the air like a setter. "What does it smell like here? I can't figure it out."

The weather was clear blue, sunny and cool. An airplane rumbled through its takeoff above us.

"It smells like grass. It smells like lawns."

"That's right! How strange. When was the last time you were in an airport that smelled green?"

The ride into town was along your typical airport-to-city freeway, but the difference was the road was flanked on both sides by more greenery and after a certain point, the Danube Canal. You sensed how far east you were when road signs said Prague and Budapest.

When we turned onto the Ringstrasse, passing Fabiani's Urania Theatre, the city opened up like a beautiful gray fan.

"It's so clean!"

"Look at those horse-drawn carriages."

"Oh Harry, there's the Opera House!"

The chauffeur was kind enough to take us on a short sight-seeing tour before dropping us at the hotel. Not that we could understand a word he was saying, but he pointed in all the right directions and we were able to get a good first glimpse of Freud's home.

Vienna had the clean, orderly, tight-assed feel of a Communist city with Western frills: stores full of goodies, every other car a Mercedes, well-dressed women. . . . A town where people were suspicious and kept secrets. How did I know all this in half an hour? I didn't, but walking around the place that night with Fanny told me things. The center of town was empty and quiet after nine o'clock. Even the drunks kept their voices down, but looking for an open bar to have a drink was tough. When we found one, the people inside were frantic with good cheer, as if they needed to store it up before going out again into those solemn streets.

I've often had interesting experiences in new cities my first day there, and Vienna was no exception. On an L.A. friend's suggestion, we hunted down a Hungarian restaurant that was supposed to be atmospheric and serve perfect goulash.

The restaurant turned out to be a tiny hole-in-the-wall with eight tables and a two-hundred-pound waitress who looked like The Fabulous Moolah's tag-team partner. We sat down and ordered the strangest-sounding things on the menu. I noticed when we walked in that the restaurant closed at ten, and since we arrived at nine-thirty, there were only a few people left. One of them was a shabby-looking old man who ate slowly while reading a newspaper in Cyrillic. By the time our food arrived, the three of us were the only customers left.

On finishing the old man signaled to the waitress for what I thought was the check. Instead she walked to a sideboard and, opening a drawer, took out a thick handful of passports. When she put them down in front of him, I looked as closely as possible without being too obvious and saw as he shuffled through them that they were all from Communist countries. Rumania, Bulgaria, Hungary. I kicked Fanny under the table and gestured for her to check it out.

The man took a large yellow fountain pen from his pocket and began to write a long time in each of them. *What*, I don't know, but I sure don't like the idea of anyone writing in my passport, particularly if I own one from a part of the world infamous for issuing passports about as frequently as hens lay golden eggs.

When he was done, he gave the pile back to the woman, who quickly put them back into the drawer. He got up, didn't pay, and left with a loud "Auf Wiedersehen!"

"What the hell was he doing?"

"I have no idea."

"Wow. Welcome to Vienna."

The next afternoon Easterling met me in the lobby of the Imperial Hotel. Although clearly in his forties, he had the young, clean-cut blond look of a Mormon proselytizer or a gay dancer on Broadway.

We walked across the street to a restaurant and small-talked our way for half an hour. Then a woman showed up, a real knockout, whom he introduced as his wife, Maris. She was the dark to his light—black hair, big marvelous brown eyes, pale skin.

I liked her even more when she said she'd been a fan of mine for years and proceeded to rattle off intelligent insights into my work. I was impressed and flattered, especially when she said she'd "begged" Walker to let her come to our meeting.

Basking in this, I didn't notice the child really until it was standing by Maris's elbow and looking at me.

"And this is our son, Nicholas. Zack, this is Harry Radcliffe."

He put out his hand, but gave a "dead-fish" shake and wouldn't look me in the eye.

"Is your name Nicholas or Zack?"

"Nicholas, but my friends call me Zack."

I'm good at guessing kids' ages, but this one was a mystery. He might have been anywhere from eight to thirteen. His face said nothing—no little-boy innocence there, but no twelve-year-old wiseguy either. Unfortunately, he wasn't a good combination of his attractive parents' features—Walker's nothing-special blue eyes above Maris's small nose and large teeth.

"How old are you, Nicholas?"

He looked at his parents and, putting a hand over his mouth to cover a giggle, said, "One."

"Pretty big guy for one."

The waiter came and we ordered. Maris took out some paper and colored pencils and gave them to

Nicholas, who started drawing, one hand over the sheet so we couldn't see what he was doing.

I talked about the shaman and why I'd wanted to meet with Easterling. He looked at me appraisingly. The food came.

"Venasque came and spoke to me after he died."

I waited for more, but both Easterlings were watching to see how I'd react to that one. I cut a potato in half and shrugged. "No surprise. His dog, Big Top, has been protecting me since the old man died." I briefly described the earthquake and how he'd led us to safety.

Nicholas was whacking away at his meal as if he were in a film on "fast forward." I paid no attention because his father was saying Venasque had appeared in their bathroom as Connie the Pig.

"Connie died the same day as Venasque."

"Right. He said she had to die for him to be able to come and talk to me through her form."

"He came back as his pet pig? How's *that* for a Jew reincarnating?"

"Harry?"

"Yes, Nicholas?"

"I'm not really one." Little Nicholas was fast becoming a pain in the ass, but I created a smile and looked his way. My eyes touched first on his plate and stopped. He'd ordered a Wiener schnitzel. He'd been eating it for ten minutes. But his food looked exactly as it had when first served: golden meat uncut, slice of lemon sitting on top; french fries piled high and smoking; a fat tomato half, a splat of red, off to one side. I'd seen him eat that tomato in one big bite. Seen him shove it into his mouth and one cheek bulge out. But there was the tomato, the meat was whole . . . his glass still filled to the top with black Coca-Cola. Instinctively my hand came up, palm out, as if it were trying to keep him away.

The boy reached down and brought up the paper on which he'd been drawing. It was of me exactly as I was at that moment: hand up just so, fingers splayed, mouth open, tongue at the gate of teeth ready to rush out and protest.

"You!" Shock rippled down my body, but rippled back up as laughter and understanding. It was Venasque! He'd come once as a pig, why not show up next as a little boy over lunch in Vienna?

How like him to tease, to draw me in my future, but wait till the present to stick it in my face.

"What's up, old man?"

The drawing became animated. Alive. Turned its head this way and that, smiled, spoke to me. It spoke to me.

In German.

But I don't speak German. My moment of truth had finally arrived! Epiphany! *Spoken to from beyond the grave* . . . but I couldn't understand a fucking word of what was being said.

Everything around us was frozen, as if in a snapshot. A woman across the room, her head thrown back in midlaugh, a waiter serving asparagus, a man bending over to pick up his dropped napkin. . . . Nothing moved. There were no other sounds in the restaurant. No other sounds in the world. Only the picture and me and the smiling boy holding up a piece of paper were alive. Even his "parents" held their fixed positions.

"Er musste jedes Gramm an Kraft und Mut zusammennehmen, um nicht auf der Stelle zu sterben."

"I don't understand. Don't do this! Please don't play games, Venasque!"

It did no good. He'd always done things his way. Whatever truths or information he had for me were hiding in a Black Forest of umlauts and verbs at the end, guttural *r*'s and a vocabulary that sounded rough and convincing at once.

However, I knew too that he was never malicious or misleading. Like any superior teacher, there was meaning and great value in his actions no matter how bizarre or obscure they seemed at first. "Whatever you learn quickly is rarely important, Harry. It might help get you through the day, like memorizing someone's phone number, but it doesn't help you figure out life. Not usually, anyway."

"Mom, after lunch can I take Harry to the flea market?"

Reality returned. The restaurant was once again noise and movement; asparagus was served with a yellow flourish; the woman dipped her head and finished her laugh.

"Sure, if he wants to go."

Ten minutes later the boy and I were out on the street together hand in hand, walking the Ringstrasse toward the Opera. His parents had been very calm about letting little Nicholas go off and play tour guide alone with an almost-stranger.

When I asked about that, Walker got an amused, there's-more-to-this-than-meets-the-eye look and said only, "Zack knows what he's doing." Maris said nothing.

"How come your parents let you go around alone like this? You're pretty young."

He swung our arms back and forth, the way children do. "Did you like my drawing?"

"Yes, but I didn't understand what it was saying. I don't speak German." As if he didn't know that! Instead of answering, he swung our arms back and forth, back and forth.

I had to assume it was Venasque holding my hand, having fun playing in the skin of a precocious child. I so believed in him and his beneficence, his concern for his students' well-being and progress. If not, if he *hadn't* been choreographing all of the demons and fairies flying around and through my life then, designing the false leads, trapdoors and fata morganas that shimmered on the horizon, I would have been very, very scared. Faith is that—you stop worrying and go on with your business.

The Ringstrasse was old-time lovely; enormous trees cast shadows across freshly painted benches. Flower stalls, clean hot-dog stands, no car honked its horn. There was no litter, no graffiti.

"You don't like it here, do you, Harry?"

"No, not much." I looked at the kid, unsurprised he'd read my mind. "It's beautiful, but it's finished. They'll put up more buildings or take some down, but it's like rearranging furniture in a house you plan to live in for the rest of your life. Cities have to have the feeling of incompleteness for me to be happy in them. Places like Vienna are perfect museums that're happy with their permanent collection. Other cities are still trying to figure themselves out. That's for me!"

As if to support what I'd said, Nicholas led us past the spanking-clean Opera House, Café Museum, and Secession Museum, which was covered with scaffolding and workers restoring Olbrich's oddity to its original condition.

On to the *Naschmarkt*, Vienna's open-air market. What a difference! Exotic and redolent, it gargled and spluttered with life and alien noise like a shortwave radio when you spin the dial across the channels. People pushed and yelled at each other in German, Turkish, Croatian. Children whined, dogs ran underfoot, bags were brusquely, expertly filled with Albanian "Paradise" tomatoes, Cretan goat cheese. One store, as large as a phone booth, sold only Hungarian paprika. Its aroma was the gift of the day.

A rude place, no one had time for you here beyond a purchase and quickly counted change. Next! But life held sway here, process, the ignored flow and stumble of people getting through, choosing the best bunch of carrots, checking a list to see what's needed next.

How do you design buildings for this life? Do you try to contain it? I thought of marathon runners and the people who race up alongside, offering them water or a slice of orange. Was that how to do it—give what's essential but stay the hell out of the way?

"That's the flea market down there, see?"

Hard to imagine a more frantic, colorful scene than where we were, but one roiled only a few feet away. In a giant parking lot adjoining the *Naschmarkt*, Vienna's Saturday flea market was in overdrive by the time we got there. Thousands of people milled and looked, bargained and dealt in an irresistible thunder of language and noise. Everything was for sale, everyone had something to say.

Flea markets remind us of how narrow and fixed our values are: What unimaginable things can have meaning to people! A man bought a bent and rusty 1983 Nevada license plate for one hundred schillings. One woman did a brisk trade selling single used, unmatchable shoes, and empty record album sleeves. Astonished, I turned to Nicholas and asked, "How much do you think she charges for that stuff?" He said nothing, but a moment later the thought came that valuing something meant understanding it better than the next guy. To me, it was absurd buying an old license plate—but what if the man who bought it knew better? Knew more about it, even if that knowledge seemed spurious or even insane to me. And even if it was worthless, didn't his wanting it make his imagination broader and grander than mine?

"Like language."

"Huh?" I looked at Nicholas, although my thoughts were five miles away.

"Like language. Listen to all this!" We stood in the midst of the flowing crowd. Putting up small hands, he gestured broadly around us. "How much of it do we pay attention to, even when we understand? It's just noise, like junk, like old license plates. But that's wrong, Harry, 'cause no matter what language, there are things being said *above* the noise. Come here."

He took my hand and led me to a building nearby that turned out to be a subway station—Kettenbrückengasse. Without stopping, Nicholas started to climb up the side of it and I went right up after him. With all the commotion of the flea market, only a couple of laughing punks noticed. A subway glided to a stop below us. Standing on one of the three graduated roofs, I looked down and watched the doors of the dirty silver train open.

"What am I doing?"

How many times had I said that when I was with Venasque? How often had I climbed out on "limbs" with him, ostensibly to get a better view or perspective of what was troubling me at the moment. We climbed to the second roof, then over the edge to the third a few feet higher. Train tracks directly below to our left, the bedlam of the flea market in front of us.

"Close your eyes and listen, Harry."

"For what?"

"Your mother's voice."

"Listen to *that* for my mother's voice?"

"Start with her. Close your eyes."

I closed them. I opened them. "My mother's voice?"

"Do it!"

For a while I heard James Brown, but not Mom. Someone just below us kept playing his song, "I Feeeeeel Good . . ." over and over. The air was so full of sharp smells (cooking meat, smoke, metal, old clothes) that I sniffed more than listened.

That changed. Somehow the noise suddenly moved a step closer. As if one moment it was out there, the next *here*, inches away, close enough to feel its breath on my face. Although my eyes were closed, I felt a kind of vertigo. My brain didn't even have to click in before my stomach wailed, "Get back!" Only here it wasn't fear of falling from a great height, it was because noise had so totally invaded and taken over. Perhaps we need five senses because singly they're too intense and concentrated. Hearing alone, for example, would drive us mad. Life lived only through sound. That's what vertigo is—suddenly life goes only through the eyes and it's too much.

I'd been told to concentrate on one, and for the

few pitiful seconds I could do it, it was a terrifying look over the edge. Was life just keeping common things like this at bay; the sound turned down, gloves on so we don't have to touch it directly?

"Maybe God is volume, Harry."

The first thing I saw on opening my eyes was a hot dog that'd been immaculately conceived in Nicholas's hand.

"What do you mean? Like sound, or size?"

Chomp Chomp. He shrugged. "Part of what you were thinking was right, but only part.

"Hey! Here comes another train! Come on, jump!"

Suddenly the boy leapt off the station roof, down twenty feet to the top of a subway car pulling into the station.

I ran to the edge, but wasn't about to take *that* plunge, Venasque or not.

"Jump down!"

"No way!"

There was a "beep" and then the car doors slid shut with a hard clunk. Nicholas crouched down, still holding his hot dog. Stuffing the rest of it in his mouth, he brushed his hands off and waved to me.

"Don't be surprised!"

The train started out of the station.

I cupped hands around my mouth. "Surprised by what?"

"That all the words are God!"

He was gone. I was on a roof in Vienna thinking about God, how to get down, and what I was going to tell the boy's parents.

That last question was answered ten minutes after I'd climbed down, found a telephone booth, and called the Easterlings to tell them their child had last been seen playing hood ornament on top of a moving subway car.

"Hello?"

"*Nicholas?*"

"Hi, Harry."

"You're home already?"

"I can't talk now, Harry. My favorite cartoon show is on." He hung up. I heard my coin drop down into the belly of the telephone.

🏴 Nervous breakdowns, earthquakes, love triangles, dead shamans, showering dogs, and magical children (among other things) *can* take their toll on one. Despite them, I walked back to the hotel that afternoon feeling vibrant but composed. Life is best when it's surprising and you're looking forward to what's next. I was convinced expectation is the best we can ever hope for. I knew we were going toward something momentous in Saru. Already enough mystery and purpose had revealed itself on the way there to indicate it was a hell of a lot more than building yet another rich man's tower.

"Christ, Harry, where've you been? We're having dinner tonight with Prince Hassan, the Sultan's son." Fanny was lying naked on the big bed watching a tennis match on television. She didn't look like she was in an extreme hurry.

"I thought we were supposed to meet him in Zell am See."

"We were, but he's flying over to have dinner with us. I guess there's a Saruvian restaurant in Vienna?"

In the midst of taking off my hat, I stopped when I heard *that*. "It's not called the 'Bazz'af,' is it?"

"Yes, I think so. Why are you yelling?"

"Oh, no reason." Hat on, I walked straight to the bathroom and ate six antacid pills.

The first time I ever met the Sultan of Saru was at the Restaurant Bazz'af in Los Angeles. Unfortunately, a rich Saruvian entrepreneur decided the world needed to taste the food of his homeland, so the sadist opened a bunch of Restaurant Bazz'afs around the world. They are very expensively appointed and purportedly use only the best ingredients, but my meal that night was a bad dream of fiery sauces, ominous vegetable dishes all of the same military consistency and color (khaki), and meat that was not nice. I won't go into it further. I'd gone to the restaurant with Bronze Sydney, who has the appetite of ten, but even she looked stricken by the time we got up off our cushions and waddled to the door. The only things she said in the car afterward were: (1) Never eat dinner sitting on a cushion, and (2) That meal was worse than our divorce.

After eating the stomach pills, I looked in the bathroom mirror, tipped my hat to myself, and asked how I was doing. My father taught me the practice when I was in high school. Look yourself in the eye and see how others saw you today. Don't check for pimples or nose hair—that's first-thing-in-the-morning or last-thing-at-night stuff.

"Some guy from the Saruvian Embassy called while you were out, sweating bullets, and said Big Top isn't eating his steak." Fanny had snuck up on me while I was mirror gazing. We looked at each other in that neutral zone. She leaned against the door frame, a small woman with friendly teacup breasts and rather wide hips. I always liked holding her body and watching it, particularly when we made love. Fanny closed her eyes and smiled angelically through most of the act, but her body, as if connected to some other woman, thrashed, twisted, and probably would have zipped around the room like an untied balloon, given the chance. I often had to hold on for dear life. She said she wasn't aware of what she did when she fucked, but wouldn't take responsibility for her flips and jigs.

"You look very edible in your birthday suit."

She smiled and checked herself in the mirror. "Thank you. Speaking of edible, doesn't Big Top eat steak?"

"No. Venasque fed him club sandwiches all the time so he likes mixed things. I usually give him chicken salad or deviled ham from the deli. Did the Saru guy leave a number? I'll call back and tell him.

"Listen, Fan, I've got to warn you that if this Bazz'af restaurant is anything like the one in Los Angeles, you'd better prepare yourself. It's the pits."

The phone rang in the other room. She turned to get it. "Probably the Saruvian Embassy saying Big Top won't eat the caviar either."

I followed her. "Caviar? You told them he liked that?"

"Sure. I told them to try it. *You* feed him salty potato chips. Hello?"

I waited for her to hand me the phone. Instead she listened a long time, slowly sitting down on the bed, the phone tight to her ear.

"It's crazy! An *arrow*? Dad, is this the truth? All right. Wait a minute. I said *wait a second!*" She put her hand over the mouthpiece. "My mother got hit by an arrow at a fashion show! She's in the hospital. Stable condition. They think she'll be okay. Unbelievable."

"An *arrow*? How'd that happen?" I started to smile. It was impossible not to.

"Not funny, Harry."

"Then why're you smiling too?"

She shook her head and went back to the phone.

Twenty minutes later she was dressed and in the middle of packing her bag again. "She went to a fashion show where the models came out in Robin Hood outfits. They were carrying bows and arrows and pretended to shoot at the audience. Cute, huh? Guess who was in the first row? My ma. Guess who got hit when one of the idiots accidentally shot an arrow? My ma. Now I know what Warhol meant by 'fashion victims.' "

"So you do what, fly from Zurich?"

"The Sultan's plane is supposed to be here in an hour. Thank God his son was flying in for dinner. I'll go right back out on it and I should be able to catch the Swissair night flight out of there.

"You know what pisses me off most? My mother never goes to fashion shows. Never. It's her goddamned friend Mary Rice who always coerces her into doing that dumb foofy women's shit. But Mary Rice didn't get hit by an arrow. Oh no! *She* got a good story to tell the girls at coffee klatsch. And they'll all be listening sympathetically but laughing like hell inside. Damn her!"

I remembered the man who'd died in the car wash. This fate was even more ignominious.

"Let's get Mary Rice with killer bees."

Fanny frowned at me, a pink bra in her hand.

"Look, when I get back to L.A., we'll go down to

Texas and smuggle some killer bees up from there, bring 'em over to Mary's house and make sure they sting her. Then your mother'll be one up."

"You're nuts, Harry. Hand me those shoes.

"I hate this! I love my mother but I want to go to Saru. I've always wanted to go to Saru! Did you know some people think that's where Christ went when he disappeared for those years in the middle of his life? Some say Saru and others India. *Damn* it!"

While packing, Fanny told me facts and stories about Saru. I often forgot how thorough a person she was, both personally and professionally. Invited on this trip, she'd gone out and read every bit she could find on the country.

"Do I have everything?" She stood still and surveyed the room. "The most important thing to know, Harry, is how wonderfully this Sultan has done since he took power. Remember how he joked one day about his enemies there? Well, the enemy happens to be his brother, a guy named Cthulu. The Sultan downplayed it, but this Cthulu is one scary number. When their father the old Sultan died twenty years ago, there was a power struggle in the family. A third brother, Khaled, was supposed to take over, but Cthulu killed him. Rumor also has it he then *ate* part of Khaled's body afterward to gain his strength."

Fanny made a rueful face and shook a finger at me. "If you'd done your homework, you'd know all this."

"I'm going there to design a building, honey, not study cannibalism. But you're right. I'm sure glad you're telling me. How did the Sultan defeat his charming brother?"

"That's where the plot thickens. The *official* history

says our man was much more popular and thus able to get together more people and firepower. But the *unofficial* word is that he had a prophetic dream—a dog came in a dream and told him everything that was about to happen, so he was ready for Cthulu when the time came."

"Ah, another reason why he wants to build his dog museum. Who told you about that?"

"His son." She picked up her suitcase and rolled it to the door.

"How come the Prince would tell you but the Sultan wouldn't?"

Certain moments pass in silence which are suddenly split by a lightning bolt of realization. Snapppp —its fatal white electricity shoots down and across you, into the earth.

Knowing a big mean revelation was at hand, I sat on a chair and said quietly, "Tell me about you and Prince Hassan, Fanny." Click click click—things started coming clear. "Tell me why they invited you on this trip and why the Prince 'just decided' to come over for dinner with us tonight."

Hands on hips, she faced me square on. "Don't threaten me with your questions, Harry! I got enough to think about. Tell you? Okay. Because he's my other lover. You want to hear that? You want to know it? Now you do! Because I met him in L.A. and we got along beautifully. And because I'm getting tired of being treated shitty by you. Did you think it was going to go on like this forever? Calling me into the game only when *you* think it's time for me? Forget it! I'm no specialty team player, Harry: I don't just return kickoffs. I want to play the whole time, Coach.

You want your Claire and eat Fanny too. Well, fuck you, you can't. Or rather you can, but so can I.

"I have to go."

Would you care to know how many curtains there were in that Viennese hotel room? How many water glasses in the bathroom? Wooden hangers, as opposed to metal, in the closet? I counted them all. After Fanny left I sat on the bed, staring at the floor, trying out the word "cuckold" in my mind. But that term applied essentially to married men: I wasn't. Plus I had a lover too. ZZZZ—static and contradictions were building in my head at an alarming rate— enough to make me swear at myself and stand up.

"There's nothing to make your desire for them soar more than to hear they're fucking someone else," I said aloud.

At the window I pulled a curtain aside and tried to catch a glimpse of the hotel entrance. Was there a limousine with diplomatic plates waiting down there, or an erection-red Ferrari driven by her royal lover?

I'd never met Prince Hassan. The Sultan spoke of his oldest son in glowing, albeit vague terms. I knew he'd gone to school in America and remembered a magazine article on the world's most eligible bachelors with him in a photo next to some blond French poodle with wowie cleavage at Cannes or Forte Dei Marmi.

From the window I stalked purposely into the bathroom but with nothing to do once there, I began counting again—two water glasses, four fat towels, and a partridge in a pear tree.

"Screw this!" Acting the hurt brat, I'd refused to go downstairs with Fanny when she left ("Do you honestly think I'm going to carry your bag down to *him?''*), but now if I hurried—

I saw him almost as soon as I stepped out of the elevator into the lobby. Sitting near the reception desk smoking a cigarette, he looked more like a fifteen-year-old skateboarder from Laguna Beach than Crown Prince of Saru. In his late twenties, wearing faded jeans, a black Purdue Boilermakers sweatshirt, and high-top basketball sneakers that were a cartoon of color, flashy arrows, lines, and zigzags. The outfit both reassured and annoyed me. This was royalty? And the man Fanny chose to share breath with? Hmm.

No Fanny in sight. Flamethrower that I am, I decided to go head-on and walked over. "Prince Hassan?"

He looked up from his cigarette and made a small amused smile. "Yes?"

"I'm Harry Radcliffe. Where's Fanny?"

"She left for the airport in my car."

"You didn't go with her?" I said with a sneer and heavy eye contact. I know what you've been doing to my girl, motherfucker.

"No. My father wanted me to take you to dinner, and what the Sultan says, goes."

Wimp! Weenie! Daddy's boy! No balls, huh? You let your father boss you around like that? All galloped across my mind as splendid things to say, but they were the jabs of a man with a kicked ass. A loser's *nyah nyah* when we both knew he had Fanny and the advantage. For the moment.

"She told me about the two of you."

An ash fell on his knee. He flicked it off with a quick finger. "Radcliffe, would you like to hear what

Fanny said when I asked her to leave you? 'Harry's a selfish bastard, but he never stops coming at you. He's like a fly that keeps buzzing around my face.'

"Imagine being me: The woman I want prefers you, a fly, to me, a prince. To make it worse, my father insists you build his museum." Stabbing the cigarette out in a nearby ashtray, he watched the embers burn down and out. "After Fanny and I first slept together, I spent two days seriously considering having you murdered, but then a frightening thought came to me: What if you are an afrit?"

"What's that?" I sat down across from him and took a cigarette out of his pack. "May I?"

"Please, be my guest. May you die of lung cancer.

"An afrit is a very dangerous jinn. Do you know what that is? Al-Qaswini says that 'the jinn are aerial animals, with transparent bodies, which can assume various forms. At first they may show themselves as clouds or as huge undefined pillars; when their form becomes condensed, they become visible, perhaps in the bulk of a man, a jackal, a wolf, a lion, a scorpion or a snake.

" 'Jinn often attain the lower heavens, where they overhear the conversations of angels about future events. This enables them to help wizards and sooth-sayers.' But Radcliffe, most important, 'certain scholars attribute to them the building of the Pyramids or, under the order of Solomon, the great Temple of Jerusalem'! What do you think of that? Everywhere I turn now, you are there to annoy me and make me crazy." He stuck a finger up in the air—EUREKA! *"But* you may be doing it all on purpose! You're listening while I explain what a jinn is, but inside you're laughing and thinking up your next torture.

"My father can't afford to build this museum. He is being attacked on all sides by his enemies and should use the money for weapons and training a stronger army. I've tried to talk him out of it for years but he is stubborn and believes he is doing God's work. All right, build the madness, but get a Saruvian to do it, or at least an Arab. No, he wants a California architect who is only recently out of the insane asylum."

I sat back in the seat, smiling. The cigarette, although I hadn't smoked in five years, tasted delicious. The Prince might've put horns on my head, but the tone of his voice and vehemence of his gestures said Harry Radcliffe was a big pain in *his* ass, and I hadn't even begun to bite.

"I suggest we begin by hating each other and hope it goes downhill from there. I don't want to like you, Radcliffe. I don't even want to know you. If you are an afrit you have great power, but know I'll fight as hard as I can. If you're not one, I still might have you killed.

"Is that fair? Do you understand?"

"I do."

He stood up. "No, I don't want to shake hands with you. There's only one other thing I want to say."

I got up slowly and took a final drag on the cigarette. "What's that, Prince?"

He spoke over his shoulder. "Fanny says I'm a much better fuck than you." A couple nearby whipped their heads around and looked at him with shocked, open mouths.

It *almost* shut me up, but not quite. "That's because fucking is for mortals, Your Highness. Remember, I might be a *pommes frites.*"

He stopped, turned. "*Afrit!* Are you stupid, or only testing me? How can I tell?"

At the Restaurant Bazz'af, Hassan told me to have a dish which, when translated into English, was Soft Bells and Hard Flowers. It was delicious. He ordered fish sticks and a Coke. When I asked why he was having that, he said it was none of my business.

We ate in silence. Savoring each bite, I tried to figure out what was in my meal. Some kind of nut, some kind of smoked meat.

"Do you believe in magic, Radcliffe?"

I looked at him and chewed.

"I don't care if you do! I'm only trying to make conversation."

"Yes, I believe."

"Fanny does not, although I know she was there when your dog saved my father from the earthquake. I visited that dog today at our embassy. He is very ugly."

" 'That dog' is also very magical, Prince. I'd be careful what I said in front of him."

"You see? This is another reason why I think you're an afrit. You have bewitched both my father and Fanny, and this ugly magical dog is further proof of who you are. I'll say this, though, you'll have competition in Saru! There is so much magic there, you snap your fingers and ten magicians appear."

I put the last bite of food in my mouth, dabbed my lips with the napkin, and smiled. "Maybe I know that already."

~ Buying a pair of shoes is one of the most optimistic acts I know, next to falling in love. I like nothing better than to see an old man wearing a brand new pair of brogues or cap-toed oxfords, preferably jaunty orange-brown, unscuffed, heels unworn. We want to be here tomorrow, but buying new shoes, like falling in love, says I *plan* on being here tomorrow.

Notwithstanding this latest Fanny cherry bomb, I still felt positive about the turns my life was taking, so my last morning in Vienna I went shopping for a new pair of shoes.

Like many American tourists, I believed that in most European cities of any size, there were still bound to be a few stores run by craftsmen or eccentrics who sold goods of Old World quality. The first time I was ever in Venice, wandering those damp snaky streets, I had the luck to come upon a small stationery store that looked like it hadn't been entered since the 1950s. The window was a desultory, sunbleached mess of once-red school notebooks, curled paper party favors, and ink bottles with barely legible names like *Bleu nuit*. Standing defiantly in the middle of this defeated jumble was a carved plum-wood Popeye about two feet high. One of those rare objects so familiar but unique that you literally *erupt* into a grin of love and recognition the moment you see it. I went in and, after pretending to browse, asked in a bored voice how much it cost. The old woman who ran the place couldn't believe I wanted the figure but said the equivalent of twenty dollars. Even more thrilling, carved into the bottom of one of the feet was the name Del Debbio. One of the reasons I was in Italy then was to see firsthand the Roman stadium and sports complex Enrico Del Debbio had designed for Mussolini in the twenties and thirties. Even to Radcliffe, convinced-atheist graduate student, it was more than a spooky coincidence.

I didn't expect to find a pair of Del Debbio shoes in Vienna, but maybe a shop with an old man in gold spectacles and his helper-elves. . . .

What I found instead was Palm.

After a couple of hours walking and window shopping, I found myself on the other side of the Danube Canal in the city's Second District. Only a ten-minute walk from the posh center of town, the personality and color of the Second was entirely different from the chic fat-cat-and-tourist-on-parade feel of the area around the St. Stephen's Church. Here were lots of dark, rough-hewed people looking like gypsies or peasants just in from the countryside. Women wore Russian babushkas and had gold-capped front teeth, their men moustaches thick as steel wool. They all seemed to be yelling at each other in hard, fast, incomprehensible words. Yet while they yelled they were often smiling, so I couldn't tell if they were happy or angry. It was clearly a worker's district, the buildings that dead-mouse brown of places where too many people live in each room and the only light in the windows at night is the smoke-blue flicker of televisions lulling the tired suckers to sleep.

Even the streets were dull and minimal. Anonymous apartment buildings and some stores, but very few and they offered only the essentials: small glum markets, an electrician, a *Geschäft* that sold toilets and bathtubs.

It wasn't the best part of Vienna to find great new shoes, but I continued walking and looking at both the architecture and people.

A street sign saying Lucygasse stopped me. One of the great loves of my high school years was named Lucy Hopkins, so in her honor I walked along her street.

Halfway down the block I saw the store. It was small and undistinguished. I wouldn't even have paid attention if there'd been more interesting sights around. The black-and-white unadorned sign over the window said "Morton Palm, Türen & Leitern." A door and ladder store? In the window was a pile of round gray stones. Lying on top of the pile was an ornate art deco picture frame around a quotation nicely handprinted in three languages: German, English, and Swedish (I later learned).

"A door is the difference between in and out."

That got my interest percolating. As if to steel myself before taking the next step, I peered up and down the street while slowly turning the doorknob and pushing in.

There was no one inside, but the desert menagerie stopped me and kept me wide eyed until Palm came out of the back of the store.

In that cramped, narrow room there must have been a hundred different cactus plants, varying from the size of a thumb to six feet high. Any time that many anything are together at once and in such a small space it's both impressive and loony, like the newspaper photographs of the woman who lives with forty cats, or the man with the largest collection of beer coasters in the world.

Many of the plants were blooming—brilliant, pastel flowers which contrasted vividly with the drabness of the store and the street outside. At first it almost felt like the room was filled with unmoving tropical birds keeping very still and silent, until the next moment when they'd just as mysteriously burst back into a havoc of screech and song.

"*Guten Tag.*"

The first time I saw Morton Palm I thought he was either dying or carved out of marble. He was so thin and his hair was shaved so close to the skull that I immediately thought of men in concentration camps. What would have been normal features on another face jutted out on his like a bunch of umbrellas beneath a sheet. His skin had the silvery yellow-white pallor of good marble. When he smiled, his teeth were the same color as his skin. Long nose, small mouth that curved up at the ends, biggish ears. Hard to tell what color his eyes were because they were sunk so deeply into his head.

"Do you speak English?"

He held up his hand like a benediction. "I speak Swedish and English. What can I do for you, sir?"

I made a sweep with my hand. "Your cactuses are impressive."

He nodded but made no comment.

"To be honest with you, I don't know why I came in. The quote in your window, I guess."

" 'Were I a door I would wish to swing out upon my hinges, and allow my room to fill with what has come from the outside.' They are both from a poem by an American, Russell Edson."

"Oh, do you like poetry?" I felt idiotic asking but there was something about this marble man that made it important to keep our conversation going. He was the strangest combination of peace and odd. His diminutive, sickly appearance was offset by the turtle-slowness of the way he moved and spoke. The skinny people I've known are usually nervous and hyper. But everything Palm did was too damned slow. His blinks must have lasted half a second; when he moved to gesture, it was with the languorousness of a sea fan under water. I'd never seen a person run at 33 1/3 speed.

"No. Someone gave me the poem because of my business."

"You make windows and doors?"

"Yes. And I raise cactuses because they're strong and funny-looking. Would you like to see my work?"

From beneath the counter he took out two wooden boxes about the size of a car battery. There were brass handles and fittings on both. He opened the first and spoke. Slowly.

"I make three kinds of doors and three ladders. These are the miniatures that I show customers. Which are you interested in having?"

"I'd like to see both, if you don't mind."

"It is my pleasure, sir. People coming in are usually in a hurry. They want a door in a day. They want to buy a ladder instantly. There *are* firms that do seven-hour service, but I must make each of my pieces from the beginning. It is the only way I can work. I must warn you of that right now. It takes many more hours than most people are willing to give." He smiled and took out the first ladder. Slowly —the smile, the hand into the box, the lifting out. Soooo slowly . . .

How I wanted them to be special! Jack and the Beanstalk ladders, doors to perception. What he showed me was good solid work but nothing special. His different ladders and doors would do the job for many years, but wouldn't open on to heaven or cause you to have an epiphany once you'd reached their top.

Palm held each miniature a long time and carefully explained their pros and cons. He was honest and dull. He did his job and the result was okay. Yet there were things about this man that made me both like and *want* to like him very much. The plants, his strange physical appearance, the great affection for his trade.

What sealed my feelings for him was the way he had returned all the small doors and ladders to their proper places when he was finished with his presentation. I forgot to mention that inside these two boxes he'd cut slots to size for each model.

"Why doors and ladders, Mr. Palm? Why not tables? Or chairs?"

"I am forty-six and not *so* intelligent, Mr. Radcliffe. There is a *finishedness* to doors and ladders that I have not been able to find anywhere else in my life. A ladder is a ladder. Once you have completed it, whether there are six steps or ten, it is there to do its job. To be a ladder. A door is the same. Hang it and it is there to open and close.

"Chairs change from one year to the next. Sometimes people want them comfortable, sometimes to look at and put in museums. But not ladders, really. They can be wood or steel, but a ladder's job is permanent and unchanging. A door too. They don't have a choice, do they?"

For lunch that day I ate fried mice. After we'd talked a long time, Palm asked if I'd like a cup of tea. We sat there amid the cactuses drinking tea and eating "fried mouse," a Viennese pastry he had which tasted like a heavy, dry donut.

We'd reached the point where we were addressing each other by first name and had begun to give certain details about ourselves. As I'd expected, Morton's story was far more interesting than he'd first let on.

He'd been a professional soldier for fifteen years with the United Nations peacekeeping forces. One would have to be either supremely tranquil or nuts to spend as much time as he did where he did: Cyprus, Rhodesia, as it was becoming Zimbabwe, the Sinai. Along the way he'd married an Austrian woman who worked at the United Nations in Vienna. It didn't succeed because he was away too often and she worried too much after he was shot the first time. They were divorced, but he'd had such pleasant times in the city that after being shot the second time, he retired and went to live there. Ten years later he had little money but liked his life.

We went into the back of the store, where he showed me his tools. Many of them were old, bought in junk stores and flea markets around Europe. He said they enabled him to work with the wood rather than against it, as happened with modern power tools. Most endearing was Palm's sheer delight in what he did. A placid, albeit good-natured man, the only time he genuinely smiled or became animated was when describing ladders and doors he'd made. I envied him that. There'd been a time when my work defined and justified me to myself. I knew there was a distinct possibility that that time had passed for me, despite the moment's enthusiasm for the trip to Saru and the new project there. I told Palm these thoughts, then felt embarrassed for crying on his shoulder.

"I'll tell you a funny story, Harry. When we were

on the Golan, there was a guy there who read without stop and was always telling us good parts out of his books. Once he read something, I don't remember from what it was, but the story was great: This old woman was in her bed and she was dying. Her family was only waiting for her to breathe a last time. She got worse and worse, so now it's really close to the end. But suddenly she farted like a cannon. You know what she said? 'Good, a woman who can still fart isn't dead yet.' " Palm ran his hand across a piece of smooth wood. "I think you are still farting, Harry."

His story kept me chuckling the whole walk back to the hotel. Evening had come and suddenly the streetlights blinked on all around me. Traffic was heavy and slow. The eeriness of faces inside cars at night. Cigarettes flicker, a snatch of music heard on a radio as you pass. Men in funny looking yellow and red coats stood on street corners selling newspapers. Loaded trolleys racketed by, their bells clanging impatiently. People wanted to get home, meals were cooking there, bathtubs filling. That rich energy at the start and end of a day; beginnings get us going.

On Vienna's main shopping street jugglers, mimes, and opera and folk singers vied for the attention and spare change of the crowd. I was in no hurry and stopped often. Whenever I saw this kind of street scene, it made me think of medieval markets, and even further back. Were there mimes in the time of the pharaohs? In Jerash I'd walked over smooth giant stones in the marketplace that served as road for the chariots and still showed the grooves of the wheels. What songs were sung there to distract and hold pas-

sersby on their way home? What tricks did the bus-
kers play? How did things smell? What did the air
feel like?

Back at the hotel I had two telephone messages:
one from Fanny, the other from Claire. Please call
back.

I didn't feel like talking to Ms. Neville, so I called
Ms. Stansfield instead.

"Oh, Harry, finally! I didn't think I'd get you. I'm
so sorry about what happened. If there's anything I
can do—"

"Wait. What are you talking about, Claire?"

"The Sultan."

"What *about* the Sultan?"

"You didn't hear? He's dead! He was murdered."

"Who killed him? Where'd it happen?"

"In Saru. Rebels shot him. His daughter was riding in a horse show and he was in the audience.
Something like twenty people died. It was similar to
the Sadat assassination years ago. The news said
other members of the royal family were killed too."

Half an hour later I was listening to the news in
German, understanding nothing but *"Sultan"* and
"Tod." The phone rang. A secretary came on and said
Mr. Awwad, Saruvian ambassador to Austria, would
like to speak with me. Awwad wasted no time asking
if I'd be willing to remain in Vienna a couple of days.
He said the Crown Prince had returned home, but
before leaving had specifically requested that I stay in
case they still might need me to go there.

"Why would anyone want me in Saru, Mr. Awwad? Especially now?"

"This is off the record, all right?"

"Sure."

"I go off the record very often, Mr. Radcliffe. I have been misquoted too often."

"Okay! Okay! Why would the Prince want me in Saru after what has happened?"

"Off the record, there are two possibilities—he would like you to attend his father's funeral because he knew how much the Sultan liked you. But more possible is because the Prince is a very headstrong young man. I would not be surprised if he had you build the museum for his father anyway."

I called Fanny, who said many of the same things as Claire. After she asked what I was going to do, I told her about my conversation with the ambassador.

"I don't know how true that is about Hassan, Harry. He's not crazy about you, and now that his father is dead—"

"Then why *would* he ask me to stay here?"

"I don't know, Buckaroo."

 Palm didn't know either. I spoke with him next and asked if he'd like to have dinner with me.

That dinner turned into two days of poking around together. I went to the Saruvian Embassy, got Big Top, and the three of us walked in the parks, drank wine in different *heurigen*, and the second evening went back to Morton's shop, where I helped make a door. What was the point of returning to Los Angeles? Vienna was something new, Palm good company, and the chance of adventure in Saru still hung like a small cloud over the horizon.

I also wanted to pay the Sultan homage. Besides what he had done for me, from all I'd heard he had been a good leader who genuinely cared and tried to do something about the well-being of his people. At different times in our conversations he had spoken with great pride about the growing literacy rate, a new hospital complex in Bazz'af, and the fact the educated young were choosing more and more to return to Saru after completing their education in England, France, the United States.

"They want to be lawyers and doctors at home, Harry. No one is forcing them back. They could make their riches in Beverly Hills or Paris, but they are coming home! This is a very positive sign."

What would happen now to his nation was anybody's guess, according to a long and detailed article in the *International Herald Tribune*. Unlike Egypt at the time of the Sadat assassination, the opposition in Saru was not splintered into warring factions. The Sultan's sole opponent had been his cannibal brother, Cthulu. Having murdered both of his siblings, it was down to a face-off between Cthulu's people and those loyal to Prince Hassan.

Another question: Did Harry Radcliffe *want* to be in a country at a time in its history when fratricide had succeeded and chaos, Arabian style, was sharpening its scimitar right outside?

The answer to that one came easy. After we'd put the finishing touches on his door, Palm and I had a couple of glasses of plum schnapps and then I got up to go. Big Top had been sleeping by the wood stove and was not happy about getting up and walking home through the chilly night.

Outside the air smelled of coal and wood smoke. It wasn't very late, around eleven o'clock, but the streets were empty and not many lights were on in the windows.

We moved slowly, like two old men trudging home after a night at the bar, because the dog's rheumatism made him limp. For the hundredth time I wondered how old he was and how much longer he would live.

His wide white ass toddled from side to side. Limp and toddle made his body move in a number of directions at the same time.

He stopped, but his tail started wagging like a windshield wiper on high speed. Another Big Top trait was that he rarely barked—only stood his ground and furiously wagged when something was interesting or a threat.

Seeing him frozen in that familiar pose, I looked up. At first there was nothing—no people nearby, no scene, no danger. Frowning, I looked down at him to see where he was pointing. Left, off to the side. Still nothing until I looked away across the wide street.

"What *is* that?"

Big Top needed no encouragement. Tail still a whipping blur, he pulled us across the street to the car.

Because many of the pieces were so savagely hacked and torn, shapeless, dangling, and wet, it took me long ghastly moments to realize that what was dumped and smeared across the length of the car had once been an animal and not a person. Brains looking like buttery cauliflower were scattered in soft blobs and red clots over the windshield. Islands of shiny purple-brown slabs lay on the white, white hood of the car. There was a rough circle of blood drawn on the roof—as if whoever had done this took one piece and rubbed it like a polishing rag there. Volvo. I saw the name half covered by a large sliver of raw heart? lung? A white Volvo.

I stood and stared. It was macabre, terrible. Most of all because it'd been done purposely. But I stood and stared. There was evil here violent as murder, mad as rape. Its intensity was as tangible as heat from a car crash.

Whoever had done this was sitting in a bar nearby quietly drinking wine and chatting with a friend. Or nearby doing worse. How could someone do this? If caught, their answers are always awful—because it was important to them or, shiver-time, *unimportant*. Oh God, at least let the creeps have been angry or getting even. We understand that. Anything else is the dark side of the moon.

Big Top pulled on the leash and sniffed crazily at something beneath the car. Jerking him back, I bent down to look. A deer's head sat near the right front wheel. A hand-size hole was in the skull, but otherwise it was intact and beautiful. If the car had driven away, the head would've been crushed. The dead eyes caught light even down there and reflected two small candle flames. Unflickering.

I must have walked around ten minutes trying to find either a policeman or patrol car. When I did and had brought the cops back, they were less interested in the Volvo than in what I was doing there. I ended up calling them assholes. They understood and I was brought to the station house.

My American passport thrust in their faces left them singularly unimpressed. I said I was allowed one phone call. They said this wasn't America and if I didn't behave myself they were going to hit me on the head. "Heet you on dee hate," as Officer Wilheim put it.

Finally they did allow me to call, but the problem was I had only two Viennese telephone numbers in my wallet—Morton Palm, and the Saruvian Embassy. Morton had had enough of me for one day, so I called the embassy at two in the morning.

Forty-five minutes later Ambassador "Off the Record" Lawrence Awwad appeared, looking ready to kill anyone in his path. He was a giant man, handsome: the kind of figure who makes people sit up straight when he enters a room.

Everyone but me got to go into another room and confer. When they returned, each spearing me with a dirty look, I was out of there in fifteen minutes.

"I asked you to stay in Vienna, Mr. Radcliffe, but I don't like trouble with the police."

"I appreciate your help, Ambassador, but don't scold me. I told you what happened."

We were stopped at a traffic light in his armor-plated Range Rover. He glared over and shook a finger at me. "Prince Hassan said you were a pain in the ass and I should punch you in the nose if you caused any trouble. I am just warning you."

"That's twice tonight someone wanted to hit me there."

The car telephone next to him purred and he grumbled something in Arabic which, by the exasperated tone, seemed to be "What *now?*"

I looked out the window while he talked. Big Top circled and circled on the backseat, sniffing and grunting in between, trying to find a comfy spot to drop on. I didn't have the heart to tell him we'd be home soon and he'd have to get up again.

Awwad hung up and accelerated around a taxi, a motorcycle. "Are you packed?"

"More or less."

"How long will it take for you to get ready?"

"Half an hour. No more. What's happening?"

"You're going to Saru."

"Tonight?"

"Yes. The Prince's plane just landed at the airport. It's waiting for you. You and the dog, that is. He was very specific about your bringing the dog along."

"Okay, let's go. What a night this has been. What a night, huh, Big?" I looked over my shoulder to confirm this with the bull terrier but he was fast asleep.

"Do you like Randy Travis?"

"Excuse me?"

Awwad slipped a cassette into the car stereo and sure enough, out came the syrupy country and western singer's voice.

"Randy Travis is very popular in Saru. George Jones too."

I didn't ask why. The more mysteries waiting in Saru the better.

🖎 The scene at Vienna airport was a stark reminder of what had just happened in the country I was about to visit. The terminal, though blazing with light, was almost empty at that early hour. Except for soldiers and policemen, who were everywhere, which was ironic because there were so few civilians around to cause trouble.

When Awwad pulled up to the front doors, two men dressed in dark green battle gear and carrying machine pistols came over. Once again I was left out of a conference in German, but while they spoke to the Ambassador, the men kept looking my way with unanimous "Watch your step, Buddy" expressions.

I got my bags out of the back of the car and coaxed Big Top to the edge so I could lift him down. Once on the ground, he shook himself violently and yawned. Neither of us were used to these hours, but unlike him, adrenalin had me pumped high and wide awake. Waiting for Awwad to finish, I imagined a coming attraction for the movie about my life at that moment: "Adventure! Danger! *Night Flight to Saru.* They sent him into trouble and he was happy to go!" Next, a shot of an old propeller plane, engines already spluttering as I boarded, runway glistening black from mist. Lift-off into the night. Then a map superimposed over the screen, a finger pointing out the route the plane was flying—across a wedge of the East Bloc, south over Turkey, Iran . . .

"We will walk to the plane. It's faster. Come on, Radcliffe." Without looking back, Awwad started through the sliding doors into the building. We followed.

Inside were even more policemen. I sang out, "What's going on, Ambassador? Why the armed camp?"

"This airport was already attacked once and many died. Since the Sultan's death, there have been threats to the entire government of Saru. People knew the Prince's plane was coming tonight, so the Viennese took precautions."

"That's why I'm flying at three-thirty in the morning?"

"Not only you. Turn around and look at my car."

Outside, the soldiers who'd met us were both on their backs under the Rover.

"Bombs?"

Still moving, Awwad gave the classic hands-up, "who knows?" shrug.

Outraged, I grabbed his arm and tried to turn him so he'd look at me. It was like trying to turn a small building. "You drove us around this whole time *knowing* there might be a bomb under your car?"

A hack of rough sounds burst from his throat. I realized it was a laugh. "You have a verz, man." He pointed to Big Top. "Do you think he'd let anything happen to you? Why do you think they want him in Saru? Why do you think *I* kept him in the car when you were in the hotel?

"You're an insect, Radcliffe. But sometimes God protects insects. Why would He give you a verz if you were not important?"

We'd reached the passport gate. Awwad breezed straight through, ignoring both stop signs and inspectors. In the narrowness of the passage, Big Top got in front of me and tangled in the other's legs, tripping him so that he almost fell down.

A moment of pure rage lit his face. But on realizing what'd happened, he bent down and patted the dog. "I guess I should not call you an insect, eh? Your verz does not like that. I'm sorry. Excuse me."

This apology was not to me, understand. The Saruvian ambassador was addressing a bull terrier who did appear to be staring indignantly up at him.

🔪 Soldiers and police, police and soldiers. The whole time we moved toward the plane—through the

building, then a bus ride across the tarmac to a
brightly spotlit Lear jet circled by official vehicles—
uniformed men with guns and hard, watchful expressions stood nearby. It made me feel significant and
panicky. What was I getting into? What was about to
happen?

The airplane door opened only after we got out of
the bus and were saying goodbye.

A frisky breeze blew and died, blew and died. I
listened to it whistle around different parts of the
plane behind us. Why do small details matter, or
catch the mind's eye, when we are about to leave?
Later, you remember them more vividly than anything: that whoosh of night wind, the lovely green of
a baggage tag, the Oriental child holding a donut in
his hand. . . .

"Are you excited about going to Saru?" Awwad
smiled at me for the first time while brushing his hair
down with a hand.

"I don't know. What's it like there?"

The splurt of a voice from a walkie-talkie nearby.
A man appeared at the door of the plane and waved
at me to come in. I waited, wanting Awwad to answer
my silly question.

"God provides the food, Man provides the cooks.
There are good cooks in Saru, Radcliffe."

As a kid I knew a girl named Fairlight. I hadn't
thought of her or her name in years, but after I woke
over the desert and looked out the window, that's the
first word that came to mind—fairlight.

Down below, endless miles of moon blue sand lay
like an unmoving ocean in early morning light. But

the dazzlers, beautiful and haunting far away above
that flat distance, were the many fires of Saru's oil
refineries. They flickered and leapt, orange and yellow over the blue earth into the graying sky. Despite
recognizing at a sleepy glance what they were, I
stared and dreamed them into the flaming gates of a
fantastic Arabian Nights city, where carpets flew and
veiled women wore real rubies in their navels.

The pilot came back and said we'd be landing in
twenty minutes. I put a hand on Big Top in the seat
next to me and stroked a thick white flank. Opening
his eyes, he grumbled appreciatively.

The plane dropped and dropped again. The dancing fires loomed nearer.

"Do you not remember me? I have been waiting
this whole trip for you to remember!" The pilot stood
directly above me grinning like a monkey on amphet-
amine. Why were so many people from Saru peculiar?

"I am Khaled! From the helicopter in Los Angeles.
I saved you in the earthquake. You must remember!"

"Oh Christ, the helicopter! The guy who likes to
fly into dangerous places, thank God. How are *you*?"

He loved that. His grin grew two inches. "Fine!
Now we are flying together into Saru where things
aren't so great. We have to come in low because I
don't know if Cthulu's bastards have missiles yet. If
they do and we get hit, it'll be worse than the earthquake!" He whistled loud and enthusiastically, the
kind of down-spiraling whistle a kid makes when his
toy airplane goes into a nose dive.

It was under these loony conditions that we
landed in Bazz'af, the capital of the country. As the
plane made its dipping, turning approach, I watched
Big Top to see if my local verz was getting nervous.

Usually when a plane touches ground, I give a happy sigh, but this time I was too busy trying to scan the horizon through the tiny porthole window.

Nothing happened.

The plane landed, taxied quickly to a far corner of the field, and shut down. On the way I saw a Luft-hansa 737 parked near the terminal. I found that very reassuring—if the Germans were still landing their businessmen and tourists in Saru, things couldn't be too bad.

Less reassuring was pilot Khaled coming out of the cockpit with a large handgun.

"So, they had no rockets, huh, Harry? Do you want to have a gun too? This one? Please, take it."

I put up a hand—no thanks. "What happens next?"

"Next they are coming for you but we must be very, very careful. The airport has been under fire on and off since the Sultan was killed."

"What *is* the situation here since then, Khaled? Who's winning?"

He bent down and looked out my window. "It depends. They have control of one city, we have Bazz'af. They have the mountains, we have the rest. But our leader is dead and theirs is still alive. It is impossible to say. I will tell you, we did not expect any of this to happen. They were much stronger than we thought. The reports said Cthulu would never try anything now because he did not have the men or the power. So now we say 'fuck you' to the reports. Everything is up to be grabbed.

"Here they come. Get ready."

A Range Rover exactly like Ambassador Awwad's in Vienna came into view across the airfield and

moved toward us. I half-expected to see it get strafed
by enemy gunfire but it made it over and stopped a
few feet away.

"Put this on, Harry. It's for the best."

Turning from the window, I saw Khaled holding
up a brown bullet-proof vest the way a clothing sales-
man holds a jacket you're about to try on.

"*That* does not fill me with confidence. Is it that
dangerous out there?"

"Put this on and it is not dangerous, my friend.
Then they have to hit your head and that is a difficult
shot."

"Yeah, but that's what happened to the Sultan,
wasn't it?" I said, slipping my arms into the vest.

"He was not a careful man. Dying was not important to him. Only living gave him interest."

The doors of the Rover opened simultaneously.
Prince Hassan climbed out one side, a big bruiser who
was obviously his bodyguard the other. Both wore
army uniforms. Bruiser toted an AK-47 attack rifle
and had a couple of hand grenades hanging off his
belt.

The copilot opened the airplane door and gave
Hassan a hand in.

The Prince looked tired but sturdy and stable.
God, how old was he, twenty-five? Twenty-eight?
What a life he had ahead of him now. Soon he'd either be dead, or leader of an important Arab country.
He'd go to war with his uncle, who he knew had
murdered his father. It was mythic stuff. Coming in,
I'd imagined the fires of Bazz'af's refineries to be the
gates of a magical city. Thinking about Hassan's fate,
it struck me I wasn't so far from the truth. "There
lived once in far Saru three royal brothers. . . ."

"Prince, I'm terribly sorry." He took my hand and shook it solemnly. "Your father saved my life. I didn't know him well but I liked him . . . and he saved my life."

Hassan looked at the floor, as if waiting for me to go on, but I could think of nothing else to say.

"My father liked you and believed you could build for him the dream he had all his life. He's dead now, so the best I can do for him is to finish what he began. What I said to you in Vienna no longer holds true: We *will* build this dog museum for him, exactly the way he wanted it." He looked from me to the pilot, then to his bodyguard. "And while you are doing that, I will kill Cthulu. I will do it personally."

The road from Bazz'af airport to the capital is a black asphalt ruler, straight across the desert, covered with the damnedest-looking traffic I had seen in some time. After a few days there, I realized the primary mode of motorized transportation in Saru appeared to be bicycles and scooters. Which made sense because both are relatively cheap and easy to maintain. But the rigors to which they were put were unbelievable and downright imaginative. Three or four people on a little Italian scooter were a typical sight: Papa, Mama, and two children covering every possible inch of the vehicle as it crawled down the road. Or a French 'velo' pulling a homemade trailer loaded with a few zillion pounds of cloth or dung or vegetables.

That first day the Royal Highway was a slow procession of these martyred two-wheelers wobbling along down the middle of the beautifully paved road, ignoring anything behind them. Add to this various ancient trucks and cars spewing exhaust smoke thick enough to melt the eyes, horses and donkeys pulling wagons . . . and you get some idea of the traffic flow.

It was long, empty miles of parched desert countryside, bedouin camps, and large goat herds wandering the sides of the highway before modern civilization began to show its face. Five or six miles out of town large billboards advertised in both Arabic and English such things as Saru Airlines, "Direct flights to Qatar and Jidda twice daily" and the Bazz'af Concord Hotel's "Casino, Olympic swimming pool, festive conference rooms."

Two images in particular remain in my mind. The first is of a small boy holding a camel on a rope standing in front of a poster for Siemens telecommunications. The picture was of a satellite in space beaming sherbet-green light down to a sexy red phone held by a sexy white Occidental hand. What did a satellite mean to this kid? Or a telephone? As we passed, the camel turned his head and gazed our way.

Image number two was of a Coca-Cola poster a few miles farther on. It was a familiar one that I'd seen recently in California. Only here the middle of the picture was gone and in its place was a blackened ragged hole where a perky girl's face should have been. Her hand, holding a frosty bottle of the world's favorite drink, survived.

"What happened there?" I asked no one in particular.

"Mortar shell," Hassan and his bodyguard said simultaneously.

"Why would someone shoot at an ad?"

"Because Coca-Cola isn't a drink, Radcliffe, it's

America. Do you have any idea how many people in this part of the world hate your country?"

"I'll tell you a secret, Prince. America isn't gaga about the Mideast either. I'm tired of being told my country is shit. Because if we *are* such shit, how come the rest of the world keeps copying so much of what we do? How come kidnappers in Beirut wear Michael Jackson T-shirts? Or the Japanese use Cray computers to forecast their weather? Why did you go to college there if it's so despicable?"

That put the kaibosh on chitchat for a while. Up in the front seat, Hassan wouldn't turn around and look at me, but his chauffeur glared laser beams in the rearview mirror. I think he wanted to evaporate me, but every time we made eye contact, I gave him a big grin, and once I said, "Did you know that a third of all architects in Finland are women?"

What little I saw of Bazz'af that first day was unimpressive and disheartening. A new-looking city built on a series of hills, the architecture was generally characterless, get-it-up-fast cement blocks. The air smelled of cardamom, dust, and grilling meat. In the center of town, among crazed traffic and the sound of tape-recorded calls to prayer from the minarets, a large colorful souk gave one of the few hints of what life had been like there in the long ago. Nearby, ruins of a Greek amphitheater sat humiliatingly surrounded by signs for Marlboro cigarettes and Jimmy Jeans as well as stained, ugly apartment buildings with laundry hanging off the balconies. You felt sorry for the old outdoor theater rather than any kind of awe or delight for what beauty remained. Please read Harry Radcliffe's article on this very subject in *FMR* magazine—"The Don Quixote Colosseum and Drive In."

However, the way the chauffeur was flying through town, I was definitely not being taken on a guided tour of the capital.

"What's the hurry?" I whined as we sideswiped our way past veiled women and ox carts, the dirtiest Mercedes taxis I'd ever seen, and a din of noise that would have given Times Square a run for its money.

"We have no time to lose. The longest you can stay in Saru is probably three or four days before Cthulu's people know you're here. Then they'll try to kill you because they know you were working with my father. You *can* stay as long as you like, but I'd advise against it." Hassan turned in the seat for the first time and smiled at me. "I have no objection to your dying, Radcliffe, but I'd prefer you wait till you've finished my project."

"That's big of you, Prince. How come you're driving around like this without protection? Cthulu's men want you dead more than me. I'm only an architect."

"We are being well protected, whether you see them or not." He gave a small nod toward Big Top. "Your verz is part of it."

"So where are we going now?"

"To Nalim. The place where my father wanted to build the museum."

Once we'd passed through the melee at the heart of town, the road climbed through narrow winding streets lined with cyprus and cedar trees and modest one-family houses. According to Hassan, this was an exclusive section of town where most of the diplomats and foreign businessmen lived.

"It reminds me of Haifa."

"I wouldn't know. I've never been there."

Oops. Not having been in the Mideast for many

months, I'd forgotten you didn't mention certain subjects in these climes, Israel being one of them. "How
far is Nalim from here?"

"About half an hour. On the outskirts of town. My
father wanted the museum to be close enough so all
people could visit. That will be different now, but the
building must be done."

After the suburbs came the inevitable sports complex with its seventy-thousand-seat soccer stadium,
swimming pool big enough to float all of Hannibal's
elephants, state-of-the-art track. Every Gulf state I'd
visited, no matter how poor or backward, had one of
these monstrosities in their capitals. The stadiums
were used maybe ten times a year, admission was
charged to use the pool in countries where the average income was sometimes as low as $150 a year per
. . . but all that was compensated for by the pride
factor involved. It was one of the first things you were
shown on a guided tour: the big bright flower in the
lapel of these countries' otherwise shabby suits.

"My father hated sports. And he hated that place
especially. He said it reminded him of Hitler and the
Nazi Youth."

"Why'd he build it?"

"He didn't—it was donated by two oil companies
who were afraid he would throw them out and take
over their wells. Originally that was where he
planned to put his museum, but gave up the land
when he heard they'd build it for free. It's ugly, but it
is a nice place. He ordered that any team, no matter
how small, can play in the stadium, and the pool is
open every day."

"How much does it cost to swim?"

"Nothing. And lessons are free."

Before we reached Nalim I'd begun to realize what a decent man and exceptional ruler the former Sultan of Saru had been. Hospitals and schools, factories that employed the handicapped . . . The man I knew in the Los Angeles hotel emerged in an altogether different light—as a pragmatic visionary.

Mohammed Idris Gharadani had plotted a course into the late twentieth century for his country with a determined mind and reasonable hopes. Saru was still struggling along despite its great oil reserves, but if the Sultan had been allowed to continue, I think his country would have eventually emerged a prime mover in the Mideast—right up there with the big boys.

Nalim was nothing—some houses, some goats, a store so small and dark inside that it could have passed for a cave. We were in and out of the town proper in roughly eight seconds. A few minutes more down the road the land flattened out into wide dry vistas and reddish earth. A silver sliver of a plane wrote a thin white vapor trail across the royal blue sky. In that open expanse around us it seemed such a hopeless and lovely gesture.

The car turned off the highway onto a dirt road no wider than the span of two arms. We bumped slowly down it for about ten minutes before coming to, of all things, a chain-link fence. On the other side, a gentle hill rose in front of us topped by what appeared to be a ruin.

The motor died. The chauffeur honked the horn once. He and his boss sat facing forward, saying nothing. Car metal clicked.

"What's up?"

"We're waiting for the gatekeeper."

I looked from side to side. "Where is he?"

"He lives on the other side of the ruin."

"Why don't we just climb over the fence? Save him the trouble of coming down here?"

"Because that's the only thing he lives for, Radcliffe. Five or six times a year someone comes out to look at the ruin and the old man has the great luck of being in charge. He walks down from the hill with his one key, opens the gate even though anyone *could* easily climb over, then he closes it behind them after they've passed through. The same happens when they leave. He will have something to talk about to himself afterward because there's no one else around since his wife died. For this he has a salary from the state and his life means something."

Properly chastised, I sat quietly in the back waiting for Godot the gatekeeper. He showed up five minutes later, walking like gravity had it in for him personally. Dressed in a robe that was once black but had faded into some obscure, indescribable color, the man was old and wrinkled and generally toothless. But Hassan was right—already coming down the hill the fellow babbled so happily and constantly that it was clear we were a sight for his sore eyes.

Opening the fence was a ceremony in itself. After long greetings, the man drew the key out of his robe and offered it to Hassan through the car window. The Prince gave a slight bow of approval. The other touched the key to his forehead in what I assumed was fealty. After unlocking, he walked the gate open and waved us through. Passing close by, I saw the expression on his face—pure bliss. He waved. I waved back.

"His name is Mahdi. His three sons all died fighting with my father against Cthulu."

"Did he have any daughters?"

"No. Every one of his children is dead. His wife too."

We stopped fifty feet from the ruin. Can a pile of stones be called a ruin?

"It was a castle at one time. One of the desert castles of my ancestors. They came to hunt out here."

"What period? How long ago?"

"I cannot tell you that, Radcliffe. I was forbidden to by my father."

What sounded like cicadas sawed the air around us. There was no other sound. Off in the distance, the far distance, were the black tents and grazing animals of a bedouin settlement. I thought I could make out two shepherds but wasn't sure because they were so far away.

"Why can't you tell me? Is it a secret?"

Hassan bent over, picked up a handful of earth, let it run down through his fingers. "When my father was alive and planned to build the museum here, he said when you came I was not to tell you anything about our land or its history. That was what you would have to discover for yourself. If you were a good and thorough architect, he believed you would find out everything about Saru for yourself. Read books, travel, talk to people here . . . He thought that was the only way you'd be able to build our museum correctly."

"Listen, Prince, you're getting on my nerves.

"*If* I do this museum, and I haven't yet said I *will*, I have my own ways of going about it.

"With all respect to your father, what he wanted is

about step three on a list of perhaps a hundred things I do before getting down to real work. I *read* books and talk to people and get the lay of the land. That's kindergarten. But you want some more? Which way does the wind blow here most often? What color does the earth turn evenings around twilight? What'll be the average age of the people who come to visit? Do you foresee a time when the rest of this land will be developed and if so, in what capacity? Will it be industry or residential? Do you want the museum to stand out, or complement the landscape—"

"All right, Radcliffe, I get your point. I only told you what my father said. But it doesn't matter now because as far as Nalim is concerned, we cannot build the museum here anyway. It is much too dangerous. Cthulu will attack any kind of structure we put up in Saru. It will be symbolic of my father to him."

"Where are you planning to build it?"

"In Zell am See. In Austria."

"*Austria?* The Sultan of Saru's dog museum in Austria?"

"Yes, that was my father's wish. There are two reasons. The first is because nothing will happen if it is erected outside Saru, even if it is my father's building. Cthulu is only concerned with the country. Knowing him, he'll even see it as a victory if we do it somewhere else. But the more important reason—"

I don't know what came first—the growl or the thud of a shot. Big Top had been standing nearby, nosing the ground. I wasn't looking but could hear his familiar snorts and sniffs. They stopped and he snarled so loud it made me jerk my head.

Way down the hill the old gatekeeper was pointing a pistol at us. His first shot went wild to the left, the next would've hit me if the dog hadn't jumped. Jumped straight up in front of me. The bullet smashed his head. The thick wonderful head I'd patted and hugged so many times. Big made a deep *huh* sound and slammed against my hip.

Hassan and his bodyguard shot the gatekeeper so fast so many times that bullet impact and not life kept him standing and jerking seconds longer.

I heard myself shouting, "You're a verz, don't die. You're a verz, don't die."

Verzes die. Their back legs shudder and what's left of a jaw click-click-clicks and they bleed so much you don't know where it all comes from. Then they're dead and you pull them across your lap and put your face down to theirs and plead, "Look at me! Look at me! Goddamn it, *look!*" But one eye is shot out and the other is finished looking. I rested my cheek on his wet face. Squeezing him tight, I rocked us back and forth.

The two men spoke in Arabic but I ignored them. The next time I looked up was after hearing a big windy "whoosh." The bodyguard stood with a metal gasoline can near the old man's body. It was on fire, one giant flame stinking of gasoline. And more. I'd never smelled burning flesh but it was there too, rising over the chemical reek. You don't know you know that smell until it's there and unmistakable. Burning flesh. A dead dog. The desert.

In Saru the greatest wrong a human being can suffer is cremation. According to popular belief, the act destroys the soul as well as the body thus giving the deceased no chance for redemption.

Before leaving the ruin that day, the three of us stood over the smoking body and spat on it. Another Saruvian custom.

"If the last to see a man alive spits on him, then he goes to God with that spit on his face. It is the first thing God sees."

I carried Big Top in my arms to the car. Dead, he felt much heavier. I hefted him higher onto my chest. His blood covered my clothes but I didn't think about that. I thought about him slowly eating potato chips on the patio in Santa Barbara; of how he'd appeared at the hotel during the earthquake. Venasque had loved the dog and never stopped talking about him.

"Big Top's not smart, but he's *got* smarts. The two of you are alike in that way. Fact is, the two of you are alike in a lot of ways."

"How so?" Normally I'd've bristled at being compared to a bull terrier, but the shaman's dog was different.

"Big Top knows a lot but isn't talking. You know a lot but aren't using it."

"I'm a famous architect, Venasque. People say I'm a genius."

"You *are* a genius, but you never built anything genius. You're like Big Top there too—both of you could contribute more but don't 'cause you're satisfied with the way things are. Him with his silence, and you with your genius."

"Satisfied? Venasque, you and I met because I was having a nervous breakdown. That's not exactly the symptom of a person who's satisfied with the way things *are!*"

"True, but once you got your sanity back you were only worried about not wanting to be an architect anymore. Big deal. It'd be more important if you were worried about whether or not you wanted to be a person anymore."

"You mean kill myself?"

"Naah. There's no such thing as suicide. Do you really think Man has a choice whether or not he can take his own life? We don't even know how to live the right way. You think God's going to let *us* decide whether or not to die? That's like getting the final exam on the first day of classes!"

"Then what happens to suicides?"

"It's like the kid who's called out of class to go to the principal's office: You think you know the reason why he got called, but you're wrong."

This conversation crossed my mind as I lifted the dog's body into the back of the car.

"Wait a minute." I turned. Hassan and the body-guard were a few feet behind me. "I think he should be buried here. Would that be all right? This is where the museum was going to be?"

The two men exchanged a look and the Prince nodded. "It would be a great honor if you were to lay him here, Radcliffe. I know my father would have appreciated that very much."

"All right. I think it's a good place. He has all this space to sniff around and explore."

There was an army spade in the car. The Prince took it and walked back up the hill to the high pile of stones. The bedouin tents were still there, the only dark marks on a reddish horizon. There was no time out here. Clocks had no place any more than this castle that had once been used for hunting. Big Top's skin and bones would fade back into this soil. For a while they'd be like the black tents out there—notice-able but then one day gone.

"Where would you like to lay him?" Hassan's voice was sympathetic and much quieter.

"I don't know. A place with a good view. Big Top liked to keep an eye on things, even when he was lying down."

"May I make a suggestion? Please let me show you."

We walked around the ruins to the other side. The world from there was one silent enormous desert flowing out in uncomplicated lines and empty space to more of the same. It made me feel sad and insignifi-cant. "Must be cold out here at night, nothing but stars to keep you warm."

"The place I wanted to show you is right over here." Hassan beckoned. We climbed over stones un-til coming to a small cleared space out on the edge of the hill.

"This is it—"

"This is—"

We looked at each other, Hassan with eyebrows raised. "You know this place?" he asked, unsurprised.

"Yes I know this place. But how?"

His eyes went to the dog's body in my arms. "A verz brings you where it wants to be buried."

It was not surprising that in whatever last testa-ment he'd written, the Sultan of Saru requested a very simple, quick burial. According to ritual, his son and two other intimates washed his body, then wrapped it in a rough white sheet and with little more ceremony than that, put it in the earth. I was one of the few people at graveside when they lowered him and although I rarely cry, I was crying that day along with the others. I was a newcomer to this man's goodness and intelligence, but besides the sadness of loss, it is both terribly frustrating and bitter to discover another's true worth only after they are gone. Like a treasure you've held but unknowingly let slip through your fingers.

However, it would be dishonest to say my tears that day were only for the dead. Lately life had been like a "Wild Mouse" ride at an amusement park; whipped from one extreme to the other, there'd barely been enough time to gulp a quick breath before the next dip, twist, or flip had me loop-de-looped or upside down, trying to figure out where I was and how to see things from these constantly new perspectives. Certainly I cried for the Sultan and Big Top, not least for the loss of their love and rightness, but also because I felt guilty, afraid, even excited. Two good and genuinely magical beings had died, one while saving my life. With little of their goodness and none of the magic, how was I to protect myself from the same world that had killed them? Throwing the first shovelful of desert earth back into Big Top's grave, then seeing the Sultan in *his*, was so awful yet galvanizing, that I could feel my spirit's temperature change almost by the hour.

After his father's funeral, the new Sultan of Saru and I stood alone in the vast parking lot of the royal compound. It was large enough to hold a rodeo. Although many cars were parked around us, Hassan and I were the only people there. Others were inside the residence paying respects to the family. Until now, soldiers and bodyguards had been everywhere but for the moment none were in sight.

Not looking at me, Hassan barked out a fake, offensive laugh. "I thought you *liked* my father! You were going to build this for him, you said. But now the real truth climbs out from under the Radcliffe rock, huh? I know how 'famous' you are, but really, do you believe anyone deserves so much money just for designing one goddamned building?"

I licked my lips and balled both fists in my pockets. "Why don't you get your facts straight before you sound so naive? *All* architects receive a percentage of a building's costs, Your *High*ness. I've done no work yet, but've already said I'll take fifty percent off my usual fee. Check around and you'll discover that that kind of discount is never, *ever* done. Particularly by someone as famous as me. I liked your father but I don't like you. That fifty percent reduction *is* for him. Whatever work I do on this project is for him, his memory. I don't give a damn about you and I don't give a damn about Saru. I think your father would've been offended if I did this for less. You want me to do it free? I don't believe in that. The only things you get for free are what nobody else wants. And death. Death is free."

"Hah! The important things in life are free. Look at love! Do you pay for love?"

"No, but after getting it, I've had to 'pay' a hell of a lot to keep it. Wait till you've been around Fanny Neville a while. You'll see exactly what I mean."

"I think it is only fair to tell you, Radcliffe, I have asked Fanny to marry me." New Sultan or not, he looked at me with a young man's doubt and insecurity.

I suppose I should've felt shocked or provoked, but the image of the viper tongued Ms. Neville as spouse to the head of state of a desert kingdom was so zany that I bit back a smile instead of calling for a sword and challenging him to a duel. "What did Fanny say?"

He straightened his shoulders and stuck out his chin. "That she would think about it. I wouldn't be surprised if she said yes."

"How come you want to marry her? She's got the temper of a badger. Plus isn't it a little soon to be proposing?"

"No. *I* think life with her would be generous and peaceful. I know she is partly in love with you, but I'm willing to accept that for now. People change. And gradually she'll see I'm better for her than you. She even said herself the only reason you want people around is to keep you busy till you get back to work on your buildings. She thinks the only thing you can love is your work."

"Fanny said that?"

"More than once." He said it simply and with the dignity of truth. He could have gloated or rubbed my nose in it, but didn't. I appreciated that. Fanny and I had fought so much and she'd said many astute things, but coming from this man who loved and wanted her so much, the words did far more damage than she'd ever managed in our tussles.

"Listen, what if instead of money, I offered you something better, something that will amaze you?"

Still smarting from his Fanny news, I caught only

a part of what he said and none of it registered. "What? What are you talking about?"

"You already have a great deal of money. What if, instead of this fee for your work, I paid you in magic?" One bird sang alone somewhere near. The sun was growing insistent above us and this man had just made a real offer—no tease or trick in his voice. There are moments in life of such importance that it feels like the day, your heart, your fate all suddenly stop and stand still, awed by what's happening or what's about to.

"I'm listening. Go on."

He stepped out into the parking lot. "When I was young, they taught me certain things a Sultan of Saru might need when he is ruling. My father and all of the previous Sultans knew them. One of these things I will show you now will prove this magic I mentioned is possible. But don't think I do it to show off! That's one of the first lessons you learn when they start to teach you these powers: If you ever use them in a wrong or selfish way to get something for *yourself* in life, then you are *fucked*. I, for example, would love to use what I know to win Fanny, but that is out of the question. Too bad for me. Point out what kind of car you like, Radcliffe." He gestured around with out-flung arms, as if he were one of those lovably rabid salesmen on television in L.A. who, wearing cowboy hats or riding giant turtles, try to get you to "come on down" to their used car lots.

Mercedeses, Lincolns, the Saru-biquitous Range Rovers, all stood around in shiny splendor. I was keen to see what he was going to do, so I scanned the ranks like a real prospective buyer. Sticking out like a gaudy bum from all of that other swanky iron was a lollipop-green Lada, a Russian automobile that looks and drives like a telephone booth on wheels.

I pointed to it. "How about the Lada?"

Hassan looked at the green car with his head slightly tilted, as if listening to secret inner voices. Then he gave the smallest nod and walked to it through the other cars.

As if ashamed, or being shunned for its ugliness and cheapness by the more formidable machines, the Lada stood apart from the others at the place where the gravel bordered the lawn.

He put his hand on the roof and patted it. "This is my car, but that's all right. It is a real car—they do not cost much, they're well built, and when you ride you feel the whole road. I like that."

"I would've thought you'd own one of these big boys—" I remembered the pictures of him in trendy magazines.

"No, no. To father's despair, I always liked Ladas. My father . . ." He said nothing else for a time, only rested his hands on the green roof and sighed.

"My father loved beautiful things. He believed in them, if I can say it that way. It was very hard for him to hold himself in and not buy more." Looking first inside the car and then at me, Hassan walked around the side. While speaking, he slowly continued to circle. One time, two, three . . . I thought at first he was checking for something—dents on the outside or whatever—but after the third or fourth go-round my eyes began to narrow.

"When you are raised with money in every pocket, and people are down on their knees to you

from the day you are born, you have a hard time staying human. My father did a very good job of being a
great ruler, but he learned a taste early for beautiful
things. I am different because I was sent away to a
private school from a very early age." Round and
round and round. My eyes narrowed more and
watched him oh so closely. Round and round. What-
was-he-doing?

"At this school I grew up with many American
kids who were spoiled, but spoiled in the way they
had so much money they could afford the luxury of
hating the school and their parents and everything
they came from. We all wore lumberjack shirts and
smoked dope when we could get it and said 'fuck the
rich.' We really didn't mean that, but we said it and it
gave us a little perspective about our lives. These kids
knew where I came from and who I was, but to the
son of the president of United States Steel or Ford, a
prince is only amusing. It was a good experience because I was not used to being treated like an equal,
but it was not what my father expected. He wanted
me to learn perfect English and Western economics
there, which I did, but I also learned Pink Floyd and
how to wear jeans with holes in the ass."

The Lada had begun to shrink.

I'd been listening carefully to him and thus not
registering what was going on right in front of me.
His tale of the poor little rich boy away at private
school suckered me into looking away while the ma-
gician started to work. But when I realized, it took
only seconds to know this man wasn't, *couldn't be*,
working an illusion or ruse: He was shrinking a full-
size automobile by walking around it. No abraca-

dabra, no zim-zams, only circles round and round a one-ton green Russian box, and every one made it smaller.

"What are you doing, Hassan?"

He kept moving. It kept shrinking. "Giving you a choice, Mr. Famous Architect. Showing you what is possible and giving you a choice."

It was down to the size of a VW Bug. He kept talking. I was watching but not listening. What car's smaller than a VW? That size. Smaller. Then it was no longer. . . . No adult could get into something that size, even if they bent like a pocket knife. Maybe a child. Yes, a child might've gotten in. But another circle and too late—too small even for a child. A dog could get in this time. A small dog.

Hassan kept walking, talking quietly. The car was now down to the size of a couch. Round once more. Too small to sit on. A rug. Round and round. A radio. A loaf of bread. Where it stops nobody knows. The two of us were still alone out there. The bird still sang. The expression on Hassan's face had turned from calm to naughty, as if he had something more up his sleeve and was about to show it.

"What do you think, Radcliffe?" He stopped when it was the size of three or four cigarettes laid side to side, a Dinkytoy, a half piece of toast. Its brilliant unnatural green spotted the white gravel like fresh paint. It wasn't so different in color from the grass. Small enough now to be overlooked in the grass. Easily.

Hassan bent down and, picking it up, held it out for me to see. When I reached for it, tentatively, he snatched it back and shook his head.

"Watch." He put it in his mouth whole, chewed not very long, swallowed. Gone.

Thank God I'd been around Venasque enough to see plenty of astounding things. Otherwise I'd have obeyed my guts at that moment and started running.

"That didn't happen. You didn't eat your car. You just ate your car!"

"I ate my car, Mr. Radcliffe. Right in front of you."

"You ate your car. It was that big and then it was this big and then you ate it! I saw. I saw you do it." I began to hyperventilate. The inside of my head grew light and pink and full of dizzy. I couldn't stop talking. Venasque said never doubt miracles—only your own reaction to them.

"This is a very fucking seriously scary situation, Your Highness. You just shrunk a big fucking *car* and ATE it! I mean, that is not what I wanted to *see* today, okay? So will you pretty pretty pretty please tell me what you're doing so my head doesn't detach in the next minute? Pretty please? I want to get out of this country. I *really* want to get out—"

"Shoosh. Shoosh. Calm. Everything is all right. I only did that so you know and can believe me. I am now going to give you the choice." He raised his left arm out to the side. "Money here." Right arm out, other direction. "Magic here. I will pay you with whatever you choose."

"What magic? What are you talking about?"

His elbows came in close to his sides, both hands pointed at me like a cowboy holding two guns. "It's simple: I'll give you the money you asked for, *or* I'll give you one wish and guarantee that it'll come true. Nothing else as payment—only one wish, but for whatever you want."

"You can do that?"

"You saw what I can do. Yes, I have that power."

"Why didn't your father use it to save himself?"

"Because it is not allowed. I told you. We can use it only to help Saru. If you build the museum, you are helping the country."

My mouth was terribly dry. I kept trying to lick my lips but without any luck. I looked at the sun. I looked at Hassan. His hands dropped to his sides and he shrugged. "Either is yours if you choose to do it."

I licked my lips with a tongue like pumice. "Promise on the honor of your father."

He put up his right hand and closed his eyes. "I promise on the honor of my father that I can do this."

"I'll also want an ironclad contract that says if you *can't*, you pay cash."

"Agreed."

Venasque, my life, the breakdown, work—all crossed my mind like the vein network seen in an eye when, looking into a light, you catch a certain angle. Everything interconnected, everything of a piece.

"I'll do it for two wishes."

He shook his head. "Impossible."

"But I'd use the first one for someone else. It wouldn't be for me. That's fair. One for me and the other for another."

"Who is this other, Fanny?"

"No, someone else."

"Claire Stansfield?"

"You know about her?"

"Fanny tells me everything," he said proudly. "You are disgracing yourself, bargaining like we are in the market! I am not selling eggplants or rugs. I will not invite you into my shop for a glass of mint tea while we discuss terms. I offer you the miraculous, Harry Radcliffe. One wish. If you're a good man, you'll accept and give it to her. Help your friend with it."

"Why give me this choice, Hassan? Why not pay money? You can afford it. Why even offer a wish?"

"Because I promised my father before he died. It was his idea. He thought you were a good man and deserved the chance to be given the choice. I argued against it but he prevailed. He was my father and I honor his wishes."

"He really liked me, didn't he?"

I said it to bait him, but to my surprise he answered solemnly, "He liked you very much. He thought you had a very talented back of your head."

"What does that mean?"

"It is an old belief in Saru. We say there are two men inside each of us, except they are not aware of the fact they share the same space. One looks in one direction, one the other."

"You mean like the Janus figure?"

"No, as far as I understand, Janus is one man alone looking both forward and backward over his life and taking it all into consideration. Here they say the point of life is getting the two 'sides' of your head, the men inside, to realize they are there and that it would be much more effective if they worked together. We believe that's why people behave so strangely—sometimes the man in front decides, sometimes he sleeps and the man in back decides. The man in the front of your head is logical and pragmatic, the one at the back is a dreamer, an artist. People say here, 'A good front,' or 'Radcliffe has a very talented back of the head.' It's a quick way to describe a person's character."

"Sounds like watered-down Freud to me."

"It's not so different, except they were saying it here a thousand years before Sigmund Freud."

"Touché. I'll do it."

"You don't want more time to decide?"

"I've decided. How do we do this?"

"Say, 'I accept the wish and will do what I can.' "

"That's all?"

"Only that."

"Sounds a little skimpy for this deal. You give me a cosmic wish, I give you a billion-dollar building, and that's all I have to say?"

"It's a deal between God, you and Saru. He does not need a thirty-page contract."

"Or a notary public, huh? One last thing—what if my wish was for you to die, Hassan? What would happen then?"

"Nothing. I am protected for now."

"You're sure?"

He wasn't. The flash across his eyes said he wasn't sure of anything.

"*Is* that your wish? That I die?"

"I don't know you well enough to want you dead, Sultan. 'I accept the wish and will do what I can.' "

Nothing happened. The sky didn't crack, no oceans roared. The only thing I felt was some sweat rolling slowly down my back. "What happens now?"

He put out his hand and we shook, hands tightly gripped, looking each other in the eye. "Now you can make your wish. Or whenever you like. It will happen."

Still shaking, I looked down at our hands and

thought how appropriate—hands. I said to Hassan
and Whomever Else was in on this, "I wish that Claire
Stansfield is given back her hand."

"Say it again, Radcliffe. Say it for yourself this
time."

"I wish Claire Stansfield is given back her hand."

We landed in Vienna about nine in the evening.
I'd insisted on a commercial flight from Saru rather
than return on the royal jet, mostly because I was
tired of being surrounded by people I had to talk to.
More than anything else, I wanted to be alone to let
my brain work in silence. Too much had gone on in
the last days without a chance to be properly pro-
cessed and considered. It was as if my mind was a file
room where recently, instead of putting things in their
proper places, people had simply opened the door,
thrown papers on the floor and walked out again. I
may be a genius and have a very talented back of the
head, but my mind works slowly and cautiously. It is
an old man, looking at ideas under a magnifying glass
and bright light, turning them every which way before making any decisions.

On the flight back I sat in first class next to a man
who kept telling me in happy bad English his name
was Rabbit Hat when translated from German. Finally I told Mr. Hasenhüttl I heard him the first six
times and didn't care what his name meant.

Either he understood or caught the homicidal tone
of my voice, which fortunately sent him back to his
Saru Air magazine. Besides his unfortunate name and
manner, Rabbit Hat also had the bad habit, or good
revenge, of sucking his teeth with foul vigor. Just

when you thought or hoped he'd gotten that poppy seed or piece of meat out and blessed silence returned, he went back to work in there with short wisps and whistles and hard sucks that kept me from doing anything, other than devising ways to torture and kill him. Luckily he got up at one point and spent what I guess was a long time in the bathroom because when he returned, I'd slipped into the sweetest little cat nap. Soon, however, dinner was served and this sucking monster, this Austrian from hell, decided I needed to be awakened for it. Tap Tap Tap on the arm. "Hello?" Tap Tap Tap. "Hello? Time to eat, Hello, you!" Tap—

"Stop that!" I jerked out of sleep like he'd stung me.

Pouting, he pointed at the table in front of me. It was down and on it sat a tray with a chicken leg hidden by a slice of pineapple topped by a zip of whipped cream, fat golden pellets of potato too geometric to be healthy, and other edibles that could only cause despair.

My gaze stopped on a fork and the idea of stabbing my neighbor in the head with it came and went. Instead I closed my eyes and prepared for the drop back into sleep.

Tap Tap Tap.

"I don't *want* dinner. Leave me alone, please."

Tap Tap— I grabbed his fingers before the third tap and held them. "Don't touch me again. Don't talk to me. Don't suck your teeth." I rang for the stewardess. She came quickly, having been warned who I was by the Sultan's people.

"Miss, this man is annoying me. I want you to find me another seat immediately."

"I'm sorry, sir, but there are no free seats in first class."

"Then I'll move back to tourist. Just get me another seat *now*."

After she scurried off, Hasenhüttl said quietly in perfect, unaccented English, "Gee whiz, Radcliffe, I'd've thought you were tougher than that. You sounded like a faggot hair dresser. 'Just get me another seat *now*.' " He imitated a swishy gay's whining voice.

"Who are you? What do you want from me?"

"That would take a long time to explain. I'm Rabbit Hat. Or maybe Air Wair with bouncing soles. I don't know—what do you think my name should be? Here comes your seat."

Our backs were turned to the stewardess so it was impossible to see her coming, but a moment after he spoke she touched me on the shoulder and said she'd found a seat for me. I looked at Hasenhüttl and moved to get up, but he stood instead.

"I'm here to fuck you up, Harry. Plain and simple. Wishes aren't free. There's always a kick in the ass that comes along with them. I'm yours." He told the worried-looking stewardess he'd be moving and not me.

As he slid past my knees, I asked, "Why are you telling me this?"

Having reached the aisle, he bent over me. "Because there's no fear without knowing. You're never really afraid until you're sure. Now you know. Now it's for sure. I'll see you around."

What did he look like? An overweight businessman in a dull suit, square eyeglasses, forgettable face. If he said he sold ink or tractors or was a politician in a Communist country, you'd believe it. Rabbit Hat was a good name for him. A big rabbit in a hat.

Several minutes after he left I got up, handed my untouched tray of food to the stewardess, and went back. The tourist section was packed but they'd found him a place between two Arabs. He was reading a computer magazine and didn't look up.

"Who sent you? Cthulu?"

He ignored me. The Arabs stared.

"Rabbit Hat, I'm asking you a question. Who sent you? What are you supposed to do to me?"

The plane bumped hard and I almost lost my balance. My man pushed his glasses up and rubbed his face. "Think you'd better get back to your seat, Harry. Looks like we've hit some turbulence."

"Answer my question first." The plane bucked again, swayed from side to side.

Pulling the glasses down, he looked at me coldly. "Answer your question? I'm not here to do what you like, friend. It was nice enough of me to warn you I'm around. I didn't have to do that. I could've just started sprinkling tacks on your path and watched you dance down it barefoot. But now you know. Look, you read the fairy tales when you were a kid. Rub the lamp and a genie comes out, but so do a lot of other things! The greatest thing that can happen in life is your wish comes true. Or the *worst* thing that happens is your wish comes true. I'm the other side of the wish, honey. The dark side of the moon. I'm the one who can walk on your voice."

I returned to my seat and watched a film I don't remember a bit of because the headphones were tuned to a classical music channel and I didn't change it.

Vienna airport is a nice piece of work. It's well conceived and small enough so it doesn't take forever to get out once your plane's landed. I was one of the first off our flight, but lagged behind so I could watch my new nemesis and size him up better. He brushed past in the flow of others and walked quickly toward passport control. After a cursory glance, an inspector waved him through but I was stopped and they checked my passport thoroughly, even turning it upside down and holding it to the light at one point.

Thus it took some time to catch up with Hasenhüttl at the baggage claim. Although my bag was already in sight, I stood five or six feet behind him and waited till he got his before snatching mine off the belt. I kept the six feet between us while we walked toward the "Nothing to Declare" door to the outside. He passed the last customs officer and the electric doors slid open.

Ambassador "Off the Record" Awwad was standing on the other side of the doors, and for a moment I thought he was there for me, but I soon realized he wasn't. A smile erupted on Awwad's face when he saw Hasenhüttl, then he stepped forward and grabbed his bag. Simultaneously, a customs officer touched my arm and gestured for me to stop and open my suitcase. Outside, my two pals turned and walked away. The doors slid closed.

"Shit!"

"Bitte?"

"I said *shit!* You want to look in my bag? Here!"

I had to talk to someone about this and the best person, if only he'd been alive, was Venasque.

Halfway back to town in the taxi I remembered what
had happened with Walker Easterling's young son
when I was last here: Nicholas's magic at the lunch
table, the way his parents had unconcernedly let us
go alone to the flea market, then climbing the roof
there, the way the boy jumped onto the train and told
me to listen for . . . the voice of God? What was it
exactly? That part was foggy in my mind. What was
most vivid and important was the conviction that
Venasque had returned from the dead that day to in-
habit this child so as to tickle and point me in a certain important direction.

Was it possible to reach my mentor again through
this child? I needed only ten, fifteen minutes to talk,
to lay it out and say "What should I do? And if you
won't tell me that, just say if I'm warm or cold here. Is
my compass pointing in the right direction?"
Venasque. If I could touch base with him I knew he
would help. I knew he would want to help. Nicholas
Easterling. I had to see that kid, talk to him, *try*.

I got to the hotel too late to call but was so wide
awake and wound up by this new possibility that I
dropped off my bag and went out to walk on the
Ringstrasse. I passed a man in a phone booth and saw
him take off his hat before dropping coins in the slot. I
wondered if he always took his hat off before talking
on the phone. My father always listened to Verdi's
Masked Ball when he did his income taxes. Venasque
had a special spoon he used only for cooking soup.
Habits. They keep us so comfortably grounded on
earth. With a jolt I realized most of the habits I'd accu-
mulated over my adult life had generally disappeared
or changed very noticeably in the last months. Walking in the cold Vienna air, I checked this idea by ex-

amining how I brushed my teeth—up and down now, when for years it had been side to side. I startled a couple nearby by proclaiming, "I was always up and down!" From there I mentally scanned a bunch of habits, as well as other personal trivia, and it became disturbingly apparent that virtually without noticing it, great chunks and blocks of what I'd been had either vanished or changed dramatically in the last year.

What did that mean? Was it good or bad? I asked Venasque that question a million times—"Is it good or bad?" At the beginning he answered because I was so confused and needed his help too much. But as I healed and got stronger he'd turn it around, "What do *you* think, Harry?" Or once when he was cranky, "Jesus Christ, that's the only interesting thing *about* life—trying to find out if things are good or bad. You want me to tell you all the time. You're like the dumb man who's never had sex. He goes up to someone and asks, 'What's sex like?' This other guy says, 'Nice, but it always gets me in trouble.' So the first guy says, 'That's all I need to know. I'm staying away from it!' "

In front of a McDonald's I looked through their beaming, gleaming window and wondered if I was disappearing. First my habits jump ship, which I don't realize till *now*, then comes a nervous breakdown that wipes most of the rest of my slate clean. . . . Carrying these thoughts, I entered the yellow/red happyland of the perpetual cheeseburger. At the counter a tired-looking Oriental girl tried to smile when asking what I wanted. I ordered a Big Mac and a Coke and took them to the nearest table. Say what you will, there's something comfortably womblike about eating at McDonald's, no matter where it is. I used to think their garish American "Midwestness"

made these restaurants as outrageous and incongru-
ous as flying saucers, especially when you saw them
plopped down and glowing on the streets of Berlin or
Bangkok. But that opinion changed too one night in
Aachen when the only thing I wanted in the world
was a burger with fries and I found a Golden Arches
and it was great. No matter who you are, sitting at
one of those familiar tables munching familiar warm
food, knowing everyone around you is eating the
same meal, is like a religious ceremony: Let us all now
unwrap and eat our hamburgers.

On the last bite of my late meal in Vienna, I realized that disappearing and McDonald's had a lot in
common. Western culture sends out so many mixed
signals it's a wonder there aren't more lunatics at
large. On the one hand we're taught to do whatever
we can to prove we're individuals. Hey, short of
death, what could be worse than being mistaken for
another person? An added benefit is, the more individual you are, the more chance you have at a kind of
immortality. Look at Gandhi. Look at Mao. Look at
Elvis.

On the *other* hand, we're expected to be Republi-
cans or Democrats, Beatles fans, members of the
Lion's Club or Kiwanis, proud citizens of the U.S. of
A., France . . . Trinidad.

What sane society screams that one must be different to be successful, then with the same breath says
anyone who doesn't like hamburgers is a "weirdo"?
To yourself be true, but if you're too true you'll be
alone. Or you'll "disappear" because the status quo
has no use for the genuine oddball. Taking out a pen,
I wrote on a rumpled napkin: "Two ways to be invisible—eat every meal at McDonald's, or be so strange

that people make every effort *not* to see you—bums, real geniuses, etc.''

▶️ Next morning the phone rang while I was adjusting the water for a bath. Telephones make me nervous and excited. Inevitably I overreact when one rings nearby. Scampering naked back into the bedroom, I lifted the receiver prepared for anything.

It was Awwad, or rather his personal secretary, wanting to know if the ambassador or the embassy staff could do anything for me while I was in town. I wanted to say yes, answer these three questions in whatever order you please: (1) Who is Hasenhüttl? (2) What's Awwad's connection with him? (3) What does he want from me? Instead I thanked them for their concern and said I'd be in Vienna only a day or two and didn't think I'd need their help.

I walked back into a welcoming cloud of hot-water steam in the bathroom. Adjusting the tap, I heard the phone ring again. This time it was Fanny.

"You told Hassan I have the temper of a badger?''

"You do. How are you Fanny? How is your mother?''

"It's nine o'clock there, right? Have you taken your morning bath yet?''

"I was just running the water when the phone rang.''

"Well, here's something for you to think about when you get in: I've decided to marry Hassan.''

There was a mirror across the room. I looked into it and raised my eyebrows, as if to say, "What can you do?''

"Aren't you going to say anything? Aren't you going to tell me not to?"

"No, Fanny. You want to marry the guy, do it. But to call up and tell me over the fucking *telephone*, does not deserve a human response from me! No, I'm not going to stop you. I will tell you I think you're a coward for not having had the nuts to look me in the eye when you said it."

"You're a genuinely dreadful man."

"Better dreadful than spineless, Toots. I would never have done it like this to you. Never."

"You'll never get the chance, Fuck Head." She hung up.

I walked back to the tub and got in although the water was still far too hot. When I got out twenty minutes later my body looked like smoked salmon. While soaking, I conjured and mouthed three or four hundred brilliantly witty and cruel lines I wished I'd been able to think up while talking to her. The French even have a phrase for it: *esprit de l'escalier*. The spirit of the staircase; what I wish I'd said a moment ago but didn't. In my case, what I wish I'd said a moment ago but didn't because I was too stunned and hurt to respond. Using the phone was her knockout punch. Like a doctor calling to say you've got terminal cancer.

"Goddamned telephone!" I moaned, rubbing my neck with a towel and staring into the other room at that guilty black object. It slid so many words from so many voices into your ear and caused so much trouble. Voices. Words. Volume. "Maybe God is volume. Don't be surprised that all the words are God." *That's* what little Nicholas Easterling had said to me, standing on the roof of that subway train as it moved out of

the station. Words. Mysterious ones from a child.
Shock words from a lover. And what had the inscrutable Hasenhüttl said to me the night before? "I'm the
one who can walk on your voice."

It took hours to reach the Easterlings. When I
did, Maris said her husband was out of town and she
had a cold. Meaning, obviously, go away and come
back at a better time. I convinced her it was important, I wouldn't stay long, and without directly men-
tioning the boy said it had mostly to do with their
"offspring." She chuckled and invited me over.

The apartment was a quick ride from the hotel. I
was there in a jiffy and despite knowing I was coming, Maris still sounded flabbergasted to hear my
voice on her intercom.

"How'd you get here so *fast?* Did you beam up?"

The door buzzed and with a very excited heart, I
pushed it open.

Standing at the bottom of the staircase, I looked up
and realized the grim fact I would have to climb more
than five flights to reach the Easterling apartment.
Americans aren't used to climbing stairs anymore. Or
more than one flight, anyway. Tedious and old-fash-
ioned, a long climb is also guaranteed to cause de-
pression because it reminds you in two minutes how
grossly out of shape you are. I was beginning to
breathe heavily by the third floor and sounded like a
dirty phone caller rounding the banister to the fifth. A
thin cat with a sweet face stood up there on the landing, twitching its tail.

"Hello there, kitty." I reached down and stroked
its head. It pushed up into my hand and purred. Very

nice. My kind of feline. Any cat that behaves like a
dog is welcome in my universe. Otherwise not. I con-
tend that an animal that thinks itself superior, yet is
content to play with a piece of string for three hours,
is lacking in important matters of the spirit.

"His name is Orlando."

Bent over to pet the cat, I twisted around, looked
up, and saw a giant round belly. Peering over it came
the beautiful face of Maris Easterling. Although she
wore no makeup and her complexion was too pale,
she still looked fine. Stupendously pregnant, but fine.
Maris Easterling had not been pregnant when I saw
her less than a week before!

My spirit said, "Uh-oh" before my conscious mind
caught up and began realizing what was going on.

"Hi. You made it up those stairs okay?"

I was staring at her stomach. She was so very, *very*
pregnant under that blue sweatshirt and stretched
pair of pants. This woman *was not pregnant* when we
met a hundred hours before.

Rudely, instead of going to her, I sat down on the
step next to the cat and rubbed a hand over the top of
my head.

"Are you okay, Harry? Those stairs can really kill.
Want a drink of water?"

"No thanks. Your boy isn't around, is he?" But
already I knew there was no Easterling child. Yet. No
Nicholas. It *had* been Venasque who led me to the flea
market that day, but only that day masquerading as a
child not yet born. Once again, my shaman had put
on one of his performances for me.

Maris continued smiling at me and then shrugged.
"You mean Walker? No, I told you, he's out of town
until tomorrow."

"No, not your husband, your *son*, Nicholas."

"God, how'd you know that?"

Purring louder, the cat pushed into my side. I hugged him into me, as if for dear life. "Know *what*? What do you mean?"

"That name, 'Nicholas'! We only decided on names the other night and here you are already knowing it! Nicholas for a boy and Lydia for a girl." She looked at her stomach. "Do you think they're nice names?"

"There *is* no boy yet, is there?" Unthinkingly I looked at her door, still hoping the child I'd met would emerge. But there was no magical son Nicholas yet. Not for months. Not till he was born.

"We don't know if it's a boy yet. I was in the hospital and they gave me that test where they can determine what sex the child is? But I said I didn't want to know. Walker agreed. This'll probably be the only child we have. We want it to be a surprise."

Venasque came as the boy for a day to tell me those things about God, volume, words. One day, no more. I was alone now. Did that mean he thought I could handle matters on my own, or was he limited to one visit, that sole appearance? Was he standing on a cloud in heaven, eating potato chips and shaking his head at how badly I was handling my life?

Maris and I spoke for another half hour. Luckily she was full of enthusiasm for my work and asked quite technical questions about how I'd conceived and achieved a certain this and that in my designs. Running as much on empty as I was, talking about the work, work I'd been listless toward for so long, lit a small pilot light in my spirit.

Before I left she shyly asked if I'd be willing to look at some of her "things," as she called them. These things turned out to be marvelous miniature cities done from a variety of materials and that showed a real talent for the stylishly preposterous and visionary. From what little I could remember of that time, they also reminded me of the city I was building when I was crazy. One in particular, and I asked if she'd consider selling it.

"Sell Harry Radcliffe one of *my* cities? Why that one, if you don't mind my asking?"

"Because it reminds me of a madness I once had and miss, in certain ways."

"You miss being *mad*?"

"I miss being obsessed. I like the weather there."

She touched my shoulder. "You sound so sad saying that. I don't think crazy people are obsessed. They whirl, but don't know it. The fun of obsession is stepping back once in a while, catching your breath, and seeing what you've been doing in the middle of your tornado. Crazy people can't step back. They just spin till they go up in smoke."

A gentle white fog/mist that had been sitting on Vienna gradually thickened into snow about an hour out of the city. The day had begun as one of those unique winter jewels where the pureness of sky and sun makes you feel life is generous. That lasted a few hours until clouds began scudding in from the west on a nasty little button-your-top-button wind. I was at the train station by then and actually preferred the idea of traveling across a day the color of stone. The express from Vienna to Zell am See was scheduled to take four hours. Leaving early, I hoped to be there by noon. A few days getting the lay of the land and a good whiff of the place was my invariable first step before returning to Los Angeles and beginning pre-liminary sketches. A professional racing driver I know says whenever he has a race, no matter if he has driven the course a hundred times, part of his fixed regimen is to walk slowly around the track before he even gets in the car. Me too. Without a hundred people around telling and asking me what to do, I visit a new site often, alone, before putting a protractor to paper or poking at a calculator.

I glanced up from my map as we swept past the immense baroque abbey at Melk, overlooking the Danube. When riding a train, I like to look at a map of the route we're traveling. First I search for any cities on it I've heard and dreamed of all my life, their names as romantic and exciting as movie stars: Salz-burg, Venice, Prague. Next comes the search for su-perbly named places I will never see but am glad to read once, and forever after know exist—Ybbs, Znojmo in Czechoslovakia, Winklmoos Alm. Bronze Sydney gave me this gift. She said it was like looking out a car window and watching someone who doesn't see you. That way, you're always one up on them, though it's unlikely you'll ever see them again. Znojmo, I know you, but you don't know about meeee. . . .

The train ride was bliss. The snow whipping hori-zontal outside only added to the feeling of cozy lux-ury and calm I felt as we flew clickity-click over the flats in the east and then began to rise and see moun-tains in the distance once we had passed the city of

Linz. I had a history of Saru in my bag but deserts, burning sand, and camels didn't fit the mood of this trip. Neither did an English translation of Otto Wagner's *Modern Architecture*, which I'd bought in Vienna but not looked at since. Although I was content to be there alone, after a few hours I became slightly restless and got up to go out into the corridor to stretch my legs. Sliding the compartment door open, I checked both ways to see if anyone was in the passageway. Not a soul. Stepping out, I bent down to look out a window and desperately wished I had a cigarette. To smoke in that empty corridor, with the noise of the train getting louder, my head pressed against the frosty glass, would have been perfect. Outside, two white cows stood in a white field looking impassively at each other as snow landed on their backs and dark noses. A farmer drove a tractor slowly down a country road parallel to the tracks. A woman sat next to him on the seat, hands crossed in her lap. Both wore green cardigan sweaters against the swirling snow. Their faces were very red and their hands were bare. I saw no buildings of any kind around and wondered where these people were going, how much longer they had to travel.

Caught up in worrying about freezing farmers, it took time to realize English was being spoken nearby. When I'm traveling in a country that doesn't speak English, suddenly hearing it again is both a treat and an insult after so much verbal static. A treat because I know those words! I can understand again. Praise the Lord! An insult because once you listen, it's mortifying to hear what people say in your language. Everything is a complaint, everything is a comparison—"I've been constipated since I left home." "You're lucky—I got just the opposite problem. I'm missing half my tours!" "How much is that in real money?" Etc. Ozzie and Harriet go abroad. "I Love Lucy" without the humor.

Prepared to listen for five minutes to grumbles and whines about food, prices, accommodations . . . I tuned my eavesdropping ears to the next compartment where the door was open and the English was coming from. A man with a resonant voice and slight accent was speaking. Curious, I walked down the hall a ways as if I were out for a stroll. Turning, I came back and looked in at the last second. A rather pretty teenage boy was facing a gray-haired man, who was wearing a black sweater and pants. At first glance I thought he was a priest. Both were nodding their heads. Neither looked at me.

"Where did I fight? I fought the Russians in Wien! At the end of the war, the Nazis were sending any boy out who could breathe and carry a rifle. My brother Klaus, seventeen years old, was killed and my best friend too. Many people hid their sons from the Nazis at that time, as later they hid their daughters from the Russians for exactly the same reason—to stop the rapes. The Nazis raped us boys by putting us in helmets and sending us to fight. The Russians raped the girls . . . Hmph! . . . in the more normal way. But what's the difference, you know? Either way it is, take off your pants and do what I tell you or die.

"I was a big shot when I was fifteen, if I do say so myself. At fifteen every boy is full of shit. So Mr. Bigshot full of shit says, 'Okay, I'll go and fight.' We boys, *children*, against the Russian army. There was nothing left of our army! No bullets, no food, all of the officers had been taken back to defend Germany. . . . Ha! It was suicide, but we big shots went to fight. Can you imagine our stupidity? It was almost beautiful."

"Was it exciting?"

"It was *boring* at first because nothing happened, then in one night it was the most frightening time I have ever known. This night they woke us up screaming 'Run! The Russians are coming, there are millions of them and no stopping them. Run. Try to get away.' "

The old man stopped talking. I was craned so far over to catch every word that my back ached. Then I heard the sound of a match popping open, a cigarette being lit, a long draw, exhaling. Not only did I want to hear the rest of this story sitting comfortably in a warm compartment, I also wanted to bum a cig from the guy.

"So we ran. My God did we run! But at night, where are you going to go? The enemy could be anywhere. Especially when you don't know an area. Up near Gmund we were, on the border. It was so dark and we were so scared. Running and falling and running again. What a night! Finally the sun started coming up, thank God. It was very quiet. We kept stopping and listening for cannons or guns, but nothing. It was a beautiful day. We got directions south toward Wien from a farm woman who was crying, 'What do we do? They'll kill us. They'll come in and kill us all!' By then we had dropped our guns and packs somewhere because they were too heavy. The Russians were right behind us, what did we care about *rucksacks?* Well, we cared the middle of that day when we were so goddamned hungry and didn't have anything to eat! Now you must remember that there was very little food around in those days. Did I already tell you that? The only available food was for the army, so when *we* didn't have any, we couldn't just go up to a door and ask someone for a bread or potato. There were none. None! The entire country was starving. The Russians were coming, the Americans were coming, everyone was coming and we were starving.

"Now I will tell you the most incredible part of the story. I have remembered this image more clearly, I must say, than many other things I remember from forty years ago and the war. I don't know why. Maybe because it was so strange and unreal.

"We had been running for twenty hours and none of us had eaten any food. Nothing. Water we could find, but food was nowhere. At the end of the day we slept again in the woods. You know how dark those forests are in the Waldviertel, eh? But we had to sleep somewhere, so we walked far into the woods and lay down to sleep in the dark and cold again. It was again the most terrible and frightening kind of night. Every sound woke us up. One boy was crying. And then early, early in the morning, for the first time, we began to hear big guns going off somewhere and we knew they were coming now. So there were three of us sitting up together in the black woods, waiting for the first light, any light, to come so we could start again running to Wien.

"But now listen, when the light did come and we'd been going maybe two hours, we came to the wonder, a vision I see as clearly this moment as forty years ago. On the main road near Eggenburg we came to a house, a farmhouse, that had bread everywhere. There were trucks in the *Hof* full of bread, the doors of the *Scheune*, the barn, were open and *it* was full of bread. I cannot explain to you what it was like. Bread was everywhere. We could smell it from the road, Markus, can you imagine? A house of bread! And us so damned hungry. We looked at each other and thought this is a trick of God. Or the devil. This wasn't possible—life was never so friendly. We forgot about the Russians and ran across the road like wild men. You have never seen so much bread in your life. Who was it for? My friend Tilo went over to a truck and climbed on it. He got up there and started throwing bread to us over his shoulder. Like this—fuf-fuf-fuf. Big round, brown breads. God! They were rolling all over the ground and us laughing, running to catch them. We were crazy with hunger but were going to eat fresh bread in one minute, all that we wanted. As we rushed over to grab them up—BANG! a gun went off. From heaven to hell in one second. We'd forgotten the war and the Russians with all that beautiful bread in sight. Then someone yelled in German, 'Don't touch that bread! Get away from it or I'll shoot you!' We looked around, I with two fat ones in my hands, and there's a boy no older than us with a rifle pointed.

" 'Are you crazy?' Tilo screamed at him. 'What do you care if we take some? There are hundreds here, thousands!'

" 'I know, but I can't let you do it,' the boy said. 'My orders are to kill anyone who takes even one. It's bread for the army.'

" 'But we *are* the army!' I screamed. Look at our goddamned uniforms, *Trottel!'*

" 'I still can't do it. I was told not to give any without orders. I have to shoot if you take any, so put them down.'

" 'All right, you have orders, but one bread—one for each of us. You have thousands. None will be missed!' I pleaded.

"The son of a whore wouldn't do it. When I started to hide one under my shirt, he saw and pointed his rifle at me. The look in his face said he would shoot me, no question. I let the thing drop on the ground. It was so soft. Never in my life have I wanted something as much as that bread at my feet. I couldn't stop looking at it. Like I was hypnotized.

"Tilo said, *'Dreckskerl*, give us one! Just one, who'll know it's missing?'

" 'Because they'll shoot me if I do. How do I know you aren't them?'

"We argued more but no use. No bread for us. *Ay Gott*, I can still catch that smell in the *Hof*. Whenever I pass a *Bäckerei* and smell, I remember that day at the bread house. Anyway, we turned around and walked away. We discussed going back and killing this guy, but none of us were capable of that yet. We were boys!

"Lucky us, we met with some soldiers who had food. They were going *richtung* Wien, so they shared their food and we moved on together. Later that day we heard the guns again and right after that we came to the next crazy place, just like the bread house. Only at this farm, there was a soldier guarding hundreds of bicycles. They would have gotten us home fast, but this *hosnscheissa* had crazier orders than the first: He wouldn't let us have bicycles because he was guarding them against the Russians! The Russians were so close we could hear them loading their guns and laughing. We all knew how much they hated us for what our army had done to them, and they were savages anyway, nightmare people—Tartars and Cossacks and *Ur-typs* from Mongolia. We yelled and yelled at this man that we should all run now while there was still a small chance. But no—he was staying and fighting and we could go shit ourselves. Houses full of bread and bicycles, but none for us."

🔊 "I sound like Donald Pobiner." Shrugging the suitcase higher into my hand, I stepped away from the train. My best friend when I was ten was a tight-assed little shit named Donald Pobiner who was no fun and even then had the infuriating habit of making pronouncements that were mostly stupid but always irrefutable, as far as Donald was concerned. "Ketchup gives you cancer" being one of his more memorable ones.

When the train slowed for Zell am See, I looked through the window and asked myself, "What's so special about this place?" There was a nice lake surrounded by medium-sized mountains, their tops covered with snow. "Switzerland's better" was my next Pobiner pontification when I climbed down the metal steps.

Outside it was snowing lightly, which gave the air that nice warmth and stillness that can come with snow. One of the small enjoyable details of train travel in Europe is even when getting off at a large stop, you often must walk across tracks to get to the station. There we were, a small group of us crunching across the snow as the Innsbruck express rolled out behind us with a skate and screech of metal on wet metal. I turned once, impulsively thinking to catch sight of the old man and his young listener.

"Harry!" Morton Palm shouted, as he stood under the eaves of the station with his bare hands up tight in his armpits and a big grin on.

"Morton, you made it!" Walking up, I dropped my bag and patted his arm. I was genuinely glad to see the man. He was the first, and after long thought the only, person I called from Saru once I'd agreed to do the job. Obviously Hassan told Fanny, but I didn't even call my partner to tell her what was going on. I contacted Palm because I wanted company when I was in Zell am See; company that could speak German well, knew something about my field, and was someone I liked being around. The fact that he was an ex-soldier didn't hurt either. In the long conversation we had before I left Bazz'af, I asked him to meet me in the mountain town and bring, among other things, a gun. When I began to explain the recent situation in Saru, he said only, "I know, Harry. I've been following it. The gun's a good idea."

We walked through a waiting room full of people wearing colorful ski clothes and the look of smug fatigue that comes with paying lots to use your muscles. Outside, taxis stood in front, puffing blue exhaust smoke into the still air. The drivers checked us out incuriously before going back to their newspapers.

"Where are you parked?" I asked Palm.

"At the hotel. It's a five-minute walk."

"Where are we staying?"

"You asked for the nicest place in town, Harry. I

got us rooms at the Grand Hotel. You'll like it—it's right on the lake."

"The Germans beat these landscapes down into postcard pictures so they can promenade around them. Look at this—it's straight out of *The Magic Mountain* or a Friedrich painting. Beautiful, striking, and absolutely wrong."

"Why wrong?" He took out a pack of cigarettes, which made me even happier he was here with me.

"Could I have one of those? Wrong because it's like topiary, or a ship in a bottle. Ships don't belong in bottles—they belong out on limitless seas, fighting storms and sea monsters. This kind of vista should be dramatic and spectacular—not prettified and docile, like hedges trimmed in clever shapes. These are the *Alps*, man! Blizzards! Avalanches! Hundred-mile views! But what've they done with this place, besides tame it? Quaint little boat docks and wide-deck restaurants on the summit, where you can drink Remy and catch a little sun before taking the cable car down. . . .

"Listen, in the Renaissance, people were so fucking *afraid* of mountains that when traveling across them by coach, they'd actually put on blindfolds so they wouldn't be driven mad by their dangerous power! People really believed that could happen. That's what I'm talking about. Where are those feelings today, Morton? I'm sure the only things that'll drive us crazy here now will be the price of the hotel room or a drink at the bar."

"How come you're forever angry, Harry? You're a lucky man. You have what you want, your business is a success, and you even went crazy for a while without losing too much. But you're always distressed, always angry. It's hard for me to understand."

Palm didn't say more than that as we walked toward our hotel, which was now in view. But coming from a man as placid and satisfied with the way his life had gone, the remark cut me in half. Was I so misanthropic and ill tempered?

The Grand Hotel am See was a nineteenth-century wedding cake properly restored. Our adjoining rooms with balconies looked out over the lake and mountains. Tame as it was, I wished someone I loved was there to share it with me. Fanny came to mind, as did our last conversation. Did I love her? Had I ever? Already many of my memories of her centered on our fights rather than the many good times we'd had together. Was that fair, or only because I was "forever angry"?

Morton opened the doors to my balcony and stepped out on it while I hung things in the closet.

"Come here, Harry. I want to show you something."

Sillily enough, I was afraid to join him. Afraid he might say something else true that would cut me in half the other way.

"Christ, it *is* pretty," I said a bit too heartily and full of false delight. Morton smiled with half of his mouth, knowing exactly what I was doing.

"Off there to the right, behind us, is the Schmittenhöhe. We'll go up there tomorrow, or whenever you're ready. I skied here and at Kitzsteinhorn once, years ago. Both of them have beautiful views from the top and wonderful long runs down. Do you ski?"

"I tried once."

His smile broadened. "You didn't like it?"

"I didn't say that! I just said I tried it once. It was okay. Very, umm, healthy."

"Uh-huh. Now across the lake, there, is the town of Thumersbach and next to it Maishofen. They are much smaller and quieter than Zell am See. What I want to show you is to the right of Thumersbach. Follow my finger? That smaller mountain there is called Hundstein. Do you see where I'm pointing? That is where your Sultan owned his land."

"*Hund* means dog in German."

"That's correct. The Sultan has the best place to build his museum—on a mountain called Dog Stone."

"You're kidding."

"No, the truth. I have talked with a man at the *Verkehrsbüro* here in town. He told me the whole story. The Sultan of Saru came to ski Kaprun once four years ago and heard there was a mountain here named Dog Stone, or Dog Mountain, to play with the translation. Since that time he had his people working to buy as much of the mountain as he could."

I asked Palm to point it out again. Instead he went to his room and brought back a detailed map of the area. By golly, there was the name in real black ink: Hundstein. Pointing to the map and then into the distance across the lake, we found it and looked in silence.

"Can you imagine buying a mountain because you like the name?"

"From what you have told me, he knew he was going to build this museum a long time ago."

"Yeah, but in Saru! Far as I know, the Sultan didn't have any plans while he was alive to make Mount Dog into Mount Museum. That's why he asked me to Saru—to see the country and the site. It was his son

Hassan who decided to do it here because he's afraid
Cthulu will blow it up if they build there."

"A fair guess to make, knowing the history of that
man. I have been reading about Cthulu since you
hired me. My room is full of books about Saru. Come,
let's get something to eat first. We have days to talk."

I don't know about Morton, but the ten days
we spent together in Zell am See were some of the
best of my life. As an adult, I have never had a real
man friend, and I use that term in all the rough and
tumble, us pals, drink into the night, talk about
women, spill your male guts way it was intended. As
friends, women interest me far more than men.
Women's minds are more intricate and labyrinthine,
their perceptions deeper, and what they tell you is
generally new stuff. Male friendships are ham and
eggs, toast and coffee meals. Men-Women friendships
are an exotic, foreign taste—delicious in odd ways,
like fresh paprika, like fennel.

But those days with Palm showed me how satisfying ham and eggs can be as a meal, how filling and
delightful in its simplicity. We went for long walks
around the lake, drank beer in the restaurant we
found at the train station, which turned out to be the
best place to eat in town, and took every cable car ride
up to look at the genuine splendor of those mountains
in winter. What made me smile was thinking how, on
that first day, I had wished to have a woman with me
there. What I'd learned was a pal of your own sex
wasn't as romantic and prickly, but the ease and natural empathy in the air around this kind of relationship
was a pleasure to know and possess.

 "Harry? Is that you?"

I'd picked the phone up without really knowing what I was doing. "Hello? Yes? Hello?"

"Harry, is that you? This is Claire. I'm calling from California."

"Claire! Hi, Claire! How are you?" I sat up in bed and tried to focus my eyes. It was four in the morning.

"I know it's very late there, I'm sorry, but I had to call when I knew I'd get you. This is so important and you're the only one who can help."

"Sure, don't worry about it. What's the problem?"

"Harry, I need to borrow twenty-five thousand dollars. You're the only one I know to ask." She began to cry. "I would never ask but you're my last hope and it's so important. It's my life."

"Claire, it's no problem. I'll call the office tomorrow and they'll have a check ready for you by the end of the week. Okay? Honey, are you all right? Do you want to talk about it? Listen, *the money is yours.* Don't even think about that. Are you in trouble?"

"Oh Harry, thank you so much. No, it's not like that. I didn't know what I was going to do. You can't just go to the bank and say, 'I want to borrow twenty-five thousand dollars for a hand.' They'd think you're crazy. Oh *thank you!* I can't tell you—"

"Wait a minute! What do you mean, a hand?"

"The Sterling Hospital in Portland has invented a prosthetic hand that is supposed to be the most advanced in the world. But it's so sophisticated that they've only made a few, and they cost. . . . The whole procedure costs twenty-five thousand, Harry. And if I want to have one soon I have to be able to prove I have the money to pay for it now. I just learned this a couple of days ago and I've been going crazy trying to think of how to get it, short of selling the store. You were my last hope. You saved me, Harry."

📯   "The Sultan is not to be reached, Mr. Radcliffe. He is still asleep. It is only seven o'clock in the morning here."

"I don't care what time it is there. You tell him that if he doesn't come to the telephone right now he can *kiss my ass about this fucking museum!* He cheated me!"

"That is not possible, Mr. Radcliffe. Call back later and perhaps he will talk to you. If you are not so rude." Click.

I was the only one in the breakfast room at seven the next morning. I'd been walking around the lobby, fuming, for half an hour when the doors opened. Not that I was hungry. I wanted something to do before calling Saru again and raising hell. I ordered coffee.

"Your tea, sir."

"I didn't—" Looking up, I was blinded by the fat face of the mysterious Mr. Hasenhüttl from my Saru flight. "What the hell are you doing here?"

"Do you mind?" He pulled out a chair and sat down. He was dressed in a burnt-orange jogging suit that made him look like a lifeboat.

"What do you want? I saw you and Awwad together in Vienna. Why are you sneaking around me? I'm doing the job!"

"I don't sneak, Radcliffe. I'm your Invigilator. Here to make sure you play this game correctly."

"Play *correctly?* What about Claire's hand? Is that

how wishes are granted? She gets something with
wires and rubber that costs *me* twenty-five grand, but
still Hassan has kept his part of the bargain?"

"You didn't specify what you wanted. Besides,
even if you had, it wouldn't have made a difference.
A wish is a dream come true. Since dreams are never
clear, when they happen they invariably disappoint.
Remember what happened to the old man and his
bread house? Claire Stansfield's new hand is without
question the *ne plus ultra* of this field. It will allow her
to be whole again."

"But it's not a real hand!" Two waiters nearby
stopped setting tables and looked at us. Hasenhüttl
waved them off and said something in German which
I took to be "No problem."

"Is this the way things are done in Saru?"

"I'm not from Saru, Radcliffe."

"Oh, the *gods* are sending a guy in an orange
sweat suit to make sure I play fair?"

"You thought the Easterling child was Venasque.
Tell me how I knew that. Why can't a fat man in orange sweats come from the gods?"

"Because all you did on the plane was threaten
me. 'I'm here to *fuck you up.*' You don't talk the talk of
a heavenly emissary.

"How'd you know Awwad?"

"As soon as you committed to this deal, all of the
people involved became aware of me. That's how it
works."

"Will Palm know you?"

"Yes. He'll think he recognizes me from when he
was with the United Nations forces in the Sinai. But
the truth is, I have never been to the Sinai. Eilat once,
but not the Sinai."

"Why'd you threaten me on the plane? You sounded like a Mafia hit man!"

"Sorry. I was in a bad mood." He shrugged. "Probably something I ate. Don't you hate airplane food?"

When can one say they're home? When the plane touches down? The front door swings open, you see someone's face again for the first time? Or is it a gradual process, like coming up from a deep dive? When I was single, I had to look through all the mail first to make sure no gruesome surprises had been sitting in the postbox, festering. That done, I was home. When I was married, it was getting into bed the first night, showered, unpacked, ready at last to have a great chat.

This time I made sure not to tell anyone I was arriving in Los Angeles. At the airport I rented a car and drove straight through the city down to the Coast Highway and on out to Santa Barbara. One of the reasons why I built our house there was for the ocean view. I was no longer particularly sad the building was gone, but almost as soon as the plane left Frankfurt I felt a junkie's hunger to sit on our hill and simply *be* on that piece of the earth for a while. It was the sensuality, and the generosity of the California light there. It was a home no longer mine, yet I felt a call to it I could not defy at that moment.

Traffic was light and I arrived sooner than expected. Driving up the familiar last hill to the place, my heart felt a delightful lift and sureness that I'd made the right decision to come. Also for two or three beats, my eyes tricked me into seeing our house still there, waiting patiently for someone to return and bring it back to life. Turn on the lights, a radio, open the windows and let warm fresh air in, dial a number on the black telephone. But nothing had changed and my sweet moment of irrational hope passed when I saw the ragged chimney standing guard like a lone, useless soldier. Some artistic trespasser had spray-painted a rather nice picture of a couple fucking on one side of the chimney, the man's cock wrapping up and around the woman like a Laocoön.

"Welcome home, Harry," I said while walking up to it and running a hand over the familiar rough stone.

I suspect you have been waiting for what happened next, having read my history this far, but I swear to you I was not. It came as an absolute surprise. Venasque said we are usually the last to become aware of our own fate and what things affect it. We are simply too busy being busy to look up and see our clouds taking definite shape around us.

They lay at the bottom of the chimney, where once a marble-and-steel fireplace had been my postmodern joke in the middle of a simple but deeply pleasing living room. Since the earthquake, some enterprising thief had made off with the marble and steel. What was left was a square about four feet high. Where once cozy fires had burned were four stones—each about the size of a man's hand. They rested against each other as if they'd fallen from anywhere and only by happenstance ended up here like this. They had no unique or memorable shapes. They were brown and white, one was sort of red. You wouldn't have seen them, much less picked them out, on a beach while rock hunting. They didn't glow or hum, buzz like neon or whistle like sirens. They were stones. They were stones. But I looked at them as one would at a woman so penetratingly beautiful that her beauty sucks up everything else around it like a black hole. A face that demands you watch it and nothing else. If you remain in her orbit, you will be forced to look at this woman for the rest of your life.

Four dull stones lying against each other on a smoke-blackened floor. They made a small pile—the kind a child builds. I saw them and part of me said no, nothing's here. The other part said everything is here, not in the stones alone but in what has come together—them, their colors and shapes, the way they touch, the fact they're here now, what I have gone through to get here, what I must do next. Everything. That was the word that held my mind as I stared— everything. The Easterling boy had said, "Don't be surprised that all the words are God." Is that what this was? "Don't be surprised that everything is God —all words, shapes, objects. . . ."? I did not believe in Tao or the Oneness of Being. If this was an epiphany or religious moment, then it was funny because what came to mind next was an old joke—a fool wants to sell his house, so he carries one brick with him to show as a sample of what's for sale. The exact shape of the Dog Museum I would build in Austria was inherent in the way those four stones lay in the fireplace. I could pick them up, take them with me, and no matter how I put them down again, that shape would remain in my mind.

"You're so *active*, Radcliffe. I thought flying to California would be enough for one day. But you have to drive halfway up the coast to visit a ruin."

I looked up from the stones and saw Hasenhüttl

making his way over. This time he was dressed in a
bush jacket and khaki pants. It was useless to ask how
and why he'd come.

"I've got a question. Come closer," I instructed.

A few feet away I caught a whiff of cologne and
sweat. The underarms of his jacket were dark.

"See those stones in the fireplace? What do they
look like to you?"

"Nothing. Stones. Should I be seeing something
else?" Neither his voice nor the expression on his face
said he was joking or testing me.

I took a pad of paper and mechanical pencil from
my pocket and drew a quick sketch. Line line line,
crosshatch, diagonal, arc, done. "What does that look
like?"

He bent down, took off his glasses, and peered. "It
looks like . . . It looks like those four stones with
wires around them. And an arc." Glasses back in
place, he rolled his head in a circle. "My neck gets so
tense and tight when I travel. What's the matter,
Harry, did I give the wrong answer?"

"You honestly don't see anything other than that?
Please, tell the truth."

"No. Nothing."

"Did you have anything to do with my coming
here today?"

"No. I thought you would go straight home. What
is it?"

I turned over the paper and started another drawing. This one took a good ten minutes to complete. It
was so easy because it was so clear and whole in my
mind. What worried me was only his influence. Was
he telling the truth? Had coming to Santa Barbara
been my choice or were my strings being pulled, both

physically and mentally, by Hasenhüttl or those behind him? I wanted this to be mine! I could accept the
mystery of where it had come from, but only if it was
from some place inside me and not Them.

We sat together amid the stillness and lush smells
of twilight. Quiet voices and laughter rose now and
then from the other side of the hill—Bill Rosenberg
and his girlfriend Vicky were barbecuing. Sketching
away, I remembered the last time I was up here was
with Bill and Bronze Sydney.

"Are you going to follow me around until I've finished the job?"

"Only if you want. I *can* do other things for you,
you know."

I looked up from the drawing. "Really? What?"

"Answer questions, most importantly. Within certain bounds."

"I thought you were here as my watchdog."

"Not only. I *can* help. There'll be times when you
need my help, believe me."

"That sounds foreboding. I thought my job was to
make this building."

"It is, but you have enemies. Hassan wasn't truth-
ful when he said Cthulu wouldn't mind if the museum is built outside of Saru. He minds a great deal."

"Swell. Look at this." I handed him the pad. He
took his glasses off again and held the paper close to
his face. My farsighted Invigilator.

"I don't understand it."

"What do you mean?"

"I mean, yes, I know it's a building but I don't
understand it."

"Gimme that!" I snatched it back. "This is the Dog
Museum."

"I assumed that. But what can I say? I don't understand it."

Claire understood it. On the way back to Los Angeles (I didn't offer Hasenhüttl a ride), I called her first at home and then at her store to say I was back and how about dinner? She said yes and we made a date to meet later in the evening. There is no such thing as rush-hour traffic in Los Angeles because the term indicates a certain time of the day when it is difficult getting from point A to point B by automobile. In the City of the Angels there is *only* rush-hour traffic, interrupted by lulls.

It was dark when I got to my apartment. The place looked as forlorn as ever and the only alive thing to greet me was the blinking red light on the telephone-answering machine, silently insisting I check the calls. Imagine my surprise when I pressed the button and heard, first thing, "You're an asshole, Harry. A selfish, insensitive asshole." Click. Fanny Neville's voice. Next came a business call, followed by, "And one more thing: Don't call me, okay? Don't even pick up and try." Then a business call, then, "I just realized you're probably gloating over those other calls I made. Which just goes to prove my point, doesn't it?"

The machine signed off and I stood there with eyebrows raised. I saw the stereo across the room and thought music would be a good way to clean out the Fanny smoke.

Big Top was never amused by dog toys but he had had a hankering for rawhide bones, and a few of them were left in strategic spots on the floor. When bored, he would often go from one to the other for a few bites. Sadly, I picked them up and dropped them in a wastepaper basket. No more Fanny. No more Big Top. Lovers, pets, and habits were all going away. The Dog Museum would take a long time to finish but what would I do afterward? There was no question about wanting to go back to work now; magic and inspiration were in the air and I was impatient to see what would happen next, even if it meant a run-in with Cthulu's warriors in the Austrian Alps. Assuming I'd get out of that alive, what would come next, I wondered.

"Stop banging your head against the wall and go have a nice dinner with Claire." It was the best advice I'd given myself in days. Roy Orbison went onto the stereo and Radcliffe went into the shower.

Besides having the appetite of a four-hundred-pound sumo wrestler, the Divine Ms. Stansfield also has a tongue that can withstand and relish any kind of sauce or cooking. I have seen her astound Indian chefs, Mexican waiters, and Korean kitchen help with her demand and delight for food as hot and zingy as they can make it. On and off I've hazarded bites from her fork and almost died regretting the bonfires she swallows with nothing more than a sigh of pleasure. I have even asked to look at her tongue to make sure it doesn't come from another planet. It doesn't, so the only possible conclusion is certain gentle souls are able to eat lava and like it. Perhaps the gentleness puts out the fire. Perhaps a gentle soul camouflages other blazes and infernos within. Perhaps I'm full of shit and she just has a cast-iron stomach.

Anyway, we met at Gunga Din's. We'd been there enough times for the staff to know the lady was asbestos as well as a bottomless pit, while the "Suh" was a picky old maid who ate dull chicken tandoori or beef curry.

Claire was at the bar when I arrived. Her arm was bandaged and held in a sling over her chest. The sling and bandage and basketball sneakers were white. The rest of her was black. Before she caught sight of me, I stood off to one side to have a close look before making contact. People are good at covering up once they're seen—faces, voices, gestures all go into cosmetic overdrive, and where they really are is known only to them.

She looked older and prettier. The clothes looked new and I could imagine her walking out of the hospital and going straight to a store for a new outfit. She normally liked color—yellow shoes, bright skirts. Here she was in black and it would have been easy to take it for mourning, but knowing Claire it was not that. She believed in life and considered it her friend. I have never known a more optimistic person. If she was dressed in black, then it was her way of saying I'm empty right now. Give me time and I'll bounce back. The funny white sneakers were a light at the bottom of her black curtain, a tired smile at the last moment. She turned and saw me. Unconsciously lifting the bandaged hand to wave, she looked down at it, then back at me. Stepping forward quickly, I took her into my arms and hugged.

"I know it looks silly, but I have to wear it for a long time."

"That's okay. You look like a tough guy with it. I wouldn't want to mess with you. I'm glad to see you, pal."

"Me too, me too, me too!"

"Are you hungry?"

"For you. I want to talk to you for the next three weeks. I'm sorry about Fanny and Big Top. But I'm so happy you're back, Harry." She took me in again and hugged me to her bones. I wanted to give it back but was too worried about doing something that would hurt her hand.

In bed later, she told me a story. It still embarrassed her thirty years later and she'd never told anyone else. When she was a girl in fourth grade, her class was taking a test one day and in the middle of it, she felt a terrible need to go to the bathroom. She was a goody-goody student and never made waves. But when she went up to ask if she could be excused, the teacher, normally her ally, said no, she would have to wait until the test was over. She tried in a child's ashamed way to let the man know it was imperative, but the answer stayed no. So good little Claire Stansfield went back to her desk, put her head on her arms, and pissed on the floor. She said she would remember the sound of the water tinkling down for the rest of her life. I didn't know what to say, but she cut me off before I opened my mouth.

"It's so ridiculous, but I made a vow to myself I'd never tell that story to anyone unless I knew they were the greatest friend I ever had. It's not only because you're giving me this money, Harry, that I told you. It's because when you were away and I was in the hospital feeling sorry for myself, I realized you are the only person in my life I have ever wanted to tell."

🐟 The last I saw of Fanny before she went over the horizon of my life was outside her favorite restaurant downtown. I'd gone there for breakfast with Pup

Longwood to discuss construction crews for the museum. I'd met with Hassan and his bunch a week before and he'd laid the first of many surprises on me that made building this thing a major pain in the ass. This first flabbergaster was that the new Sultan had decided he wanted at least a third of the construction crew to be made up of Saruvian workers, even though the museum would be built in Austria. That way, when it was finished, he could say it was built by and for the people of his country. It was no use explaining to him that by satisfying his request, it would make the job even more difficult, since another third of the crew would have to be Austrians, and there were many Americans I wanted to bring along because we were so used to working with them. At the end of the evening I asked if His Majesty was secretly hoping to win the Nobel Peace Prize for International Cooperation. He brushed me off and said Saru would foot the bill for whatever complications arose.

When I told Pup about this, he nearly choked on his pancakes and said it was the goddamnedest thing he'd heard in a long while. Arabs in Austria? It would be bad enough working with Austrians who, by law, were allowed to drink beer on the job. I concurred. He was in the middle of repeating it was the goddamnedest thing, while we walked out of the restaurant. Then, a few steps from the curb, I looked across the street and noticed the Sultaness-to-be with her Hergé hair and "Don't tread on me!" look. I guess I could have steered us in a wide detour around her, but I wanted to see what she'd do when we passed.

The light changed and we started across. I knew she'd seen me because her face set like cement, but as we approached she looked over my head. I started to smile, thinking she'd give me the cold shoulder and nothing else. Longing for something ripe and brilliant to say, I couldn't come up with a thing. At the same time, I knew five beauties would come to mind half an hour from now. As a result, I didn't say a word but kept looking at her eyes to see if she'd give me a second's contact. No luck. As I walked on, thinking *At least I had the balls to look,* something stopped my feet and I went down like a chopped tree.

"That bitch tripped you, Harry! Hey, you!"

On all fours I touched Pup's ankle and, laughing, told him to forget it. That bitch didn't turn around once to see what she'd done, just sailed right on across the street and around the corner, looking good the whole way.

PART THREE

"Quidnunc"

*"I began to think of the soul
as if it were a castle
made of a single diamond."*

St. Teresa of Avila

WHEN FULL-SCALE CIVIL war broke out in Saru, even the experts seemed taken by surprise. In the beginning it got little play in the media. They saw it as only another one of the fifty or so wars rumbling in another obscure and backward part of the world and thus tended to deem it either an "uprising" or "revolt"— their patronizing terms for no big deal.

There is nothing like horror to move you up to the front page. When Cthulu's forces shot down the Lance Airlines 747 with three hundred passengers, scattering bodies, luggage, and electric guitars (the rock group Vitamin D was on board) across forty miles of Saruvian desert, the headlines roared and experts were consulted. Obscure scholars from forgotten colleges and universities who'd spent their measured lives studying the history and customs of this small country were suddenly quoted as if their every word were both gospel and gold. Professor Gernert from Muskrat State University disagreed with Professor Herring from Aloha College about the seeds of revolution which had abruptly bloomed into bloody blossom in a country heretofore best known for its membership in OPEC. Dr. Kufferle at the Sorbonne said it was a question of economics and would blow over. Professor Oppenheimer at Shirley University said it was a family feud and wouldn't. While these folks preened and pontificated in their fifteen minutes of fame, Cthulu shook hands with Libya and Iran, allowing his freedom fighters to trade their popguns for Kalishnikovs and hand held rocket launchers.

You had to hand it to Hassan, though. With no more than a bachelor's degree in business from UCLA and little experience actually running a country, much less commanding it in war, he hung tough and fought back impressively. People from his government flew in and out of Zell am See to check on our project and brought with them facts, rumors, and lies about what was going on in Saru. What we heard most often was the young master was doing things right, and although he didn't have the enemy on the run, he was more than holding his own. Morton Palm, ex–professional soldier and clever questioner, spent a good deal of time talking to these dignitaries and heard a different story.

"The Americans don't want Cthulu in power," Palm said, "because he represents the kind of fundamentalism that is so frightening to the West. They are sending military advisors in to help Hassan's army, which is neither strong nor well organized. It would be difficult training them seriously for a year to go into battle and do well, but since no one expected

Cthulu's forces to strike so fast and so hard at the same time, they are confused and badly maintained. Also, as you know, the Americans have not done well fighting in guerrilla wars. They even had trouble when they went into Panama where most of the terrain was known and they had many friends. Even more, you cannot bring American battle tactics to the Mideast and expect them to work anymore. The same is true with what happened to the Russians in Afghanistan. There is the geography to think about, the customs of the people, and most important, there is the total passion of the soldiers. The American and Russian soldiers are very professional, but they are not passionate. They do their job and want to go home. That is the reason why your Superpowers have done so poorly in these regional conflicts. The enemy not only lives on the land where the war is being fought, they are generally poor people who believe in nothing more than their God and the country He gave them to live in and protect. I will never forget seeing the television pictures of the Ayatollah Khomeini's funeral. Do you remember that? More than a million people came, Harry, and many, many of them were crazy from the sadness and shock of losing their spiritual leader. There aren't spiritual leaders in the West. We don't understand the concept. Iranians were screaming and tearing at their clothes, throwing themselves toward the body. In the West we look at this and shake our heads as if they are totally *blöd*. But they are not crazy—they are believers, in the greatest sense of that word. Cthulu has an army of believers full of courage and extreme love for him. Hassan has the professionals, the Western advisors, a better supplied army. But study what has happened in that

world over the recent years: such combinations of
forces do not work successfully there anymore. It is
passion that wins now—Iran, Afghanistan, the PLO
uprising on the West Bank. We have returned to wars
fought for the Grand Ideas: God, Home . . . instead
of wars for more money. I think this is very interesting. It makes the West very uncomfortable. Poor peasants rising up against the rulers in their castles.
Simple people who believe in God and their land.
And it is so embarrassing! I saw this again and again
in the eyes of the Israeli soldiers when I was there.
They had the guns against the Palestinians' stones,
but it was equal, neither side was stronger than the
other. These soldiers could feel it—you saw it in their
faces. Like having a fight with a child but their little
arms and legs are as strong as yours, the way they use
them."

"Do you think Hassan will lose?"

"Not yet. It's too early to tell. He still is stronger
because he has the weapons and tactics, but if the
fighting goes on a long time, the other side learns.
Then it is dangerous—because they have their God,
their passion, *and* strategy."

The fighting went on a long time. The war, settled
down into a comfortable endlessness, was once again
relegated to the middle pages of the newspapers and
sixth item on the television nightly news. Broadcast-
ers had trouble pronouncing the names of locations
and fighters on both sides. There were reports of Russian weapon caches, photographs of bodies sprawled
like pinwheels and starfish after major offensives.
When film reports of life in Bazz'af were shown,
merry children jumped up and down and waved at
the cameras. One teenager, ostensibly being inter-

viewed about the loss of family members, was more interested in showing how he could break dance. How could there be a war on with these people so happy and bubbly? In photographs Hassan looked young, strong, and capable. He'd been educated at UCLA, knew his way around the Western world, and was even about to marry an American journalist. It sounded like the plot to a romantic movie. Who wouldn't guess he'd be the eventual winner?

His prospective bride began showing up more and more on the news, smiling less, sounding terribly serious and intense. One day her short blond Neville hair was gone, replaced with a more sedate brown that I guess better befitted her upcoming position.

In contrast to this Dream Team, Cthulu looked like one of those old paranoids with nasty eyes who sits in the public library all day and hogs the good magazines. What he said too was your usual "wretched-of-the-earth" tripe. Which was another confusing part of the picture: Why would anyone get riled up about the ho-hum stuff this old bum was spewing? How could *he* have raised and rallied an army of thousands of zealous loons who appeared to want nothing more in life than to give it up for this old squinter?

When the city of Sa'Hiq fell to Cthulu's rebels, it became clear the government was in real trouble. Strangely enough, four days after the battle Hassan appeared in Zell am See. The transformation was powerful. Whatever he had been through in the last months had made him a different man. Quiet and dignified, he toured the construction sight asking the kind of questions that made you think and even sweat a little. He had done his homework and plainly knew what he was talking about. When we were alone I asked how he'd learned so much about the subject in so short a time. He smiled like a statesman —amused and world-weary—and said he'd taken up the study of architecture as a hobby. It took his mind off his work and allowed him to think about the future rather than the difficult right now. "Some men take mistresses. I have Fanny so I don't need that. She has been telling me what books to read."

What encouraged me was how much he enjoyed talking about our mutual friend. Despite what was happening in Saru, he used any opportunity to bring the subject around to her. Now that she had committed herself to him, he was even more lavish in his praise and devotion. With her at his side he could do anything. Since "the trouble" began, she'd been his best advisor and confidante. There was no end to the woman's abilities. How could I have been so blind to this combination of Diana Von Clausewitz, Marilyn Monroe, and Jehan Sadat? How could I have let her escape? The man knew that if he lost the war to Cthulu he was guaranteed dead, but because he had the best woman at his side, everything would turn out for the best. I remember thinking things couldn't be too desperate if he had so much time and inclination to wax rhapsodic about his not-so-coy mistress.

Anyway, we had our own troubles which kept me fully occupied. Any architect will agree that there are buildings which go up like dreams. You dig the first hole and the thing is done in what feels like five minutes. The earth doesn't shift, the molding fits, there are no crippling strikes or need to send for bizarre replacement parts for the machinery that, on the whole, runs dependably. It is analogous to going to bed for the first time with someone and discovering that everything you do, every gesture, every sound, every shift, is exactly what they like. And vice versa. When you are finished and lying there in a happy heap, you think back on the act and the only word that does it justice is "Wow." There are times too when the earth and steel, stone and plastic, are so empathetic and . . . eager for each other in the design you have created for them that it is as if you're partners and what you do with each other is a true consummation. When you're finished, Wow.

Not unreasonably, I figured that with all the forces at work in the planning of the Dog Museum, its construction would be a breeze, if not downright spooky. Wrong. The only breeze came from a hundred different people and companies trying to blow smoke up our asses. We were not innocent when it came to the normal payoffs, padding, and deceits involved in international building, but soon it began to feel like every crooked, greedy son of a bitch in Europe and the Mideast had gotten attached to the project and were trying to squeeze as much out of it as they could before the police descended and threw them all in jail for extortion. No one appeared to feel or show any shame either when asking fifteen times the proper price for materials or labor. Bronze Sydney did a preliminary cost per square foot at these new inflated prices and told Pup and me. The three of us simultaneously grew exactly the same "You've-got-to-be-shitting-me" expression on our faces. Then Pup took a Sunday ski-lift ride up to the top of the Schmittenhöhe and came back down in a helicopter with an IV in his arm and a stroke in his head. Those two things happened as the credits were running; our movie had yet to begin.

The most maddening problems had to do with language and culture. The Saruvians spoke Arabic, the Austrians German, the Americans English. Some people spoke one of the other languages. A few people spoke some of each of the languages. Most people spoke only their own and got frustrated the more complicated things became and the less they were understood. Any building, either in its construction or when completed, serves as a visible microcosm of society at work. Since human beings have a natural tendency to live and work in groups, I've always felt a crucial part of my job is designing structures that allow people to group comfortably and productively. I knew from the beginning it would be natural for the different nationalities to hang together while working on the museum and in their free time, but what we didn't figure on was the xenophobia and racism that stood in the shadows waiting until the right moment to spring out and sink their teeth into the flesh of what we were trying to create.

The main meat staple of the Austrian diet is pork. They eat pork like Arabs eat lamb and Americans beef. The first night the Saruvians arrived in Zell am See, they were treated to a big welcome dinner of new wine and delicious pork Wiener schnitzel. Unfortunately, Muslims don't drink wine or eat pork. The result was an ugly shock of recognition on both sides and a lot of salad eaten. At the end of the evening I heard the German word *Tschuschen* for the first time. I heard it more than once coming out of mouths that were curled with anger and disappointment. I asked Palm what it meant. "It would be the same as your word 'nigger,' Harry."

The Saruvians didn't like the Austrians because

they were pork-eating infidels who were getting a museum that rightly belonged in Saru. And they didn't like the Americans because of the recent aggressive American foreign policy in the Mideast.

The Austrians disliked the Saruvians because they were unappreciative *Tschuschen* who shouldn't have been in their country in the first place, despite the fact that they had brought in a gigantic building project that created a hell of a lot of new jobs for the Austrian people. And they didn't like the Americans because they were too confident and condescending and impatient.

To round off this cheerful circle, the Americans didn't like the Saruvians because they did things "differently," meaning they functioned like Arabs— slowly, good-naturedly, but not always effectively— which kept the process from moving forward at a brisk American pace. Austrians were stodgy, bad-tempered Nazis who grumbled and drank on the job. Welcome to the Pleasure Dome.

One weekend I had to go to Vienna to confer with one of our Austrian construction companies. I was thoroughly depressed and empty and didn't want to do much besides sit in the hotel room and mope. That did little to raise my spirits so I took a walk and ended up at the Kunsthistoriches Museum looking at paintings. True to my nature, I avoided the Brueghels because that's the first thing people do when they go to that museum, like beelining for the Mona Lisa in the Louvre.

Painting has always influenced my building, particularly those great vast ones of battles or the big processionals where it seems the whole world has gathered to welcome Christ, a King, or a Pope. I love the idea of the painter scrunched down close to his ten-foot-by-ten-foot canvas for months painting individual faces and uniforms on the soldiers, blood on the mouths of horses, skies erupting with the most dramatic clouds and light. These paintings work to capture the whole of life and humanity in one glance. It's the totality of those moments, the distillation of light and emotion, life and death, God and possibility that should be the goal of any artist.

I sat down in front of one by Jens Juel. It depicted the building of the Cathedral of Maastricht. Hundreds of little workers swarmed over and around the building like ants over a half-eaten chocolate bar. Hod carriers, stonemasons, fat priests, women selling food from baskets, scampering kids, and barking dogs covered the canvas and made the scene look like the center of the universe, or at least like the building of this cathedral was the most important and vital event man has ever known. What struck me most deeply was the order and gladness of the chaos. At first glimpse people appear to be moving in all directions at once, accomplishing nothing. But look closer—the stonemasons carefully check their plans, the women sell beautiful brown breads to workers with hungry, appreciative eyes. The children and dogs play under the watchful tender eyes of adults. This *is* a great event because it is their lives. The kids will grow up and take their parents' place and that is as it should be. Men will work until they grow too old to handle the tools. Then they'll sit on the edge of the grass like those old-timers there, on the small hill, and watch the slow progress of this building until they die.

Compared to what was going on a few hundred miles to the west, the building of the Maastricht Cathedral, however many hundreds of years it took to complete was bliss.

I began to talk to myself. "It's language. The difference is there they understand what the others are saying." An old Oriental man sitting nearby looked at me and nodded. I asked if he understood English. He shook his head and pointed at one ear. Whether that meant he was deaf or didn't speak wasn't important. I continued. "They work together so well because they have a common goal. They *want* that church to be built, so they all do their separate parts. In fucking Zell am See . . ." I looked at my neighbor to see if he was listening. His eyes were closed. That seemed a good idea, so I closed mine too.

When I got back to fucking Zell am See who should be waiting there for me but Claire. She couldn't have come at a better time. God bless women. Spinners of countless webs, the world's best company, the only rabbits out of a hat, point-blank range, dreams-become-flesh most of us will ever know in this life.

Similar to my first days in the town with Palm, Claire and I walked around and ate and talked. Unlike me, she was full of energy and confidence. Things were going well with her store, her new hand, which she wasn't embarrassed to show, was a wonder to see and use. Her enthusiasm wasn't infectious but, more important, her presence was. Three days into her stay I realized I'd gotten so dispirited and mired in the work that I'd forgotten there were good small things around that could balance, take the edge off, smooth out my life. She made me laugh. She laughed at me.

She asked odd, telling questions that made me think and feel exhilarated with the answers when they came. The people on the project liked her and sought her out. They wanted to talk and be in her presence a while.

One night we walked by the lake when it was windy and cold. The thought of hopping into a warm bed and snuggling kept us outside as long as we could bear, just to put off and appreciate that treat a bit longer. I told her about the paintings in Vienna.

She was silent a while and then asked, "Did you see the Brueghels? No? I thought you would. I was sure you'd go see his *Tower of Babel*. It's just as you described that other one. The whole world milling around, everyone industrious and getting their job done. When I was in the hospital I read the entire Old Testament because I'd never done it and always wanted to. Do you know the story of the Tower of Babel? What surprised me was how short it is. No more than a few paragraphs."

"The Tower of Babel? Sure. 'Come, let us build ourselves a city, and a tower with its top in the heavens, and let us make a name for ourselves, lest we be scattered abroad upon the face of the whole earth.' "

"How'd you know that word for word?"

"Impressed? My father read to me from the Bible every night when I was a boy. It was one of the few times I got to have him alone with me so I pretended to be fascinated. All those 'begats' put me right to sleep usually. Doctors have to take the Hippocratic oath before they begin their practice. Architects should use 'Come, let us build ourselves a city . . .' as theirs."

There was very little light out there but enough so that I could see a look of firm disapproval on her face.

"What's the matter?"

"I don't think that's funny. The whole point of the story seems to be Man got too big for his britches and decided to challenge God with this building. To see if he was capable of making something as magnificent as God's Work. The Hippocratic oath says a doctor will serve Mankind. I don't think architects should pledge to confront God with their work."

"True, but what interests me about the story is that God stopped them because they used what He gave them to the best of their abilities! He said, 'Behold, they are one people . . . and this is only the beginning of what they will do, and nothing that they propose to do will now be impossible for them.' And he went down and scattered them. The same as if I were to give you a Ferrari, but when you drive it two hundred miles an hour, I get mad at you for flooring it like that and fix it so it doesn't run anymore. That makes no sense. Those people spoke one language and could understand each other perfectly. God gave them that gift. That's why they could even conceive of building something like the Tower. So far, so good. But then, quite logically, one of them got the absolutely valid idea to use this wonderful ability to build something extraordinary—"

"To show off how wonderful they were. Pride comes before a fall."

I slapped my head in frustration. "But then why'd God give us a Ferrari if he doesn't want us to use it to its full potential?"

"Maybe Ferraris aren't supposed to be driven a thousand miles an hour. Wyatt Leonard told me something interesting at that dinner we went to. Someone he knew was studying karate with a sixth-level black belt. The man was a real master. One of the pupils asked him what he'd do if a bunch of tough guys came up to him on the street and tried to pick a fight. Know what he said, Harry? 'I'd run away.' Isn't that great? The whole point of that self-defense stuff is once you reach a certain level, you know you can kill anyone with one punch, but you've got such inner confidence and self-esteem that you don't have to. You run away."

"How does that apply?"

"Look at you. Everyone knows you're the best. You've won all the awards. You've built great buildings."

"Venasque didn't think so."

"Venasque was your karate master. I think he was telling you the next step is not trying to make a name for yourself anymore. Isn't that why you had your breakdown—because somewhere inside you knew that was true but couldn't accept it? Remember saying one of the reasons you stopped designing was because you couldn't see people inside your buildings anymore? Because it had reached the point where you only worked for yourself? Just you, your buildings, and your ego? I can understand why you couldn't see people in them. You'd filled every room with yourself."

"You sound like a new-age guru."

"Oh knock it off, Harry. You resent me because I'm essentially content with my life. That doesn't mean I don't want things or . . . I don't know, wouldn't want a better hand if it were available. But yes, I like my life and . . . You say you're happiest when you're working. Okay, but it isn't true—you're the itchiest person I know. Even when you're working you can never sit still. That's happiness? That's contentment? What good does it do you if you live every day as if you were standing barefoot on a burning floor? Aren't we here to find some kind of peace?"

"No, to struggle. I think you're lucky if you're at peace, but I wouldn't be at peace with your peace. If I'd lost a hand I'd try to design another that was the best ever made. Is that bad? Is it wrong to struggle to be the best?"

"It's wrong if you never find it, sweetheart. You keep picking up things and saying, 'I think I found it!' You get excited, but when you hold it up to the light it's the same as you had before. That's so depressing.

"You said this was the first time in your career you ever had a real inspiration for a building. It came by magic. But shit, Harry, you're taking that magic and working with it the same way you've always worked. And you're feeling the same tightness and frustration you did with the other work. Shouldn't we use magic differently? Look at the people who built the Tower of Babel and how they misused their magic: Maybe if they'd built it as an homage to God, or simply for the joy of building, the joy of being able to work together with perfect understanding, then God *wouldn't* have stopped it. Language is there to help us understand better, not to make us competitive."

The first death brought the first magic, although I didn't realize it until much later. A welder from Saru named Mahmoud turned on a defective acetylene tank and, exploding like a bomb, it blew the man ten feet back. When I got to the scene, Hasenhüttl, whom I hadn't seen in a long time, was on his knees over the body doing something frantically with his hands. People stood around with strange looks on their faces, staring like spectators at a car crash—not moving, not talking. Palm came up behind and put his hand on my shoulder.

"Dead?"

"From what I saw, there's not much left of him to be alive with."

"What's Hasenhüttl doing?"

"No idea."

"I didn't know he was a doctor."

Turning to Morton, I was about to say something to the effect I didn't know what Hasenhüttl was, *period*, but kept my mouth closed. More and more people crowded in to look and after a while the silence that comes after sudden, violent death passed and they began talking quietly among themselves. Three languages were going at once but a few moments after I'd heard it, I realized someone nearby had said the English word "quidnunc" in an unmistakably hoarse bass voice. I'd used that show-off word for busybody more than once to describe any number of people I knew. The exact sentence it had been used in this time went something like, "Who cares? He was a quidnunc anyway." Unaccented English. Native American.

Assuming whoever spoke was referring to the blasted dead man in front of us, I turned to see what insensitive bastard had such a nice vocabulary. In the spot where the sentence had come from stood a rather infamous member of the Saruvian crew—Sharam. Infamous because he weighed about three hundred pounds and looked like Bluto, Popeye's nemesis. Another thing about this cartoon scary was he spoke no English and, from what I heard, rarely opened his mouth in Arabic. But I knew his voice because we'd had a disagreement once—through an interpreter. Quidnunc had definitely come from that voice.

"Did you just speak English?"

Looking at me like I was a dead fish, he said something in his language that made his companions snicker and avert their glances. Palm translated my question into Arabic and Bluto shook his head.

"Why'd you ask, Harry?"

"Because he said the word 'quidnunc.' It means busybody in English. I know it was him."

"I don't think so. The man doesn't talk much. I doubt if he has been studying English. He sleeps when he is not working."

The company helicopter came fluttering in and the moment passed, but it stuck in my mind and I thought about it often later.

The body was put on a stretcher and lifted aboard. We watched the machine take off again. Palm patted me on the back and walked away. Hasenhüttl came over looking notably distraught.

"That wasn't supposed to happen. I don't understand it."

"What do you mean?"

"The agreement. When you made the agreement these things were not supposed to happen."

"What were you doing to him over there?"

"I can't tell you, other than looking at him to see if there was any indication of why it happened. There wasn't. I'm very confused."

The words chilled me more than the man's death.

If this special Invigilator didn't know what was going on, where did that leave the rest of us?

"Do you mean the project was blessed, or whatever?"

"Yes, but I wasn't allowed to tell you that. Now, there's no telling." He licked his lips nervously. "It's a whole new ballgame, Radcliffe."

"I thought you'd been sent to help me!"

"I was, when I knew the rules. Now I don't."

"Anything's possible?"

"I'm as much in the dark as you."

Pardon me, but I like horror films. Some of my best childhood memories are of sitting in a dingy movie theater with a bathtub-size popcorn, alternately stuffing my face with those greasy snaps, or letting my mouth hang open, eyes squinted almost shut, waiting for the girl to open the wrong door or for baaaaad noises to come out of the laboratory. My father likes professional wrestling, I like screams and scaly creatures.

The latest *Midnight* movie came to the Zell am See theater at the end of a good week. Contrary to Hasenhüttl's fears, the death of the Saruvian welder marked the beginning of a calm productive period that allowed us to move forward at surprisingly good speed. There were problems but nothing that couldn't be handled quickly and effectively. The different nationalities got along better and slowly appeared to be adapting to each other's work habits, if not cultural differences. When an Austrian steelworker had a birthday, he was given a surprise party by his American and Saruvian co-workers.

The weather was friendly; the sun blazed Tuscan light over the mountains, lake, and spring snow as if it approved of what was going on. It contributed to the kind of weather that makes you stop what you're doing several times a day and lift your head, smile, look around. Grateful, you return to work replenished and refreshed.

Claire's lecture had an effect on the way I saw and did things. The more I thought about what she'd said, the more I realized she was right. Telling yourself to go to hell and/or get a new lifestyle is easy, but the follow-up is a different kind of hell. Like New Year's resolutions, they sound good and sincere until you have to start living them. Who knows where to begin? I chose the slow route—adjust the temper, be kinder and more patient, remember my standards and hopes weren't the same as others'. It worked half the time but I was proud of that half and it gave me hope I might tip the scale in my own favor if I kept at it. An unexpected reward came the day one of the contractors walked in and said it was impossible to do something I'd considered crucial to the look of the building. Instead of going into warp factor five, I closed my eyes, managed a smile, and asked what he suggested. His answer was ingenious and a real improvement over my plan. I congratulated him and from that day others were much more willing to share their ideas as well as hesitations and it made things work better. Palm was at the meeting and afterward said he was proud of me. Normally I'd have growled at that, but Morton was proving himself invaluable and his compliment made me puff my feathers. He was the perfect person to go to when you were stuck. Although he didn't know much about building, he

was so reasonable and broad-minded in his perceptions that his ideas, insightful and compassionate, invariably had a grain of something in them that helped
plow snow off the mental runway. After I'd gone on
and on about him to Claire, I introduced them and the
three of us spent a warm evening together. Later she
said he was open and forgiving. A bell went off in my
head and I realized out loud, "I like him because he's
like you!"

It had been a productive, interesting week at
work. Claire was coming over again to visit in a few
days, and Morton and I had downed a good meal
before going to the film. Walking to the theater, I told
him I knew Philip Strayhorn, the man who wrote the
Midnight series and played the villain. To my surprise,
Palm asked many questions about Strayhorn. Besides
wanting to know what kind of man he was, he
seemed most interested in why an intelligent human
being would spend so much time working on a product the sole purpose of which was to scare people. I
gave the Radcliffe theory on horror films, which was,
Society is so jaded that nothing normal entertains
people anymore so we've moved to the next level
down, which is to choke, maim, and electrocute.

"Do you think that's the best way to entertain people?"

Feeling expansive, I jammed my hands into my
pockets and decreed, "Shoot five thousand volts
through a beautiful blonde and you've got a guaranteed interested audience. It's the same with my field.
There are three principles basic to architecture—order,
logic, and beauty. I don't care how many eggheads
refute that, it's really the essence of what we should
work for in any design. Fuck the theorists. But now

there are some very successful architects who do things like dig a hole and drop the house inside it. We're not talking about bomb shelters here either, we're talking home sweet home. It's like a clever, wiseguy idea; an intellectual joke you think up the first year of graduate school. But because it's new and has never been done before, there are actually people flocking to these idiots now to have them design their homes. Home, Morton. 'Hi, welcome to my home. Just climb down the ladder and put on this miner's lamp.' To *me* these charlatans are the equivalent of *Midnight* movies—a real conscious attempt at finding and heralding everything ugly, unfriendly, and disordered in life. One guy even calls it 'making visible what exists between stability and instability.' Bullshit. It's the land of the wiseguy and cynic and death of the soul."

Palm said nothing and I realized my face was hot. "Do I sound like an old fart?"

"No, like you believe in what you're doing. But maybe I am not a good judge, Harry, because I make doors and ladders. I believe in things that serve their function well and can be used again and again with trust. I have read about an artist who makes ladders that cannot be climbed—the steps go every which way. It's an interesting idea, it challenges our sensibilities, but only for a minute. Then it's just what you said—the work of a wiseguy. What I still can't understand is why someone would put so much of their life and imagination into doing that every day. Building a ladder that goes nowhere is the same as making films about people hurting each other."

I reached over and punched his arm. "Then how come you're going with me tonight?"

"I like being with you. I like to hear what you
have to say. Even at a stupid movie you'll probably
say something that will make me think when it's
over."

Since the Dog Museum crew moved into town, the
Zell am See *Kino* on Saturday night was bedlam.
Packed to the gills with Austrian, American, and
Saruvian construction workers, as well as good-hu-
mored townspeople who knew what to expect, all
films were dubbed in German, which meant only
about a third of the audience understood what was
being said. This made for interesting uproar. On
screen someone would say something important. A
Saruvian would ask in loud broken English, "What
was it that this fellow has said?" Then either an Austrian would answer in equally broken English, "He
tolt heem he's going to shoot out his family, so watch
out," or an American would say, "I don't know,
Salim, how 'bout translating for me?" Which would
then be rendered into two other languages and a few
seconds later the laughter or the counterwisecracks
would begin. You didn't catch a whole lot of what
was said in these movies but it was fun being there
and I think it helped bring people closer. Often when
they were done, we would walk out laughing over a
comment so-and-so had made or how much better the
repartee had been than the movie itself.

The opening shot of *Midnight Always Comes* is of
two lovers hotting it up in a graveyard. The light is
blue-black, the music classic Bernard Herrmann—
creepy. No credits yet, only the two kids groaning
and wrestling each other's clothes off. Usually at the
three- or four-minute mark the cracks would start flying in the audience, but either because of the impend-

ing sex or violence, things were quiet. Strayhorn is clever, though, and knows you're waiting for the worst. So he doesn't give it to you, although the music builds and we're shown foreboding shadows, or once in a while the kids look up from their tussle and say, "Did you just hear something?" In fact nothing happens in that first scene until the kids, smug and in love, walk out of the cemetery hand in sweaty hand. Then the camera moves to a monument three feet away from where they did the dirty deed and bingo— there's Bloodstone having his dinner. It looks like he's eating spare ribs but when the camera moves in close you see those ain't no spare ribs. Gross enough, but to make matters worse, he eats daintily and even has a large white napkin to wipe his lips. Sighing, he gets up and walks the short distance to where the kids had lain. On the ground is a used condom. Smiling, he picks it up and puts the gray thing in his pocket.

"Maybe he's into recycling!"

"*Was hat er gesagt?*"

"*Eine saubere Umwelt!*"

The Saruvians got their version of the translation and things were off and running.

Months before, Palm noticed that if things were going badly at work, the men tended to say more and be louder when they went to these movies. You could judge a work week on the number and volume of their comments. I thought of this as the evening went on because it was quieter in there and when someone did say something it was funnier and less barbed than in recent memory.

It was this relative quiet that led to my next step. A third of the way through the story, Bloodstone is in a telephone booth calling the heroine. The phone rings in her bedroom, she hesitantly picks it up.

"Hello?"

"Hello, Heather. I want to tell you you were very beautiful today. I watched you. I watched you the whole day. I liked the way your blue slip showed under the skirt. I liked the smell of that yellow gum you were chewing. I liked your smell."

This went on until the girl was so terrified that she dropped the receiver and ran from the room. But what jolted me was that halfway through the creep's monologue, I began to understand every word he was saying. I do not speak German. I learned as much as I had to in school but forgot it immediately after examinations because I wasn't interested. Watching Bloodstone's impassive silver face, I heard what he said in a language I did not understand but from one instant to the next I knew the exact meaning of every word, every phrase. What's more, there were a group of Saruvians sitting behind me and I understood what they were saying as well. I do not speak Arabic either.

Astonished, I whipped around and stared at them as if to verify the fact they were Arabs speaking Arabic and I understood. They were. I did.

Palm laughed at something in the film and said a line in Swedish under his breath. I understood. I didn't have to think, figure out vocabulary or sentence structure, syntax, or fine points. I simply understood everything that was being said around me in every language.

I turned to Palm. "Say that again."

"What?"

"Say what you just said again."

"It was Swedish. I said—"

I stood up. "I know what you said. I have to go. No, stay here, I just have to go. I'll see you later. It's okay, I'm okay, I just have to go."

Stumbling sideways out of our row, I all but ran for the door. I had to get out of there and get some air and clear my head and try to understand and just get out of there. I saw surprised faces look up as I blew by but it didn't matter.

Outside, the icy night air felt good but it wasn't enough. I jogged down the main street not knowing where I was going, but knowing that I needed to move and empty my brain a while until I had some sanity back and could think about what had just happened. I passed an old man and woman speaking loudly to each other. He said to her in German he was goddamned sick of being constipated. I understood. Farther down the street a Saruvian worker walked along with a small boom-box radio under his arm playing Arabic music. A woman was singing in the high, swaying way that makes Mideastern music so instantly recognizable. I understood the words she was singing.

Without being aware of it, I'd aimed myself at the hotel and when I got to the parking lot one of the first things I saw was my car. The key was in my pocket and in a minute I had started the engine and was moving down the road by the lake.

When Venasque was helping me to come out of my madness he taught me a trick. "When you can feel the bad waves coming over you again, Harry, fix on a word, any word that has to do with how you're feeling and say it over and over to yourself until it makes you sick. Concentrate on it till you forget everything else. It can be anything, but make sure it has to do with your craziness. That way your mind won't think you're trying to trick it out of how it feels. It'll just think you're trying to work out one little part."

The trick had worked well after I learned how to do it, so riding along through that tremendous night, I fixed on the word *Langenscheidt*. The company makes a little pocket computer that does instant translations from one language to another. Type in *amour* and out comes "love." However, my word became "I'm a *Langenscheidt*. I'm a *Langenscheidt*." Like a weird mantra, I kept saying that again and again as I wound in and around the Austrian countryside, the mountains their own darker shadows, the knowledge of what had happened in the movie theater knocking away at my brain like a jackhammer. I *was* a *Langenscheidt*. I could understand every word in the world. I was sure I could pick up instructions in Swahili and understand, a phone book in Japanese, a recipe in Portuguese. I'm a *Langenscheidt*.

I kept looking at the green digital clock on the dashboard, seeing what time it was and then wondering what time it was. Nothing went into my head; it was too full, too scared, working too hard to sort and file, to understand, to insist it *would* understand if only I gave it another minute or two.

Near Kaprun I stopped the car and opened the door so I could get the light inside to go on. Whenever I'm reading, I mark words I don't know, copy them down, and look them up the next time I'm near a dictionary. It's rare when I don't have one of these lists in my wallet or pocket. The one I had that night was on the inside of a matchbook cover. "Lenitive." "Epigone." "Garboil." I closed my eyes and recited.

"Lenitive—alleviating pain or harshness. Epigone

—an imitative follower, an inferior imitator. Garboil —a confused, disordered state. Mother of God, I know them. I know those words."

What did it look like, driving by that car parked on the side of the road, the man washed in small yellow light looking at a slip of paper in his hand, eyes closed, talking to himself? Was he lost and looking at his instructions? Had he forgotten something and was trying to remember? Or resting after a long drive? How many times have we passed scenes like that and not given it a second thought or glance? I can tell you though, firsthand, sometimes it is much worse than that. Sometimes the road is the only solid thing beneath the man's feet and he stopped because he must look at it, right now, to reassure himself it is there. Because nothing else is.

Hours later I pulled up to the building site and got out of the car. The driving had finally calmed me down but I knew I couldn't return to the hotel until I was exhausted and incapable of thinking anymore. I drove to the museum because I understood now and had to look at it with that knowledge, no matter the time.

Behind the chain-link fence the skeleton of the structure, floodlit from all sides, looked very much like a rocket ship on its launchpad. The lights, so harsh and intense, refused to admit darkness was behind them, beyond them. But the beams quickly disappeared once they flooded out past the museum and into the Alpine night. You would think so much candlepower could shine well up into the sky, but it can bully night only so far, which is not far at all.

I opened the fence with my key and slowly trudged up the hill. Had Venasque known when he was treating me? He must have. What *didn't* that old man know? As I walked, I tried to bring up different conversations we'd had, searching for hints or clues in what he'd said to verify what I now believed to be true, to be the purpose of what I was doing. Clues. There had been so many of them! The dream of Robert Layne-Dyer and his edible house—"Everyone has a house inside them. It defines who they are. . . . You think about it all your life. . . . But only once do you get a chance to actually see it. If you miss that chance, or avoid it 'cause it scares you, then it goes away and you'll never see it again." Venasque showing me my music, written properly, under the water of the swimming pool in California. Big Top sacrificing himself in Saru, my conversation with Claire in Vienna about Brueghel's *Tower of Babel.* Like the floodlights on the building, my own intelligence and insight shone brightly against the superstructure of my life, but once it moved past it was lost. I knew that was true about many other people, but the realization did nothing to comfort me at the moment. I am not a humble man because I don't believe humility is the key to heaven. If you do a job well you are allowed to admit it, to agree with others' positive assessments. We have enough demons hopping around inside, hurting and goading and helping us to do wrong things, why not applaud (as well as appreciate) the few angels in there too? I had been comfortable with that attitude until that night.

Because no single human was capable of what I had done, *which* meant that what stood in front of me on the hillside, "my" building, was not my doing, my brainchild, but rather the creation of the powers that had moved me here and there to do and draw this,

this, and this. And the whole time I thought it was mine. My own wonderful mine. It was like putting a twig in front of an ant and watching it move up the piece of wood as if that were its plan the whole time, rather than your moment's silly diversion. Was I more angry at being manipulated, or frightened, having realized what I'd been manipulated into doing?

Looking at the structure, I could have bitten through steel. Because when it was finished, this was going to be one fucking lovely piece of work. Many times I'd wished the old Sultan had lived long enough to see his dream made real. One night I even lay in bed and imagined leading him on a tour of the finished Dog Museum. Showing him how certain materials worked together, the subtle touches and inspirations that combined to make the place whole yet eccentric in the best way.

The most important question, and the one I've asked myself repeatedly, is whether it was the best building I ever designed. It was not. That is not sour grapes either; I don't say it because the concept was not ultimately my own. After years at a job one develops a good, fair sense about one's work and knows what is good and what isn't. The Dog Museum was original and substantial, with a sense of humor that wasn't common in my work, but it was not the Radcliffe *pièce de résistance.* No way. With the amount of inspiration, magical and otherwise, that went into it, I'd thought at the beginning it would transcend everything else, but it did not. It was a prize winner, the kind of building that makes people turn their heads, stare, and perhaps even ask what it is or who designed it. But it was not the work I'd take to my grave held tightly in my dying hands because it best defined me. It would be talked about because people would love the space it created, the way it complemented and accented whatever light entered, but it was not my final say. It was not. Claire said it was. Palm said it was. Even fatso Hasenhüttl said so, but who's the expert here? Me.

As I approached the lights, a large form slipped down from a pile of lumber and came slowly toward me. Hasenhüttl.

"You're out late, Harry."

I could have cursed him but I wasn't angry. I could have yelled at him for hiding essential information but what was the point? He might have told me if I'd asked earlier. Hadn't he said he would answer certain questions? I just hadn't known to ask. Now I did. Now I could have embraced him, my own private angel, and said, "Let's have a drink. I understand. Let's celebrate." What I did instead was rather odd. When we got close enough, I reached out and took his hand as a child will its parents'. He seemed to think that was okay because he smiled and let me hold it.

"I know what's going on here now."

He nodded but said nothing.

"It *is* what I think, isn't it?"

"Tell me what you think." Although it was cold enough for me to be wearing a down ski jacket, he wore only a dark suit, white shirt, and dark tie. Our breath puffed out in gray clouds that went away as soon as they appeared.

I looked at him in his suit and over his shoulder at the museum. A moment of embarrassment passed before I spoke again, as if what I was about to say was risky or shameful.

"It's the Tower of Babel, isn't it?"

"Yes it is. It's an attempt."

"We're building the Tower of Babel here."

"Yes we are."

"Okay." I let go of his hand and looked at our feet. "I'm not even shocked by it. Why not?"

"When did you realize?"

"Tonight, at the movies. I went with Palm to see the new *Midnight*. Suddenly, twenty minutes into the film, I began understanding every word on screen. Then every language around me."

"You can, Harry. I'm speaking to you in Arabic now. Tell me what happened after that."

I noticed no difference in how he spoke. The words sounded the same, as did the tone and inflection. For the rest of our time together that night he'd stop every so often and tell me what language he had been speaking for the last five or ten minutes. There were many of them. Never once did I notice a difference. It never sounded as if he shifted from one to another for better emphasis or word choice. He simply spoke and I understood. I know someone who works as a simultaneous translator. Totally fluent in French. She says that fluency notwithstanding, there is always a moment's pause between what is said in one language and her translation into the other. There has to be because there must be moments for the mind to work through the puzzles of inversion and declension so as to make the "jump" not only accurate, but as close to the original as possible. "Jump" was her word and it's a good one. She compared it to jumping from one rooftop to another. But there was no need to jump with Hasenhüttl that night. There was a path, a straight path of language that was no effort to follow.

I told him about leaving the theater and driving around, trying to keep sane and figure out what was happening at the same time. When he asked how I'd "connected the dots" and reached my understanding, I said there was no connecting—only the unmistakable obviousness of what *was*, once I had the breath and calm to step back and think the whole thing through.   ·

"But why me? Because I'm good, or because I was a student of Venasque's?"

"Neither. Because you had the right mixture of belief, talent, and arrogance."

"But what did I do? From what I see, I didn't come up with zilch. It was all given to me. The inspiration came from outside. It isn't my building, my design; it's yours, or your boss's."

"No, Radcliffe, it *is* yours. It has to be yours or else it couldn't be. The inspiration was yours, the concept, the design. The dream of Layne-Dyer was yours too."

"Come on, man, you've been jerking me around for months! Ever since we met on the plane from Saru. What about that conversation I had with Claire? We just happened to talk about the Tower of Babel, but you tell me it wasn't set up? I'm not *such* a fool, Hasenhüttl!"

"Believe it or not, we had nothing to do with that conversation. We've interfered very little in your life."

"Well, tell me how you *did* interfere. Let's start there. Now that I guessed the right answer to the big one, why don't you just land on earth a while and give a few of those answers you *said* you'd give me. How 'bout cluing me in a tad as to what's going on, okay? It's my night, pal! Tonight I realized not only can I speak every language in the world but I have, *I* have, according to you, single-handedly recreated the Tower of Babel for the dead Sultan of Saru . . . as a Dog Museum! That sounds damned reasonable to me. Does it sound damned reasonable to you?"

"What do you want to know?"

"*Why*. Why me? Why this? Why the Tower? *Why?*"

Instead of answering immediately, he tilted his head back and looked at the sky. Suspicious that something with a halo or pitchfork might be about to land, I looked up too. Nothing there but a plane's twinkling lights as it moved north. Without lowering his head, he spoke. "While I was waiting for you, I watched two dogs talk to each other. They do it through pissing, you know. One pisses his message on a wall. The other goes up, smells the first, then pisses his answer back. These guys must have lifted their legs to each other four times.

"Communication, Harry. Everything is talking to everything else, trying to get heard, but without much success. Remember in the seventies when that book came out about how plants had feelings too and how, if you tear off a leaf, the thing screams? One big talking world. Dogs piss on walls, plants scream, dolphins whistle. . . . Everything talks at everything else, but nothing understands. We can't even understand our own groups! Think of how many languages we have, yet how few we speak. Or how few people speak their own well or with any clarity. Mankind is only now beginning to realize the enormous diversity of languages outside his own, and already it scares him terribly. Look at how he scoffs at the idea of screaming plants or messages from outer space.

" 'Now the whole world had *one language and few words*. And as men migrated from the east, they found a plain in the land of Shinar and settled there.' Remember that part of the story, Harry? 'And they said to one another, Come let us make bricks, and burn them thoroughly. And they had brick for stone, and bitumen for mortar. Then they said, Come, let us build ourselves a city, and a tower with its top in the heavens, and let us make a name for ourselves, lest we be scattered abroad upon the face of the whole earth.' " The fat man turned and pointed at the museum. "It's peculiar how painters invariably picture the Tower as a ziggurat or something that spiraled upward. The only thing that spiraled upward then was the language. Right to heaven. Man's greatest failure was in trying to create something as complete and perfectly realized as the language he already possessed. A language understood by everyone and every *thing*, Radcliffe. It's nearly impossible to imagine now, but you had a small taste this evening when your ears opened to every word spoken around you, no matter what language. Imagine *that*, times a thousand, a million. Not only did those people comprehend the language of humanity, but also that of water, of blood, of sand and bees and color. . . . Everything spoke the same language. That's what it was like in the time before the Tower. That's why things were harmonious enough for Mankind even to conceive of building something from 'brick and bitumen' that might be the equivalent. But they didn't want to build it as thanks to God for giving them this sacred gift of understanding. No, they wanted to build it be-

cause they were confused and dissatisfied with the
opulence of God's language and wanted to create
their own—a language of objects. The Tower was going to be its beginning. The *A* in their alphabet. The
stupidity! How dare they think they were capable of
that. The *nerve*, imagining they could accomplish it in
stone. . . ."

"What's a 'language of objects'? I thought God
was all powerful! How come He didn't know that
would happen when He created Man?"

"God is a parent, not a dictator. He's very proud
of His children and very optimistic. In this case He
realized that optimism was unfounded, so quite
rightly took the gift away from the children. He didn't
do it because they challenged Him, but because He
was worried for them. They took His gift, this infinite
information, and wanted to use it to isolate themselves from the rest of the world. Do you realize what
a disaster that would have been if they'd succeeded?
An utter waste of energy and spirit. Why *build* when
they could have put that knowledge to such better
use?"

"Like what?" My question stopped him short. His
mouth opened and closed once, and he looked at me
as if I'd spoken in a language he didn't understand.

"What do you mean?"

"How could Man better use this 'understanding'
than to create the best thing he knew how with it?"

"Radcliffe, the whole point is not to create, but to
understand. The only reason Man's here is to learn
what God is, and then deal with that knowledge. In
the beginning, God had such confidence in our powers that He gave us full understanding. 'Now the
whole earth had one language and few words.' Man-

kind was capable of comprehending *everything*: his own species, the wind, a goat, the mountains. . . . It was God's way of saying, 'Listen to the world, study it closely, and it'll tell you how to find Me.' But what did Man do, instead of listening and studying? He set out to isolate himself. He built a Tower above the earth. The first part of a language of objects only he would be able to perceive and understand. You don't have to build if you understand."

"Thanks, Has, I'm sure glad to hear the whole purpose of my life has been for shit. I *don't* think, therefore I build. The fact I've built some damned valid buildings doesn't matter, of course."

"Be quiet and listen to me. I'm answering your question. God took away the gift of language and left Man to his own devices. The confusion that followed led to the scattering. But it wasn't 'abroad over the face of the earth,' as it says in Genesis. Things stayed where they were, but when there was no longer mutual understanding, it was as if they *had* been scattered." His voice lost its power and an octave. "Am I boring you?"

"I'm not bored, I'm confused. I also feel like a kid in Sunday school hearing Bible stories for the first time." I tapped the front of my head for emphasis.

"Don't worry, I'm almost finished. If you're confused, think of it this way: A parent wants his child to learn how to play the violin so he goes out and buys the best, a Stradivarius. But not understanding the value of the thing, the kid treats it terribly. Bangs it around, leaves it on the floor, whatever. The parent knows the child is capable of playing beautifully, but then finds him using the instrument to shovel dirt. That's the end. It's taken away and the boy's told if he wants to play the violin he'll either have to buy one himself or build it.

"Now comes the best, most endearing part. Instead of being sold, the Stradivarius is put away. Some time later, the child misses having an instrument so much that he actually does make one himself. A very bad, rough thing but playable. He practices more and more until one day he notices the great one on a table. When he asks where it came from, the parent says it was borrowed for the night. It's been so long since the boy saw it he believes the lie. He picks up the beauty, plays, and realizes how great the difference is between it and the one he built."

"So Daddy gives him the Stradi and they live happily ever after?"

"Wrong, Radcliffe. Very wrong. Daddy lets him use it for a night but takes it away the next day. As the child improves, the memory of playing that beautiful violin grows until he becomes dissatisfied with his own and not only wants, but needs, a better one. Periodically the Stradivarius is brought out and lent to him, but always taken back. It only makes him hungrier both to play and own something better.

"Half a lifetime later, the child has grown into an accomplished violinist *and* instrument maker."

"The father never gave him the great one back?"

"No, but he knows the child has developed the potential to build one as great as the Stradivarius."

I took out a handkerchief and blew my nose. "You mean *God's* willing to let us build the Tower again?"

"Yes, but so far no one's done it. They've come close, but not close enough."

"Where? Where did they try to build the Tower again?"

"They didn't know it, but they were trying. The pyramids, Chartres cathedral, Hong Kong bank—"

"Hong Kong *bank?* You mean Norman Foster almost rebuilt the Tower of Babel with that billion-dollar heating duct he made? You gotta be kidding. What about my work? Did I ever come close?"

"No, but it's possible this time. When it's finished there is a very good chance you will have done it. The signs are right."

"What's a Language of Objects?"

"I can't tell you that."

We stood and listened to the silence. It wasn't deafening, but sure was packed.

"I still don't get why *me.* There are lots of obnoxious, talented architects around."

"Essentially for two reasons. You are a descendant of Nimrod, the King of Shinar, where the original Tower was built, and 'the first on earth to be a mighty man.' He also built Nineveh in Assyria. Only his descendants are allowed to try building the Tower."

Suitably impressed to find I was a great-great-great . . . of King Nimrod, I couldn't help asking for the second reason. What my Invigilator said shut me up good.

"The second is because you love God, Radcliffe. Your whole messy life you've been stumbling toward Him."

The second, third, and fourth deaths made no sense to anyone except Hasenhüttl and me. Sense or not, they did cause an increasingly large ruckus once a local zoologist discovered a dead rat that wasn't really a rat but a silvina, a rodent that had been extinct for fifty thousand years. People from newspapers, Greenpeace, natural history museums, *National Geographic* . . . came down on us like locusts with clipboards and wire-rimmed eyeglasses. Why so much attention for a dead animal ten inches long? Because it was still alive when they found it, despite the creature supposedly having disappeared around the time of the lost continent of Atlantis. It looked to me like a combination of a rat and a sun-bleached shoe when the worker brought it into the office and said he'd found it near the woodpile where Hasenhüttl and I had spoken about the Tower weeks before. I paid little attention other than asking the guy why he wanted to keep a sick rat. He said it was his hobby to nurse sick animals back to life. Preoccupied, I didn't think to mention it to either Hasenhüttl or Palm. But it was Morton who came in very excited four days later to tell me about the zoologist's discovery. Not being a big fan of flora or fauna, I thought it interesting but not the news of the decade. I had rarely seen Morton so wound up, and thought that was more intriguing than The Rat from Beyond Time. My normally calm friend couldn't get over the fact the thing was still alive when found. It had since expired, but not before living in the twentieth century.

"Why's that so special? Aren't they often finding extinct species in hidden corners of the earth?"

"Dead, Harry. Partial skeletons and fossils of what was, but never alive. If this animal survived into our time, think how many other beings are still around that we thought were gone!"

His wish was someone's command—during the next few days, two more supposedly extinct creatures were found barely alive on or near our construction site: the Dorn snake, and a kind of dwarf owl called a Tarkio. Even I got the heebee-jeebies after the owl was discovered, and I went looking for Hasenhüttl to find out the connection. Unlike most people's guardian angels, mine was not on constant call. When I suggested he carry a beeper so I could reach him when necessary, he gave me an expression I'd seen more than once on Venasque's face and said, "You'll find me when I think you need to find me."

Luckily this time he was at one of his favorite places—the *Eisstockschiessen* court next to the lake. The familiar gang of Zell am See pensioners and assorted kibitzers watched the slow progress of the game with their retired red faces and smelly cigarettes in hand. Hasenhüttl had taken to hanging around down there, although I never saw him playing. "Old men tell good stories, Radcliffe. No one enjoys talk as much as them and they're happy to wait their turn."

When I found him that morning he was standing alone off to one side, ignoring the game and looking instead at the lake.

Without turning to me, he said, "You came about the animals?"

"Yes. What do they mean?"

He had a bottle of Austrian rum in one hand. It was half-empty. He brought it to his lips and took a long pull, his eyes squinting as it went down. "I don't know what they mean. I mean, I don't know what any of the deaths mean. That welder, these animals. I don't know. Such a beautiful vision too—the return of the animals." He took another big drink. "The silvina was the first, but it wasn't supposed to die. None were! Now they're dying everywhere. In flight, under the ground . . . The three they found here are the only ones to have made it. They'll be finding rare creatures around the world for years but won't understand that they were all on their way here." Looking at the bottle as if it were an affront, he put it down carefully at his feet. "This is a very interesting place to be right now."

"Come on, Hasenhüttl, you know everything. What do you *think* is happening?"

"Obviously I *don't* know everything. What do I think? I think things have fucked up, to put it succinctly."

"Who fucked up?"

"I don't know. That's the problem. Maybe you, maybe your building, I couldn't say."

"What are we supposed to do?"

He bent to pick up his bottle again, looking happier to see it this time. "What do *you* do? Keep going, I guess. Keeeep on keeeepin' on. . . . Do what you've been doing and hope it fits.

"I, on the other hand, am feeling very ill. I thought this rum would help but it hasn't. Not a bit. Have you ever heard of a sick spirit, Harry? That sounds like a contradiction. But we've seen weirder things than that here lately, eh?"

🐾 Weirder still followed. Tools disappeared in clear view of their owners. The night watchman swore he saw it rain inside the building on two successive evenings. Like Hamlet's pals waiting with him for the ghost, Palm and I sat with the poor frightened watchman the next few nights waiting for this wraith rain to return but it never did. Then a Saruvian said the lettuce in his salad came to life. When some wag asked what it did, he was told, "It breathed."

Other things, but my own eerie summit was reached the day I saw Big Top again. Living in the mountains had not made a hiker or skier of me, but a good two-hour walk when the day was free and the weather nice made me feel virtuous and *sportiv*, not to mention justifying a princely meal afterward full of cholesterol, salt, and sugar. Burp. Spring was around the corner and the day of this walk, although mid-February, was sunny and about fifty degrees. There had been little snow that winter, which had effectively KO'd the Austrian ski season, but also permitted us to move full speed ahead. The local construction companies had a tendency to want to hibernate during the winter months, but after we told this to the powers in Saru, they greased certain wheels and we forged on.

So Hiking Harry, in his genuine leather Austrian knickers and hiking boots, set out alone for the heights on one of the many dirt tracks that began just above the town. The sun gives only so much of itself to the mountains, but gives it all. The rest, even midday, are the coldest, most distinct shadows I have ever seen. Walking up that hill, I kept crossing back and forth over the sun/shadow line and the temperature difference was amazing. Once I laughed, just to feel the sweat that had just popped out on my face stop running down and grow icy cold on the bridge of my nose a minute into the shadows. Birds chased each other in long arcs in and out of the light and dark. The air smelled of damp stone, spicy pine, and the oily tang of fresh asphalt being laid somewhere. In my knapsack was a yellow apple, fresh bread, and a green bottle of fizzy mineral water. Turning, I could see the skeleton of the museum on the other side of the lake. The sun struck it here and there, sending back white pinpoints of light reflected off glass or polished stone. I could have stayed there and looked at it from that new, far perspective, but too much of every day was given to looking at that building. These mountain walks were intended as part of my withdrawal cure. Other parts included two-hour telephone calls with Claire, meals with Morton or others in our crew, reading the Koran, and rereading the Bible. When I told Claire about that, she began the Koran too and many of our subsequent conversations were about the latitude and longitude of virtue and sin, the separate paths to God. I hadn't told her about my Tower of Babel chat with Hasenhüttl because I was waiting for her return when I could tell her eye to eye.

Austrians have a nice custom when they're building. Once you've gone as high as you're going to go, there is a ceremony called the *Dachgleiche*, during which the top of a spruce tree, festooned with red and white rags, is mounted with great solemnity on the highest beam. Symbolically it means that's it, folks— all we need now is a roof and we're done. Not that you really *are* finished, but it's the perfect midway pause and excuse for a *Dachgleichen Feier*, when everyone involved gets together for food and drink and mutual back patting. Good job, gang. Claire would be coming over for that and, post-*Dachgleiche*, we planned a week together driving slowly around the country, taking in the sights and each other's air after being apart for so long. I wanted to tell her the whole

story, top to bottom, and hear what she had to say.
After that, I wanted to ask if she would live with me
when I returned to California. Absence hadn't made
my heart grow fonder, but had taught it the value of a
woman who was braver and more singular than I'd
originally imagined. I thought about her constantly;
sometimes talked to her when I needed an ear. In the
old days I had usually talked to myself, but I was
getting so used to her perspective that it was usually
better and more fruitful to talk to an imaginary her
than a too sympathetic or agreeable me. Claire was
soft, but the soft of a panther's coat.

Where was I? Hiking toward Sonnalm, crossing a
meadow and moving toward a shadowy wood. A
sagging shack for storing tools sat on the border between the meadow and forest. He stood next to the
shack. I noticed him mostly because he was the only
white in that climbing landscape of browns and
greens. I didn't know it was he then because of the
distance between us but I stopped and watched this
animal turn and disappear into the woods. His white-
ness in that dark would have stopped me anyway,
but seeing the bright blur, it crossed my mind,
"Wouldn't it be funny if that was Big Top?" The moment and thought passed and I kept moving.

At dusk, tired and aching, I returned the same
way at the time when the sun was giving its last hur-
rah, making the contrast between light and shadow as
gorgeous and dramatic as it ever gets. On the lower
end of the meadow I stopped to take in both the view
and light. I'd saved the apple till then when the wea-
riness was total and the inside of my mouth tasted
gummy and bitter. Taking off the knapsack, so I could
get the apple, my mouth had already begun to water

thinking of the scrape, crunch, and sweet explosion about to come. It was when I had the apple in hand that I turned to look back uphill and saw the dog not fifty feet away. He stood stock still facing me. There was no question it was Big Top. The three big black freckles on his mouth that made it look like someone had dripped ink on his face erased all doubts. I felt he'd been waiting for me to notice. After I did, *he* turned and started back toward the woods.

"Big!"

He began trotting away.

"Big Top! Wait!" I didn't move. "Big! Stop!" When he didn't, I lobbed the apple toward him, not trying to hit him but wanting him to at least turn around once more. Maybe death had made him deaf. But maybe death didn't want us any closer either, so I continued standing there. He kept trotting. I shouted but it did nothing. I'd seen him; he'd come from another world to show me something I'd have to decipher for myself. He moved away across the darkening meadow, bright white against green like a moving pile of snow. I could see him for some time even after he'd entered the trees. Quick white sewing between the black verticals. Glimpses, hints, flashes of white, there, there, and there. Looking harder, I saw him even farther into the dark. I knew there were miracles on earth, enigmas like this dead white dog, wonders as great as my being able to speak every language on earth for one night of my life. It was easy to be stunned by them and stop there. That was wrong. Venasque said most people see ghosts and (1) scream, (2) shake, (3) later tell the story a hundred times without once thinking, why did it appear for them? What was it telling them? "Magic and ghosts don't just happen.

They don't happen in empty deserts or show up in the middle of the Pacific Ocean for a fish that happens to be passing. They need an audience. All miracles need an audience. One that'll appreciate them. Frank Sinatra's not such a hit in front of deaf people. What *we* gotta do when they happen is figure out what's the connection between them and us. Find that, my man, and you're on your way."

When I knew Big Top was gone and our encounter over, I could think of nothing else to do but raise my hand high over my head and wave at him already gone. That felt good, but it wasn't enough. "I love you! I love you, Big!" I shouted across the meadow, into the cooling air, across time and death and all the other obstacles to my friend. "I love you!"

🔪 "That guy's such a creep, even his clothes don't want to wear him!" I was talking about a certain American foreman who was becoming more and more of a problem. Palm looked at the ceiling but his silence said he agreed. The door opened slowly and a head appeared that took me a couple of seconds to recognize. Hasenhüttl, looking two thousand years old.

"Jesus, man, come in!"

Morton jumped up and offered his chair. Hasenhüttl smiled a quick thanks but the grin was gone instantly, and the way he plopped down said this guy was really at the end.

"Should I leave?" Palm moved to go.

Hasenhüttl looked at him and nodded. "Thank you, Morton. I won't be long."

From the way he looked and the almost-whisper

of his voice, that sounded like the understatement of
the day.

When Palm was gone and the door clicked,
Hasenhüttl and I watched each other over the expanse of my desk.

"I'm dying."

"Angels don't die."

"I'm not really an angel. First you have to be an
Invigilator. It's a very complex process."

"I'll bet. You gotta start at the bottom, huh?"

"Why are you always a pain in the ass, Radcliffe? I
come in to tell you I'm dying, a sort-of angel is dying
in front of you, and you make cracks."

I threw up a hand. "Because I find it very hard to
believe. You've been throwing tests at me ever since
we met. How do I know this isn't one too? From the
very beginning I found you hard to believe, but I got
used to the idea. Now you come in looking like Lon
Chaney and tell me you're *dying*? Wouldn't you be
skeptical if you were me? I thought things like immortality were a given where you come from."

He picked up my stapler and began clicking it. "I
did too. Shows how much I know. Listen, I know
about your seeing the dog again. That's a good sign. I
can't tell you why, but it is. I also came here to tell
you I won't be around anymore. I don't understand
what's happening to me, and it's not really death, but
it's like that. You're going to have to get along on your
own now."

We looked at each other. He clicked the stapler. I
wanted to take it out of his hand and put it down. I
took it out of his hand and put it down. He picked it
up again.

"If that's the truth, I don't know what to say. Do you hurt? Does anything hurt?"

"No, but thanks for asking. I look like a Dead Sea Scroll, don't I?"

"No, you look, uh, very distinguished. Like an old Indian chief."

"Bullshit, but thanks for lying. If you're not careful, Harry, you'll turn into a nice man before you know it."

"God forbid. Hey, is this really it? I'll never see you again?"

He touched his face in a way that made it look like he was trying to cool it. His lips were dry and wrinkled. "This will be my last day here."

"Where do you go now, Has?"

Looking straight ahead, one side of his mouth went up in a weak smile. "If I knew that, I wouldn't be so afraid."

"How come we never stop being scared? Even you, even angels are afraid."

"You're not afraid anymore, Harry."

"That's almost true. Ever since our talk and then seeing Big Top up on that hill, I haven't been fearful or worried. I just want to see what happens."

"You're lucky." He started to get up, lost the strength, and sat down again. "Would you mind if I stay here awhile? I'll go as soon as I can."

"Sure, stay. You want a drink?"

He shook his head. "No. I only want to sit with someone who isn't afraid. Maybe it'll rub off."

"Hasenhüttl, I'm . . . I'm sorry. I also want to thank you for telling me what this is about. You don't know how excited it's made me."

Nothing about him changed; he didn't shrink

down like the sprinkled wicked witch of the west, but nevertheless the longer we sat there the more he seemed to fade or diminish or lessen. It was as if he were using up all of his gas or air in front of me.

"Listen, I want to tell you something last. My speech is coming apart, everything is, but stay with me. I'll try to make it clear enough to understand for you. Mankind's always paid too much attention to the dead. It's been a fundamental part of life itself. Don't you do this, Harry. Forget the dead. Forget dying. It was never part of God's design. Man invented death, and so long as it continues to fascinate him, God allows it to remain." The next time the big man tried, he was able to get up again and make it to the door. "Threaten the dead. Make them afraid with what you create. Any man who loves his work forgets the dead, even his own. Any human work that is finished shows them again how incomplete they are."

 The meeting with the people from the Creditanstalt Bank had gone on too long and the majority of us in the room were beginning to slide down in our seats like fifth graders in arithmetic class. Luckily I was called to the phone by a secretary who appeared very impressed by the caller. It was the Sultan of Saru's spokesman. I was informed that His Majesty and his betrothed had decided to honor us with their presence at the *Dachgleiche*, as symbols of their support both for the Austrian people and the museum. "When will Their Highnesses be joining us?" I asked.

"In a week, God willing," the spokesman said. Then I heard the evil little click that comes from a telephone when you're being put on hold.

"Harry? Is that you?"

"My goodness, if it isn't Frances Neville herself. How're you doing, Queenie?"

"Don't pull my chain, Harry. I just want to make sure you're going to be there for this thing because I need to talk to you. And don't get any ideas about what I want to say because you'd be dead wrong. Are you going to be there or not?"

"Hey, Toots, it's my building. Sure I'm going to be there."

"How is Claire?"

"Claire's good. She'll be here for the festival too."

A silence that lasted a good long time.

"What do you want to talk about with me, Fanny? The last time we met, you tripped me. I was under the impression that was your final say."

"It was, then, but now we have to talk about something else. I've got to go. We have to leave this place. I'm not used to getting bombed in my hometown."

The late twentieth century has been the era of the Underdog. In example after example the Davids, whether they are the North Vietnamese, the Ayatollah Khomeini, even the New York Jets, have been defeating the Goliaths—the United States Armed Forces, Shah of Iran, Baltimore Colts—right and left until there really are no more "givens."

The Saruvian Army flattened Cthulu's resistance fighters in every strategic battle they had for six months. That was that. Time for Cthulu to haul ass back to his mountain hideouts and glower down at the winners. That made sense. But mythically, like a phoenix, the rebels kept climbing out of their own ashes and going back to fight again. At first it was to

be expected—typical never-say-die revolutionary
verve and passion. Next it became annoying—when
are these guys going to quit? We won the battle didn't
we? Finally the phoenix turned into the monster from
the horror film who, no matter how many times you
shot/stabbed/burned it, the bastard kept raging back
stronger than before. They captured Wadi Zehid,
where they butchered any prisoners they took. At
Cheddia it was worse. Their tactics and beliefs were
compared to the Murngin of Australia who believed
that the spirit of the dead victim entered the body of
his killer, who then grew twice as strong and physically larger. When it was discovered by a French journalist that many of those closest to Cthulu had
castrated themselves as acts of homage to him, the
Skoptsy or "White Doves" of Russia were brought
into the discussion. A lovely little sect whose men cut
off their plumbing while the women cut off their
breasts for the sake of their faith, these Doves said
God told them to do it. This same journalist, before he
disappeared forever under extremely suspicious cir-
cumstances while on assignment with Cthulu and his
monsters, asked the boss how his soldiers could act so
barbarously. "There are only heroes and the dead,
monsieur. If you know the man you are about to fight
might eat your body after he has killed you, there is
less chance you will want to fight him, you know?
Besides, our enemy are not human beings. They are of
the devil, the sperm of the dead moving toward life."
If this old nutbag stood on a corner in New York saying the things he said in his interview, people would
take one look and steer around him PDQ. But here
was Cthulu leading a successful revolution against
the government of Saru.

Back in Zell am See, when the subject came up of what that cannibal would do if he ever gained power, people tended to look down or away like someone had farted. We *knew* what he'd do if he won, but who wanted to talk about it? Particularly in light of the fact that we were the ones making a great big building for the other side, also known as the sperm of the dead. When the Saruvian ambassador to Qatar and his family were machine-gunned in front of the embassy there, Palm went to Vienna and came back with seven more security guards who had allegedly been trained specifically in counterinfiltration techniques. Their presence made us feel both more secure and more vulnerable. After a week on the job, these guards were seen infrequently and didn't say much. Palm told me they were the best of their kind but also gave the vibration he didn't want to answer questions about them, so I shut up and did my work.

Hasenhüttl never reappeared. The night before Claire arrived I went to the woodpile where we'd spoken and had a chat with him, wherever he was. I told him I was growing more confident every day about the museum. I told him ideas and questions that had come from reading the Koran and the Bible, and how I was going to ask Claire to live with me. I shared a mixed jumble of passing thoughts and enthusiasms, hopes, worries with him. When I was finished and feeling sheepish about having spoken to the ghost of an angel, I realized I had told very few of these things to Morton Palm. Not that I wouldn't, or that I was trying to keep any of it from him. I just hadn't told him. Getting up from the pile and brushing my hands off, I said to my invisible Invigilator, "Now that you're gone, you've become my friend!"

➣ If I hadn't ducked, she would have smacked me right across the face. Perfect movie scene—Clark Gable waits with a bouquet of roses at the airport, Carole Lombard appears at the arrival gate and smiles hugely when she sees him. Darling! They come together for the kiss to end all kisses. Only Carole slaps his kisser rather than kisses it.

Claire came through smiling and looking fabulous. Her hair was shorter and she wore jeans and a baseball warm-up jacket that showed off her legs and wide shoulders. She also wore more makeup than usual. I imagined her standing in the tiny airplane toilet putting on mascara with one hand while leaning against the wall with the other. I imagined her seat in the airplane; no Styrofoam cups jammed cracked and ugly into the seat pocket, no mussed blanket on the floor. Her magazine or book would be unwrinkled and in a safe place. That was Claire. She was emotional but neat. She chose vibrant colors and designs but knew where to put and order them to their best advantage.

"Hiya, sweetie!" I offered the bouquet at the same time she swung. I ducked. My mother used to belt me once in a while when I got out of hand, and the radar you develop as a child stays. Claire missed but the wind was strong. I thought it was a joke, but one look at her expression and it was clear the punch was no joke.

"I don't even know why I'm here! I don't even know why I left L.A., you creep! Why do I have to love you? It'd be so much simpler if I didn't!"

"Claire—"

With a backhand flick, she sent my flowers flying.

Red and green splashed across the air. We both watched them go, as did everybody else in the neighborhood.

"Claire—"

She walked to the nearest group of flowers and stomped a foot down on them. "You're a pain in the ass, Harry, and it's bloody fucking hard putting up with you and your ego a *lot* of the time. But I do, because I love you and I think there's greatness in you. But all that aside, you betrayed me, you son of a bitch!"

"What? How?"

A policeman came up to us and asked in broken English what was wrong. I took Claire's arm and said over my shoulder to the cop my wife had just had a hard flight and wasn't feeling well. She jerked her arm away and said, "I feel fine. Get your hands off me." She strode off. I gave the cop a "gee whiz" shrug and ran after her.

At the baggage claim she wouldn't talk. When I tried to say something, she tapped her foot madly and said, "I don't hear you. Don't even try. I don't hear you." So I shut up. I don't know what I'd have done if, after getting her bag, she'd refused to come with me. Hit her over the head and smuggle her into the trunk of the car? Thank God she came, but for the first half hour of the trip she was silent. I asked if she wanted to hear music. Silence. Was she hungry? Silence. Did she want to kill me? She was sporting a look that could have frozen the sun. It might have been better if I'd pulled off at a rest stop and confronted her square on, but there's something hypnotic about driving along at a speed that I hoped would gradually work to calm her down. I was so glad to see her. I wanted to hug and kiss her and tell her many things, but I kept quiet.

About forty-five minutes later, I caught a movement out of the corner of my eye and knew she'd turned to look at me. "Fanny called me, you know."

I nodded. If I spoke and said the wrong thing it might send her right back into silence.

"She called and said she wanted to talk about you. Now that she's getting married and you two are finished, she said she wanted to tell me some things."

I saw a sign for a roadside rest two kilometers away. I put the blinker on to move into the slow lane. If I was going to hear what I *thought* I was about to hear, I wanted to be off the road and looking at Claire. Fanny was capable of many things, one of them being fang-toothed nastiness. When she'd been hurt she rarely listened to the other side's point of view. *She'd* been hurt and now someone was going to pay for her pain. Pity the poor fucker she targeted. After we broke up, despite that being her decision, I had a lingering hunch she would do something unpleasant. As the weeks passed, that suspicion evaporated and I felt she'd manifested her hurt by originally being the one to say our relationship was over. I was wrong. Telling me to go away *wasn't* enough for her. That's why she'd asked after Claire the day we spoke on the phone. Knowing something I didn't, she was waiting for it to go off like a timed fuse. Isn't there some kind of bug or snake that sleeps under the ground for years and then wakes, only to stick its head out and bite whatever happens to be passing? If not, there should be because science could call it the Neville adder.

"Do you know what I'm talking about?"

There was the roadside stop. I decelerated more

and turned the wheel. "I don't know. Tell me what you mean."

"What do I *mean*, Harry? I mean the night you and I went to Lowry's for dinner. Where did you go afterward? Remember you said you had work to do and I believed it? Stupid, trusting me. I needed you that night! And what about the wonderful leather bag you bought me? You went back and bought *her* one too? You drove all the way back to that store to buy her the same bag? You didn't even get a different color. That's what I loved most about it. That marvelous sexy blue! Did you ever go back to a place you'd been with her to get something for *me*?"

The answer to that was yes, but I wasn't about to say it *then*. Her list went on. Lies, gifts, meetings, things said and not said. Fanny had decided to "come clean" with Claire Stansfield because now that she'd told me to go to hell, she wanted the other woman in my life to know exactly what had gone on between us so that Claire could decide whether she wanted to be involved with such a black-hearted, megalomaniacal, deceiving villain. She was as complete with her report as a tax auditor. Claire listed at least twenty rotten things I'd done behind her back, between the lines, in broad daylight, et cetera.

"Are they true, Harry? Did you really do them?"

"Generally, yes."

"What do you mean, 'generally'? Don't play word games."

"I mean yes, I did them with some little differences. I assume you know Fanny told you about them with just the slightest *slant* in her favor."

"I assumed that. I'm not so dumb. And I'll tell you right now that when she was finished I said, 'Thank you, Fanny. Now I understand why Harry chose me and not you.' And I hung up. She can drop dead. But that has nothing to do with *us*. These things are all betrayal, Harry. They're shitty and wrong and selfish, and people who love each other just *don't do them*. That's all. It's as basic as that. So I want to know why you did. And why you did them so often to me. I don't care about you and her."

A truck zoomed by on the autobahn. A car with Polish license plates pulled into the rest stop. Two small people jumped out and ran for the toilet. When they emerged a long time later both of them wore the smiles of the just. I still hadn't spoken. My mind's computer had placed all its programs into RAM disc and skimmed each for possible answers. But in the same nanoseconds, I discarded each response because they were either too clever or evasive or simply not true.

"I wish I could give you the answer you'd like to hear. I'm sure there's one that'd soothe you or make you feel better. But you know the only word that's in my mind, Claire? Struggle. I'm not getting political on you and I'm not trying to avoid the issue. I'm talking about the truly difficult, everyday struggle to do the right thing. You're a genuinely good person and because of that . . . gift, I don't think you know what it is to have to work *hard* to simply do the right thing, especially with the people that matter to you. You have it innately, and sometimes I'm very jealous. It'd also be easy to say 'lightning only strikes the highest peaks,' meaning, if you're going to love me, you've got to take the whole package and accept the way I am. But you have every right to reject that too. Maybe I do have greatness in me, and I can honestly tell you that in the last months I've been working like never before to do right, not only for the moment, but for all concerned. Did I do those shitty things before? Yes. Would I do them again? I hope not. I hope not. I hope not. Right now I want you. I want to treat you the way you deserve. I want to treat you as well as you've treated me all along. And I *am* trying. Please know that I'm trying. But I am not a character in a novel or a television series. Things always make sense there and we get used to thinking life should really be like TV or a Dickens novel. The bad guy has a terrible experience, gets brought up short by life and boom—he changes everything and becomes a good soul. I'd love to be a good soul. I'd love to be a good soul for *you* and I'm trying. That's the only thing I can say with any certainty: I *am* trying."

"That sounds good, Harry, but you did betray me."

"I betrayed you. A hundred percent."

"Which means you're not to be trusted."

"I doubt if anyone has ever trusted me."

She jammed me in the arm with her elbow. "Oh goddamn you, Harry, I trusted you! I knew your shortcomings and how deeply involved you were with Fanny, but I still trusted you. That's what's so hurtful about this—I gave you so much rope because I knew you needed it, but you took that rope and twisted it around my neck, not your own! I'm the one who's choking here, not you!"

I put my forehead on the steering wheel. "I will try. I will struggle, I—will—try. I can make no other guarantees."

"You're in no position to make guarantees."

Cars passed. Thin gray clouds looking like racing greyhounds came in and moved out again.

"Even if I believe that you're trying, I *hate* the fact I can't trust you. It's like having sex but always stopping just before the orgasm."

"Huh?"

"Because when the orgasm comes, a good orgasm, you click everything else off and just fall into it. Because you know your love will catch you. When it's over, you're on safe ground again. How do I get back to that with you?"

The few days we had together in Zell am See before the Sultan arrived were fragile and sad. Like a person with a new scar, we'd just begin to function normally when something was said or done that stretched our "skin" too much, and instantly the new weaker tissue would scream. We were formal, I talked too much and tried too hard to keep her entertained. One afternoon we were feeding ducks by the lake and she started to cry. I asked if there was anything I could do. She held out her mechanical hand, palm up, and without saying a word, opened and closed it again and again. Coming when it did, the gesture was so odd that it made me too uneasy to ask what she meant.

Another time, apropos of nothing, she told me her parents' favorite Claire-as-child story. When she was four, her mother asked her what were her favorite things. "Love, zebras, and my husband."

We screwed too much, and frequently it was the same variety: crazy-aggressive, hot but without any closeness; look up at the wrong moment and you were likely to catch a cold eye watching you. I was very glad Morton was around because he quickly

sensed the tension between us and did what he could
to lessen it. We ate meals together where he entertained us with wild stories about his days soldiering
for the United Nations. He and Claire went cross-
country skiing one day and into Salzburg one afternoon. When he asked what was wrong I told him,
trying carefully to give as fair and balanced an ac-
count as I could. He seemed sympathetic, but distant.
For the first time, I asked him if this was the sort of
thing that had caused him and his wife to break up.
"No, Harry, I was true to her. I did other things
wrong, but I always believed one person was enough
for a lifetime."

The day before the Saru contingent was due to
descend, Claire left without telling me. I returned to
the room after a morning meeting and there was a
note on the desk propped against a vase holding a
single red rose.

"I owe you more of these for ruining yours the
other day. I'm sorry to chicken out, but I can't be here
now with you, my dear. I'm going to Vienna and will
stay there until after Fanny leaves. Then we can see
how we feel and talk about what to do. I keep saying
to myself, 'Forgive him,' but then I realize I don't
want to forgive you, I want to love you. Since I can't
do either now, I'll go and be alone in a pretty city and
hopefully clean out my cluttered head. I'll call when I
get there and tell you where I'm staying."

Although it surprised and hurt me, on the one
hand I was glad she'd made the decision. She deserved my full attention, but I couldn't give it to her
until the formidable Neville had come and I'd had it
out with *that* bitch. Actually, now that I knew what
had happened between her and Claire, I didn't think

of Fanny as a bitch so much as a. . . . No, I thought
she was a bitch. A fang-addered, holier-than-thou,
back stabbing bitch who hadn't gotten the world's
best deal from me, granted, but did *not* have the right
to repay me by trying to pump venom into the arter-
ies of my life. She was a bitch all right and would get
hers. Naturally I had a plan.

I wasn't at the small airport in nearby Schüttdorf
to greet the royal duo when their helicopter came in. I
was back in the hotel room asleep, having an enter-
taining dream about buying Mormon literature. Palm
said my absence was an embarrassment for people
who didn't deserve to be embarrassed.

At the reception that night, held at the Sultan's
Schloss, half of the western part of Austria seemed to
be in attendance, so it was not until I'd milled around
for an hour that I saw or talked to either of them.

Both wore black. Way on the other side of the
room talking to a bunch of attentive politicos, Hassan
stood in a silky double-breasted suit that made him
look taller and older. Nearer to me, Fanny had on a
billowing silk blouse and slacks, and a pomegranate
red belt. Were women in Saru allowed to wear such
slinky garb? What happened if mere mortals lusted
after the Sultan's wife? Furious as I was, it pleased me
to undress her in my mind and remember what she
was like in the sack. I'd seen her asleep. Heard her
pee. Watched as she stood in front of a mirror and
patrolled her face for blemishes. She was mean but
vulnerable. I knew what she'd done came of caring
deeply for me but not getting what she wanted in
return. Now I'd give her exactly what she had
wanted, but too late. It was no longer hers to touch.

When we made eye contact I was the one who went up first.

"Hello there."

"Hello, Harry." Her eyes were a complete meteorological station of dials, meters, and wind socks programmed to read the weather in me, and between us. I gave her enough time to take a first measurement: (1) He came up; (2) he looks friendly; (3) he hasn't tried to kill me.

I knew what she was expecting—a hundred-megaton Radcliffe blast, or at the very least, gale force winds that would blow her back to Saru. What she got instead was Harry Radcliffe at his indisputable best. Gentlemanly, witty as only I could be witty, but most important—*kind*. I "kinded" her right out of the room. I could go into detail and quote what I said/she said/I said to show what I mean, but suffice it to say Fanny Neville never knew me to be so gosh darned wonderful. From the first minute, I could see it was driving her crazy. When she asked if Claire had arrived, I said yes and how important a talk we'd had in light of their recent conversation. When she pumped me on who said what, I lied like a car dealer and brilliantly made it sound like Claire and I and our love had all had epiphanies/insights/breakthroughs galore because of that momentous chat between the two women. But I did it so smartly, and underplayed things so well, that even the hyperperceptive Fanny didn't see the wool being pulled over her eyes. The trick was not to smooth it over. Sure, Fanny's exposing my badness had caused a crisis, shouting and tears. Sure, we'd come close to breaking up. Sure this, sure that, but in the end we realized there was a great sturdy bond between us that, though shaken violently, had revealed itself to be so much stronger than either of us had thought. How fundamentally we cared!

What Fanny saw was the Radcliffe she'd always wanted—as a direct result of her trying to ruin him. He was much the same man, only better now because of her shameful, unnecessary act. By being a small, tattling rat, she had helped Claire and me to find the mother lode in our relationship.

I had a part two of my revenge plan but put it on hold after seeing the result of part one that night. After fifteen minutes of intense conversation, surrounded the whole time by peeking, sneering, snooping people from the reception, I could see the damage seeping through to Fanny. When finally she asked why Claire wasn't there that night, I looked her in the eye and said, "She went to Vienna. She left because she needs time away to think whether she wants to stay with me or not. It's very possible she won't, Fanny."

"Even after all you worked through? I thought everything was all right."

"Everything is *understood*. It's not all right." I took a breath to say more, but found I couldn't. Because I was telling the pure truth and was terribly afraid I would now lose Claire because of the old me—a me I could no longer stand. *He* had done these things to her. The same Radcliffe bullshitting Fanny right now into believing her contemptible behavior had been such a help to us. You might never see her again! In her note she'd said let's talk after Fanny leaves, not let's see each other! I wanted to rush off and call Claire, beg her not to leave. To give me even half a chance to try to do it right. I was glad I'd used my

Saru wish to get her a hand, but if I had that wish again, I'd ask for another chance with Claire, because nothing was more important than another chance with her. Any kind of chance.

I looked at Fanny and felt dizzy. I touched my head to still it. I was hyperventilating badly and couldn't stop. Be calm. Excusing myself, I walked quickly away to find a bathroom where I filled the sink with cold water and stuck my whole head down into it as deep as it would go. I might lose Claire! I probably had. Call her immediately. No, leave her alone and let her work it out for herself. Beg her. Don't bother her. Crawl. Don't call.

I pulled my head up from the water, gasping, dropped it in again. Call Vienna. Don't you dare.

My head up again, I looked in the mirror over the sink. My face dripped and shone. I was panting. "You win, Fanny. You win."

One last story before I finish. Philip Strayhorn and I were having dinner at Venasque's house one night. The subject had turned naturally and comfortably to the many different ways there were to die. I was not so far away from my days of madness, and normally talk of death made me jittery. But these two men, particularly together, made even the land of no return an intriguing place to hear about. Strayhorn, who knew something about everything, told us how in the Middle Ages executions were quite formal, absorbing events. Often the condemned would get up on the platform, his final podium, and give a stirring speech to the crowd. He told them how worried he was for their souls and how he'd arrived at this pitiful place himself. Beware, folks, don't follow my path or you'll end up here. The crowd loved hearing these last-minute autobiographies while the doomed had his last earthly moment of camaraderie with those who'd come to see him die: We're all in this together and the only trick I've learned, brothers and sisters, is do not do it my way.

Venasque spoke while finishing the last bit of spicy potato salad on his plate. "Harry did that once."

Shoveling in pastrami on rye, I almost missed my cue. "Say what?"

"That was you. You got up once and gave a terrific speech and then they cut your head off. One of the only times in your whole history you ever admitted to being wrong."

I looked at Strayhorn. "When was this, Venasque?"

"Oh, in France, before the revolution. They got you for stealing a priest's pig."

"A priest's pig?"

"That's right. Who wants another pickle?"

"How much 'before' the revolution?"

"Don't worry about that, Harry. Listen to what I said between the lines that you didn't happen to read. I said it was one of the few times in your history that you admitted to being wrong. Hint hint, darling."

 I loathe oompah bands. Fat guys marching pompously around in Tyrolean hats with pheasant feathers leaping goofily off the side. Quasi-fascist, paramilitary loden costumes that look like uniforms, and the *music* they play! What sadist ever thought up

that music? What circle of hell has he been committed
to?

There must have been five oompah bands on hand
that day. And when they stopped for a breather, Austrian folk groups would come leaping up from some
other part of hell to yodel, do ass- and foot-slap rou-
tines, howl and prance through dance after traditional
Austrian folk dance. In between, a famous television
personality served as master of ceremonies and kept
up a patter of jokes and comments and a parade of
pretty girls in dirndls cut so low you could see their
belly buttons. Welcome to the Dog Museum *Dachgleiche*. Actually, it was terrible but not that bad. Once
you got used to the fact that the purpose of the whole
thing was to get drunk and congratulate anyone
nearby, it was nice in a sort of George Grosz way. My
only real problem, aside from having to listen to "The
Radetzky March" six times, was too often I'd be looking at these people having fun and remember many
of the older ones were doing this same cavorting back
in the 1930s and '40s, and then when the festivities
were peaking, a guy in a brown uniform would get
up and give a ringing speech about Herr Hitler. That
realization put a damper on my becoming too involved in the party. But it was fun. The Saruvians
drank apple cider and orange juice. Lamb had been
brought in for them. Barbecuing lamb and sausage
smells filled the air, along with the oiliness of fried
potatoes and tartness of new wine and mugs of beer. I
have no capacity for alcohol at all, and knew if I had
two beers I'd be dead drunk fast, so I took a glass
here, had a sip. Put it down and, wandering on to the
next group, took a glass there, sipped. . . . That way
I would be able to make it through the ceremony and

what followed in reasonable shape. I also knew if I got drunk I might very well call Vienna and end up saying the wrongest things to Claire. My newest plan was to leave her alone for another day, if I could bear it, then call and tell her how bad off I was and ask if she would please see me, even if she'd already made up her mind to go. That was fair, wasn't it? I held onto the scheme like a bird with a broken wing: Maybe I could keep it alive with care and concern. Maybe it would heal and fly again if I did things right.

I was staggering through a pidgin conversation in German with the *Bundeshauptmann* from Salzburg when Hassan came up, followed by a small army of minions.

"We're very proud of what you've done, Radcliffe. I know my father would have liked it." He put out his hand and we shook firmly. I was the one who broke the clasp. What would he think if I told him it was not only a nice building, but would be the Tower of Babel when completed? Knowing his opinion of me, he'd sigh at my limitless arrogance and walk away. Best to leave it alone and let future events speak for themselves. "Thank you very much. How're you doing otherwise?"

"Terribly, thank you. I am tired to the bottoms of my feet. But you know, when we have beaten Cthulu I am going to be very happy. Right now, life is not much fun."

"He sounds pretty unpleasant."

Hassan lifted his head and scratched his neck. It suddenly dawned on me he was unshaven. "One day last week a briefcase was discovered outside my office. It was full of enough plastic explosive to blow up half the palace. But there was no fuse and no timer, only the explosive. Next to it inside was a note from Cthulu. Handwritten. Do you know what it said? 'This is for your children, Hassan. You are already dead.' "

"That must have made you feel warm all over."

"It frightened me, but I am frightened often these days. My father taught me that fear is like food—you eat it and shit it out. Sometimes I am constipated. Sometimes I would rather watch a football game than think about war. Take care of yourself. Oh, and by the way, Fanny told me last night after the reception that you two had talked? She said you were very nice. It seemed to make her sad that you were nice. I found that very interesting." He gave me a royal wave and walked away with his gang in tow.

My *Bundeshauptmann* zoomed right back in to tell me many things I could only smile and nod knowingly at without knowing a word he was saying. Luckily we were soon called for the ceremony, and I was able to escape with more smiles and a few dozen *Auf Wiedersehen's*. Only us bigwigs went up to the top of the building to actually put our hands on the tree and be photographed together as one big happy family, Hassan and Fanny in the middle. The real ceremony took place after we'd all descended again and walked over to a hastily erected stage in front of the site.

Anyone who sat up there had to give a speech and when my turn came, I said, "The former Sultan of Saru did two wonderful things for me. First, he was generous enough to save my life during an earthquake. Almost more important he also convinced me to become involved with this project. Although I did not know him well, he is a man I both admire and miss to this day. From what I can understand of him, he was the best kind of human contradiction: a visionary who kept his feet on the ground. A pragmatist who was not afraid to dream and hope. His Majesty, the new Sultan, told me earlier that his father would have liked this building if he'd lived to see it. I can only hope that when our Dog Museum is completed, it will serve the functions all good museums do, which is to inform, enlighten, and finally to delight."

Short and sweet, it drew a nice round of applause although I wondered how many people in the audience spoke enough English to have understood what I said. The Austrian dignitaries talked forever, which was a double bore for those of us who didn't come from that land of inverted verbs. The speeches ended with Hassan thanking everyone in both German and English, and then going on to give the rest of his short speech in perfect, unstilted German, which surprised me. The fellow had tricks up his sleeve. I hoped he had enough of them to fight off the bad guys in Saru.

Ceremony completed, the bands oompahed up, and out rolled the food and drink again. While I was on stage listening to speeches, I scanned the audience and sat straight up when I saw a woman whom I initially mistook for Claire. Even though our mind *knows* it isn't them, a pernicious little beast inside keeps insisting, yes it is, till we get confused. I first saw the woman when she was applauding and it was quite plain she had two healthy hands. But my beast said no, that's Claire! She's come back! And for that thrilling jump of time, I believed it. When reality returned moments later, my adrenaline was critical and my heart was running the sixty-yard dash. I wanted it to be her but was petrified at the same time. I wanted this concrete, miraculous proof that she had returned. Yet if it was Claire, I didn't know what to say. No matter, because it wasn't her, and I realized that after a second, more focused look. But the false alarm left me shaky and depressed for an hour afterward, and finally, bored with these blues, I grabbed a big beer when a girl passed with a tray. The drink did nothing to help and instead sent me in urgent search for a place to piss.

My tongue was out, my eyes were closed in bliss, and I was breathing pure relief when I heard the first shots. Opening my eyes, I looked at my unit to see what was going on down there. Shots? Screams, more shots, automatic weapon fire. Short spitting bursts, stop, another burst from different places. The pissoir had open windows on the left and right sides. I heard firing from one side, then the other. Sticking myself back in and zipping up, I looked out the left window but saw nothing. Firing again. I looked out the right and saw a man, an unfamiliar Arab in jeans and a black ski jacket run by with something held up high in his hand. A gun.

More shooting, and before I could get out of the toilet, I heard two very loud explosions and the screaming of the terrified and the hurt. A woman shouting someone's name over and over, "Ferdl. Ferdl. Ferdl."

Outside was chaos. People lay on the ground, people ran, people were scared. Some were bleeding, others were already dead. It was impossible to get my bearings. I'd seen it before in Vietnam. No one ever had the right advice about bullets. Run toward the fire. Move straight up through the Killing Zone. Get down. You did what you could and prayed. Luckily this time one of Palm's special security men was bandaging a child. I ran over and asked *who?*

"Cthulu's men. We thought they might come today. Do you have a gun?"

"No."

"Then get one. Or run. Running is better."

More chaos. What do you do? Before I could decide, more explosions, a series, very close by. Boom Boom Boom. The hollow thump of mortars. They had fucking *mortars?* On the other side of the site a high cloud of black smoke and jetting flame rose evilly. I remembered that was where Hassan's helicopter landed. Hassan. Fanny.

Jesus Christ, Fanny!

I ran low, low as I could, a squat, a crab. People were shooting, an Austrian policeman lay on the ground, part of his neck and shoulder blown away. His gun lay nearby. I picked it up but didn't look at it. I just had it. At least I had a gun. It was light. Some kind of plastic and couldn't do much good but it was a gun and I had something lethal in my hand. I kept running toward the smoke. Fanny.

My feet knew before my brain. Or my brain told my feet before they told my conscious mind. Whatever the process, I stopped before I knew I was going to and the instant paralysis threw me way off balance. Stumbling forward, I was barely able to keep standing. The museum! The motherfuckers were going to blow up the museum. First make havoc, then set the charges and run. I knew it. I was sure of it. The idea had come to me again and again the entire time we'd been working here. One day Cthulu's going to try to knock this beauty down. It was so logical, but like the thought of my own death, I'd pushed it away. Why spend time thinking about something so final and inevitable? Inevitable. It was inevitable that this would happen and I'd known it all along. I stood there until I had my balance back and then turned around toward the building. It was still there, far away, but still reachable if I tried. The thought came and left in the same second. If I could still reach Fanny maybe I could help. If there was even the smallest chance, it was worth it. I turned back, away from the museum, and ran again toward the helicopter.

Moving, I noticed there was less machine noise, less firing, and now more human sounds. Cries for help, shouts, the bizarre and ominous babble of the seriously wounded. I ran harder toward my friend. Maybe I could help.

I heard a "la-la-la-la-la" sound and immediately after, the Sultan's black helicopter rose slowly up through the smoke and flew away. Was Fanny there? Someone was firing an automatic from inside the cockpit. Zip-zip-zip-zip stop zip-zip-zip. It looked like a number of people were in there. Fanny too? Up and gone.

Then I heard three gigantic explosions from behind. So strong that the ground reared and knocked me down. I knew what it was. I knew it was done. I looked at the earth five inches from my face. Such a rich brown. So alive.

One last thing. Later, when it was almost over, I saw this. Very far away, toward the ruins of the museum, one of Palm's men was chasing one of Cthulu's. Both had guns and were running fast. Abruptly,

Cthulu's man changed shape entirely and became a large deer. It is the truth. I *saw* it. Without stopping the chase, Palm's man changed into a dog. A brownish red dog. On eight flying legs, they were out of sight about the time I realized what I was seeing and what had happened. I saw it.

➤ As if to apologize for what had happened during the day, the weather that night was full of spring. It was warm, the air was a bouquet of wonderful smells; it was perfect strolling weather.

You can imagine what it was like after the attack. Police and doctors, sirens, the addled confusion and never-ending screams of shock or pain of the survivors. There was no way to logically put any kind of order back into this universe. Seventeen people were dead. Many more wounded. The museum was a total loss. The only good piece of news was that Hassan and Fanny had escaped. Not, as I'd expected, in the helicopter but in a secret getaway car that was always kept nearby the royal couple, just in case. I rejoiced to hear that my friend had survived.

I did what I could to help but there wasn't much because I was neither doctor nor priest. I was only the architect who'd designed a building that was no longer there. Once long ago, I'd smiled to think "The Man Who Built the Dog Museum" was a good epitaph to put on my gravestone. I stayed around and tried to help, tried to comfort where I could, but it was useless. Once a grieving woman, rocking back and forth over the covered body of her husband, saw me and gave me a look I will never forget. It said, "This is your fault. This is all your fault."

After that I talked to the police, telling them whatever I could. They seemed bored with my story. Then I went back to the hotel. Zell am See was bedlam. Fire trucks, ambulances, helicopters, television trucks, and hundreds of people overran the place in a fury of macabre excitement and made it feel like an ant farm. Some of them were there to help, most to gawk or take advantage of the tragedy. What surprised me was how quickly they had arrived. How quickly the news of blood had traveled. It was easy to hate them all.

Back in my room the telephone rang until I thought it would drive me mad. One of the callers might have been Claire or Fanny, but I had no heart to answer. I'd told the people at the desk where I was and that if anyone important needed me they could come to the room. No one did. The phone continued to ring until I could stand it no more and, calling down, told reception to say I was not around.

Hours later I was lying on the bed when there was a gentle knock on the door. Suspecting the police, I wearily got up and opened it. It was Morton Palm. Hating myself further for not having once wondered whether he'd survived, I stepped forward and took him into my arms. "Thank God, Morton."

Our embrace was long and needed. Once he tried to let go but I wouldn't let him. "Not yet. Please, not yet."

"Harry, I want you to come with me."

"Where? To the police?"

"No, I want you to come with me back to the site."

"Why?"

His face was exhausted. "Because it's necessary. You have to come with me."

"Really, Morton? Now?"

"Yes, we have to go now."

"All right." When I moved away from him, I felt such a smash of emptiness and loss. What could be left? But I owed it to him, whatever the reason, and I would go.

A few steps out of the hotel I stopped and looked around. "What a beautiful night. What a shitty beautiful night."

Both of us were silent during the ride around the lake to the scene of the crime. Morton drove slowly and the expression on his face said nothing.

Expecting a media circus of klieg lights and television cameras, I was stunned to see no one there when we arrived. Not a single person. I looked at Palm for an explanation, but he only held up a hand for me to wait. What was going on?

We got out of the car where the fence had once been but was now only a tangled spin of metal. No one was around.

"Morton—"

"Just wait, Harry. I'll explain when we get there."

There was no *there* left. Cthulu must have sent along the most brilliant explosives expert in the Mideast because *everything* appeared to be destroyed. I'd seen it that afternoon but with the commotion going on and my own frazzled state of mind, I hadn't absorbed the full extent of the defeat. Wires and pylons, concrete posts and steel girders, all an exploded razed ruin. Someone coming on to the site for the first time would have no idea what had stood here only hours before in the midst of so many people's happiness and pride. One of the only things remaining

above ground was the smoke and flame from small
fires still burning here and there.

"Harry?"

"You know what I saw today, Morton? In the middle of all this, do you know what else I saw? A man
turn into a deer and another man, who was chasing
him, turn into a dog. On my word of honor, I saw
that."

"I know."

I turned slowly toward him. "You *know?* How do
you know?"

"I brought you here to tell you. That's why there is
no one else around. Did you ever wonder why you
walked into my store those months ago? Or why you
happened to walk down that street and stop in front
of a dull ladder store? Because you were supposed to.
Look at me, Harry. Not like that—look at me closely.
Now touch my face. Don't be afraid—touch my face
here."

Hesitantly, unsure of what was happening, I
reached out and touched him on the cheek. As my
fingers made contact, I felt something touch my cheek
in the same place. Both of Morton's hands remained
at his sides. Frightened, I took mine away. The touch
on my cheek went away.

"Do it again, Harry. Put your whole hand there."

I put my open palm against his face and felt the
same thing on mine.

"What is this?" I whispered.

"You came to my store because you needed me.
You've always needed someone to help you see
things more clearly. Sometimes it was women, and
for a while you thought it was Hasenhüttl. You

thought it was your choice, but it wasn't. I had been waiting for you."

"And Hasenhüttl? You *know* about him? The Invigilator thing?"

"Hasenhüttl was only you. You needed someone like that for that time, so you created him to help you through. All of his fears were yours but so were the confidences. He was only another part of you, made of flesh. He "died" when you didn't need him anymore. When you knew, innately, you could do it yourself."

Waves of inconceivable emotion poured through me like water. I felt like I was giving birth. Or dying. When I could speak again I could barely ask, "And *you?*"

"I'm something else. What he told you about the Tower was true. You've known that since the moment you were conceived, but needed to make up someone like him to tell you, rather than find it in yourself. That's all right. You know now and that's what is important. What happened here today had nothing to do with your work, but how you reacted has a great effect on it."

"What did I do? I didn't try to stop them! Maybe I could have, but I ran the other way."

"No, that's wrong. Instead of being selfish and trying to save your building, your creation, what mattered most to you was trying to save the life of your friend. A friend who had treated you terribly. That was the test. We had no idea how you would handle it."

"*Test?* You mean all this was a set-up? You were giving me a final *exam?*"

"No. We didn't know this attack would happen,

but when it came we did what we could to stop it. At the same time, you were being watched. How you reacted was perhaps more important than saving the Tower. It proved you were worthy of building it. Now you have to decide whether you want to try to do it again."

"Do *what* again? *I don't understand this!*" I put my hands over my face and tried to breathe. It wasn't easy. Palm touched my shoulder but I stepped quickly away. "What are you doing? What is all this?"

"It is the Tower of Babel and you were here to build it again for the reasons Hasenhüttl said. Since the first tower failed, Man has been trying to rebuild it. But there have always been people like Cthulu who don't want that to happen. Peace is not their concern. Here you have the results of their work."

"Then why don't you stop the fucking Cthulus of the world! The Hitlers and the Stalins? Why don't *you* and all your flights of angels and fucking cherubim just put a goddamned *stop* on those bastards and let the rest of us poor jerks live? Huh? Why don't you do that?"

"Because it is Man's responsibility. You've been given what you need to do it. Like the Tower—Mankind has every tool it needs. The intelligence, the insight, the vision—"

"And once it's done?" I was so angry. I didn't care who he was. I hated him for his calm free will and patronizing pep talks.

"Once it's done you return to paradise. But only if *you* do it. Come here. I want to show you something."

"Wait! What about the dog and the deer? What was that?"

"Come here, Harry. One thing at a time." Without waiting, he walked toward the ruin. I followed. When we got there he bent down and put his hand on the ground. He signaled for me to do the same.

"Do you feel it?"

"What?"

"Wait and feel with your whole hand."

It was some time before it came. When it did, I felt a kind of slight vibration. It did not increase nor did it go away. "What is it?"

"The earth beginning to rebuild the Tower. It will do it tonight. By tomorrow morning it will be only as high as you were correct in your design. About one third and no more. Then it will stop. No one will be aware that this has happened besides you. The world will only remember and assume what stands is all that was left after the attack. That is a gift from God. He will do that much for you. Then it will be up to you or other men to go on until it is finished correctly."

"I don't believe you."

"Feel the earth. Stay here as long as you like tonight and watch it happen."

I touched the ground again. The vibration was stronger. It was frightening and enthralling. "What if I don't want to do it anymore? What if no one does?"

"Then it will stand as it is, unnoticed and forgotten, until one day another man realizes what it is and begins work again."

"Why me?"

"You never tire of asking that question. Because you are a child of Nimrod and because you are an inspired artist. But most of all, because today you chose to help rather than save yourself. That's why you will be allowed to go on, if you want.

"Yet I must also tell you nothing will be given. Cthulu will now win his war with Hassan and it will become very dangerous and difficult for you to go on, even if you choose to. It's also very possible that working on it for the rest of your life, you will still fail. There are no guarantees. There is only the sweetness of work and the undying hope of achievement."

I stood up slowly. Palm did too. I reached over and, touching his face again, felt the invisible hand on my own. "What about Claire? Will she leave me now?"

"I don't know." He grinned and put his hand over mine on his face. "They don't tell me everything."

"Is it true, Palm? Everything you said?"

"Yes, Harry. It's all true."

"Who were the deer and the dog?"

"The world is full of other things. Some are friendly, some aren't."

"What are my chances of succeeding?"

Grinning wider, he shrugged. "Knowing you, more than fifty fifty, I would guess."

"What if I—"

"Ssh. Watch now."

ABOUT THE AUTHOR

JONATHAN CARROLL is the author of *The Land of Laughs*, *Voice of Our Shadow*, *Bones of the Moon*, *Sleeping in Flame*, *A Child Across the Sky*, *Die Panische Hand* and *After Silence*. He lives in Vienna.

The following is an excerpt from Jonathan Carroll's new novel, *After Silence*, which will be available in hardcover in April 1993, wherever Doubleday books are sold.

The scene begins as Max Fischer is watching his lover's young son Lincoln practice baseball with his little league team. The bond between Max and Lincoln is an unusually strong one, and Max is basking in the moment until an accident occurs on the field . . . an accident that is destined to begin the unearthing of a secret that has been buried for many years.

LINCOLN WAS CRAZY ABOUT baseball. I had been too as a kid, so we had real empathy there. The difference between us was my obsession had centered on the gods of major league baseball—who played on what team, their batting averages—whereas Lincoln only liked to play. For him, going to an L.A. Dodgers game was fun, but nothing beat going to the park and having a catch or hitting pop-ups and grounders. He believed deeply in sports. Reputations made in an afternoon, adulation or total failure always near. The great thing about them, especially for kids, is they *are* immediate black and white: good if you win, bad if you lose.

He played on a little league team and practiced two afternoons a week in a schoolyard a few blocks from our house. What I'd do those days was finish work as quickly as possible, then clip Cobb onto his long leash and the two of us would walk over to watch our friend play. Once there, the dog sat next to me on the lowest bleacher looking like a sphinx with a nose. When he got tired, he'd climb slowly down and lie on his side in the sun. I relish the memory of those afternoons. In retrospect, they were when I felt most like a father to Lincoln. Being there for him, watching him play, walking home together afterward talking about how he'd performed made me feel a bond with him that was solid and true. We had baseball on our minds. Both of us listened and considered carefully what the other said.

Inevitably one of his sworn enemies played on his team. Inevitably the kid was better than Lincoln. Andy

Schneider. I can still see his small lips curling in utter disdain and dislike when he said Andy's last name, as if it were a rare disease *and* another name for "fart" all in one word.

When it happened I was thinking about what to cook for dinner. Cobb was stretched out on the ground watching a bee buzz his head. Lincoln was playing shortstop, pounding his glove in anticipation of whatever was about to come off the bat of Andy Schneider.

"Strike out, turd!"

Lincoln's voice? I looked up. If it was, I wasn't happy. He could hate Schneider, but razzing him that way was low-rent behavior and I'd tell him as soon as—

CRRRRRACK!

Andy hit the next pitch so hard that the sound of the ball making its second impact came only seconds after it left his bat. The second sound came when it struck Lincoln in the face. He dropped where he stood.

I leapt out of the stands and ran onto the field, empty of any thought other than to reach him. He lay in a heap, one arm covering half his head. Herb Score. The first other thing in my mind. When I was a boy, Herb Score was a famous pitcher for the Cleveland Indians who was hit in the face and almost killed by a line drive.

There was no blood. I bent down and gently moved Lincoln's arm so I could see.

"Mother of God!"

His right temple was already swelling. Apparently he'd been able to turn his head a moment before impact and thus avoid being hit square in the face. But his temple was blowing up so fast that it was already the size of a golf ball and a hideous purple blue. His eyes were closed. He didn't move.

From behind, I heard a boy's voice yelling, "What'd I do? Is he dead? What'd I do?"

The coach squatted down next to me and tried to speak but kept dropping his sentences halfway through.

"We called an ambulance. It's not that far to . . ."

"Do you know anything about medicine?"

"No. My father was a doctor but . . . Hey, listen, maybe there's a . . ."

We spoke to each other but never made eye contact. Both of us watched Lincoln for signs of life. There were none. I kept bending down and putting my head against his chest. I needed to know his heart was still beating. Somewhere inside that still body, work was on to keep him alive.

"Do you think we should do artificial . . . ? Look at the damned swelling!"

There was no blood. That scared me most. I kept thinking of all the angry exploded blood blocked up inside his small head. If it could only burst out somewhere in one horrid flood he'd be okay. He'd wake up screaming with pain but be okay. But there was no blood. Swelling and swelling, but no blood besides the lethal purple beneath the skin.

"Did I kill him? I didn't do anything! I only hit the ball!"

The worst moments. He is alive but hurt so badly and there's nothing on earth you know to do. Only watch and pray and clench your fists at how stupid and inept you are. Why didn't you ever go to a first-aid class? What if he dies and you did nothing but watch? What will his mother say? What will the rest of life be like? Everything in your head is terror. Everything in your heart is dread.

There was a mobile telephone in the ambulance but I was too busy watching the attendants work on Lincoln. I didn't think to call Lily until we'd already arrived at the hospital and they were wheeling him into the emergency ward. A doctor strode into the room and brusquely told me to leave.

"He's my son, Doctor."

"Good. I'll treat him like he's mine. Now please go. I'll tell you what I can in a few minutes."

At the reception desk I filled out the necessary papers and called Crowds and Power. Lily wasn't there but I told one of the waitresses what had happened and she said she would find her.

What do You want? A few years of my life? Let him live. What can I do to save him? Let him live. I felt ten years old. I wanted to get down on my hands and knees. Oh, God, please help him out of this and I'll be good forever. I swear to You. Just let this kid live and I'll do whatever You want. I'll go to church. I'll stop drawing. I'll leave Lily. Let him be all right. Oh, please.

The look on people's faces in a hospital emergency ward is both broken and yearning at once. Part of them is prepared

for the worst, the other part shows the sneaking hopeful-
ness of a dog you've hit but which sidles up to your leg to
see if their coast is clear.

One man leaned against a wall chewing his finger like
it was a spare rib. He looked only at that hand. A child in a
beautifully ironed yellow dress tried to play peekaboo with
a woman who rocked back and forth with closed eyes. The
child hid her face behind an arm, then popped it up again,
looking delighted. Peekaboo. She saw me looking and
quickly hid at the woman's side.

"Stop it! Stop it, will you?" She grabbed the astonished girl by the arm and shook her hard. I wanted to go
over and stop *her* but knew I'd caused enough damage.
"Just stand here and sit still. *Please!* Will you just please
stand *still,* for God's sake!"

The child's face was all shock and fear. Nothing that
happened in this hospital, nothing that happened to the
hurt person she was waiting for, would be worse than this
scold from her guardian. They'd tell her, "Daddy is dead"
or "Mommy's very sick," but it would touch her far less
than the other's scared fury. *That* was the end of the world
as far as she understood it. Standing still, she stuck her
thumb in her mouth and looked at me with absolute
hatred.

A hand touched my shoulder, and before I turned, a man's
voice said, "Mr. Aaron?" For an instant I knew they'd mistaken me for someone else. Aaron? Then a weird unnatural rustle, like leaves before a storm, went across me when
I realized they thought I was Rick Aaron.

Turning, I was about to correct them when it came to
me they thought that because I'd brought the boy in and
said I was his father.

The doctor's name was Casey. William Casey. Faced
with the moment of truth, I looked at his name tag too
long. William Casey.

"Mr. Aaron, everything is going to be all right. You've
got one lucky boy. The ball hit him on the temple and
knocked him out. We've got a large hematoma there and
he's going to have a hell of a sore head for a while, but
other than that he's okay. No fracture or serious concus-
sion. He regained consciousness right after you left."

"YES!" I punched both fists straight up into the air and closed my eyes. "YES!"

"We'd like to keep him here for observation overnight, but that's only standard procedure. I'm sure nothing is wrong."

I shook and shook and shook Dr. Casey's hand until he gently pried himself loose and told me to sit down, take a breather.

"But his head will be all right? There'll be no after-effects or—"

"Not from what I can see, and we checked him thoroughly. He's going to have a bad headache and won't be able to wear his baseball cap for a while. That's it. He's going to be okay."

"Thank you, Doctor. Thank you so very much—"

"Mr. Aaron, when I was a young doctor and *very* pleased with myself, a patient would say thank you and I'd accept it as my due. In twenty-five years of medicine I've learned to stop taking credit for only doing my best. I'm happy for you. Happy I could give you good news. I must go now."

I sat down and inadvertently looked directly into the eyes of the woman with the child. She smiled and gestured toward the other room. "They're okay?"

"Yes. Yes, a very bad hit on the head but he's going to be okay. It's my son." Tears came to my eyes. My son.

"I'm glad it worked out."

"Thank you. I hope . . . I hope yours is well too."

"It's my daughter in there. This one's mother. Know why we're here? Because that Miss Smartso daughter of mine got her fat tongue stuck in a Coca-Cola bottle! It's the truth. Don't ask me how. We're all sittin' around comfortable and happy at the girl's birthday party. Her mama's drinking a Coke and the next thing we know, she's wavin' her arms like she's drowning or something. But no, it's not that, it's she can't get her tongue out of the damned bottle. Can you believe it? We had to take a cab here because my car's broke and the cabdriver laughed at us the whole way down. What the hell, I was laughing too."

Whether it was because of the relief I felt, knowing Lincoln was going to be all right, or the way the woman was smiling at the end of her story, whatever, I smiled, then tee-heed, then cackled openly. She did too. Each time we looked at each other we laughed harder.

"How do you get your tongue stuck in a Coke bottle? The opening's so small!"

"Don't ask me. My daughter's always had special talents."

A doctor bustled by but stopped abruptly when she looked in and saw all of us laughing so hard. Even the finger chewer was going by then. How strange we must have looked. Who laughs in the emergency room? Were we ghouls or madmen? The little girl didn't understand why we were having such a good time but it was fine with her. She started skipping around the room singing, "Coca-Cola. Coca-Cola."

And that's what Lily saw when she flew around the corner with Ibrahim right behind: everyone laughing, skipping child, Party Time.

"Max! Where is he? What's going on?"

Between the laughter, the surprise at seeing her, and relief still rolling around in my stomach, I only waved and smiled, which was appalling behavior. She didn't know her son was out of danger. As far as she knew, he might have been dead.

"Max, for Christ's sake, where's *Lincoln?*"

I stood up, still smiling. "Lily, he's all right. You don't have to worry."

"What do you mean? Where is he?"

"In the other room. But the doctor was just here and said he's all right. He got hit and was knocked out—"

"Knocked out? They didn't tell me that. They only said he was hit. Knocked out? Oh Christ—"

I took her by both arms. "Lily, listen to me. He was hit on the head and knocked out. But he's all right. He'll have a big bruise there and his head'll hurt for some time, but they did all the tests and he's all right. He's *all right.*"

"Why did you bring him here? Why didn't you call and tell me?"

"Wait, calm down. He got hit and was knocked out. We were afraid, so we brought him to the hospital. We had to: it could have been very bad."

"Jesus Christ, you shouldn't have brought him here." She broke off angrily and shook her head. "Did you have to fill out papers? What did they make you fill out?"

Ibrahim was standing right behind her. He shrugged as if he didn't understand what she was ranting about.

"What did you fill out, Max?"

"Papers, Lily. You have to give them general information. It's normal in a hospital, honey."

"Normal for who? What did you say on there? What kind of information did you give?"

She was very angry. I slid it off to the pressure of what had happened. I spoke as calmly as I could. "His name, how old he is, our address. And whether he's allergic to anything."

"What else?"

"Nothing. Just the standard form."

"Standard form, huh? Shit on the standard form."

"Lily, *calm down*. That's what you do in the hospital. You gotta give them certain information—"

She grabbed the front of my shirt and pulled me to her very roughly. "You don't give them *anything*, Max. Nothing ever." Her voice shrank down to a gravelly growl.

Ibrahim had his hands on her then, pulling her back, talking quietly, pulling her away from me. It was bizarre and very disturbing. She had every right to be capsized by her son's accident, but her facial expression, voice, what she was saying all had to do with something else. Something way far away from this situation. What she said next confirmed that.

"Do you think they take fingerprints?"

"Of Lincoln? No! He's a patient, not a prisoner."

She listened, then turned to hear what Ibrahim thought.

"Lily, come on, please. Don't get cuckoo now. They don't take fingerprints in the hospital!"

"We don't know for sure, but all right. Now I only want to get him out of here. When can we take him home?"

"Tomorrow. The doctor said they'll keep him here overnight for observation. He can go home tomorrow."

"Tomorrow? Where's this doctor? I have to talk to him. We're leaving here."

What she meant by "we" was she wanted her son out of there that instant. We found Dr. Casey, who first tried to calm her, but grew insistent and coldly professional on realizing this distraught woman wanted to take her child home *now*. He said it was unwise, then not a good idea, then dangerous. There had been cases where—

"I don't care, Doctor. We're leaving. I'm his mother

and I want to take him home. If there are any problems we'll come back."

Nothing he said could dissuade her. Nothing, that is, until they'd ended their face-off and he'd lost and was leaving to go arrange the necessary papers to release Lincoln.

"You are very peculiar, Mrs. Aaron. I don't know why you're so set on this. It's certainly against the better interests of your son and what you're doing makes me extremely suspicious."

Because he was scanning his clipboard, he didn't see her face change. In seconds it went from Fuck you! aggressive to "uh-oh" to cringe. Before speaking again she looked at me. Behind the cringe was something awful at work—rats under her floor, a hidden knife in the palm of her hand.

"Dr. Casey, I'm so sorry. I just—I can't . . . It's how this happened . . . Yes, let him stay here. You're right, of course. I'm sorry."

Doctors know the tone of the confused and desperate. It is part of their human agenda. When he spoke again, Casey was all sympathy and quiet power. "I fully understand, Mrs. Aaron. But it really is the best thing to do. Let us keep him here tonight, and if you want, you can stay in the room with him. But it's best if he's here overnight."

"Right. Absolutely. I'm sorry."

"You needn't apologize. I'll tell the nurse you'll be staying with him."

I watched her throughout this weird exchange. What the hell was going on? Which Lily was real here? Which Lily was the truth? Like the doctor, I might have fallen for her line if I hadn't seen her face working, or the fear and loathing in her eyes, the wriggle and pull of her mouth fighting against itself. She was a good liar if you didn't watch closely.

How could this be her? The woman who was so helpful and generous to others, so good in emergencies, the first one to run and help strangers out of trouble. Part of it was the fact it was her trouble now, her son. But not all of it, not all.

"Lily?"

Her eyes stayed on the doctor as he strode down the corridor.

"Lily?"

"Hmmm?"

"What's the matter? What is the problem?"

She looked at me as if I'd slapped her face. "Big mistake, Max. You made a very big mistake. Very stupid."

"What? What did I do wrong?"

"I don't want to talk about it now." She walked away.

"Ibrahim, what is going on?" Besides being upset, I felt like such a fool: I lived with the woman, but now that our first crisis was here, I had to ask her boss why she was behaving so oddly.

"I don't know. She is very strange about the boy. It is more than protective. Gus thinks that she is—" He pointed to his head and gave the universal sign for loony.

"Have you seen her like this before?"

"Yes, but only when it is about Lincoln. She is a good woman, but with him she is a little crazy."

The shock of the accident, the confusion events like that can cause, emotion pulled and released like rubber bands . . . any of those were good reasons for her outbursts and contradictions. But none of them were satisfying because I had seen that terrible sneak in her eyes. There was no other way to say it. Sneaking. Lying. Not to be trusted.

"Ib, can you stay with her for a while? I'd like to go get a cup of coffee and cool out."

"Yes, sure, go. But, Max, don't be hard on her. Remember, before you, she had only this child."

"I know. I understand. It's only . . . Don't worry. I'll be back in a half hour."

I sat in the hospital coffee shop five minutes. Long enough to buy coffee, but once a cup was in front of me I knew what I really wanted was air, some space. I paid and left. There was a park a few blocks away and I gratefully went in. Late-afternoon people strolled around. Women with baby carriages, old couples in bright clothes, kids on skateboards and bicycles. A few feet from where I was sitting, a woman played on the grass with a young Boston terrier. They're sweet little dogs and this one was having the time of its life chasing after a bright green ball the woman had brought along. I concentrated on its funny play because I needed mental space from Lily and what had been happening that day. The dog dropped the ball and barked at the woman to throw it again. I never had a dog do that. The ones I'd known, you threw the ball, they fetched, then ran with it in the opposite direction.

This ball flew, the puppy scampered off, snatched it up while it was still rolling, ran back. This went on until the pigeons arrived. A large flock of them dropped down out of nowhere and landed nearby. It was unusual: fifty birds suddenly there, preening and fussing, flapping their wings. People looked and pointed. The dog was staggered by it. He stood a moment in shocked surprise. Then, classic canine, lowered his head into attack position and tiptoed toward them. There's nothing dogs like more than charging birds. Slink-slink-slink POUNCE. They rarely catch one but who cares? What must feel good is having all those scared lives leaping off the earth because of you.

Slink-slink-slink. The terrier got to within a few feet of the flock, stopped, poised to jump, one paw hanging in the air. I was ready for its triumphant spring when an odd thing happened. Almost as one, the birds turned. Lots of cooing and fluttering wings, but they moved in a grayish-pink wave at the same time. As if understanding he was outnumbered, or that something was wrong when so many things moved the same at the same time, the little dog slowly relaxed its body and, watching them closely, lay down on the ground. Maybe next time.

The world is full of mysterious connections, especially when we're going through strong times in our lives. The puppy's reaction to the birds made people laugh. Isn't that cute? It made me shudder. Frisky and sure of himself, he walked up to what he knew by all rights was his. Done it before and had great fun. This time, though, these fifty heads, one hundred wings, sudden same movement . . . All said Stop! It isn't the same, doggie. Don't even try.

It isn't the same, doggie. What was happening with Lily? Her behavior at the hospital stopped me hard. Birds are birds until they turn as one small army. Lily's familiar face gone bad, her words, this strange mistrust and paranoia that had surfaced for the first time since we'd been together. It stopped me. What was happening here?

I am not a trusting soul. I don't even trust myself. Often I have no idea what I'll do in certain situations. Who does? If one cannot say I trust myself, how can one say I trust you and genuinely mean or feel it? Because of that, people hurt but rarely wound me. When Norah Silver admitted she was sleeping with another man it was a brutal blow to my spirit, but was neither crippling nor unexpected. Somewhere in my soul is a two-foot-thick door with a giant sumo wrestler standing guard outside, not letting anyone in. It's the door to Command Center, Mission Control, the heart of the matter. Whatever your credentials, the sentry keeps you out. I am not sorry it is like this. My parents are trusting people who raised my brother and me to be that way too, but we aren't. Saul is a finagler in business, a libertine, and an all-around truth stretcher. He likes scoundrels because he is one himself. Between us, we have enough trust to fill another person three-quarters. It is one of the few things we agree on.

The night Lily spent at the hospital with Lincoln I went through our house like a burglar. I had never had any reason to question what she had told me about herself and her life, but I felt I did now. Snooping around your own home looking for clues about the person you love is perverse, but I felt totally detached doing it. I thought only that this is her place, this is where her life is, so this must be where *it* is—a sign, a lead, the key. I knew what I was looking for might be so obscure and indecipherable that even on finding it there was the distinct possibility I wouldn't recognize what I had. A photograph or a ticket stub, a letter from a friend with one unimportant sentence that, once deciphered, told all.

I began in Lincoln's room. Through his closet, through his dresser, his desk, toy trunk, books. Flip through the pages of each one, turn them upside down and shake. The clue could be there—a bookmark, something written on a piece of scratch paper. Under his bed, in all of his boxes, the obscure corners of his room where things could be hidden or taped. I kept a pad of paper nearby. Anything that said something to me I either noted or put in the middle of the floor to be considered later when I was sifting the information through my mind.

I found nothing, so operations were moved to our bedroom. Same approach there—over, under, around, through. I even checked my own belongings to make sure they hadn't been used as new hiding places. Lily kept a diary, which I read, but I found nothing other than small gripes and triumphs, philosophical musings. Events and ideas that meant something to the day but would be quickly forgotten if not recorded. A touching note, but one that did not deter me, was how many times she wrote about us and how much better life had become since we met. There was progressively more nothing as I worked through our home from room to room, object to object. What was I looking for? Often I held something in my hand and stared at it as if I were the first archaeologist to discover hieroglyphics. You *know* they are of the greatest significance, there are stories and information, whole worlds here, but all of it is a million miles away from your understanding although only twelve inches away from your eyes.

Working for hours, I cut my hands and tore a fingernail reaching and pulling, twisting things apart. I stopped to make a sandwich and ate it looking at the small pile I'd assembled on the floor that might mean something. None of it meant anything. I knew it. I knew Lily was hiding something. The more I worked and thought about it, the more I was convinced her outburst was only the tip of one big iceberg of a lie. The proof *was* here, but I could not find it.

In the end, at three o'clock in the morning, when I had filled the pad with notes, checked and double-checked that everything was back exactly as I'd found it, finished cursing, finished double- and triple-checking . . . I had come up with exactly two things: There was absolutely no trace whatsoever of Rick Aaron. No letters, no diary entry, no old shirts shoved in a back drawer with his name tag sewn in, no photographs, nothing. How could that be? How could you love someone so much and, despite a bitter end, not keep something of theirs to remind you of a time in your life when you thought of nothing but them? I knew couples who'd thrown each other's clothes out the window when they broke up, or gave the other's belongings to the Salvation Army, but *all* of these people kept something. Not Lily. To judge by what I had "excavated," the only proof of Rick Aaron or Lily's relationship with Lincoln's father was the stories she had told.

The second thing I found was a couple named Meier. Gregory and Anwen Meier. At the bottom of her underwear drawer was a small clipping from a dog magazine announcing Somerset Kennels, home of champion French bulldogs. Proprietors Anwen & Gregory Meier. An address and telephone number were given at the bottom. Lily loved dogs, so at first I thought she'd saved the paper because she was planning on buying one of these bulldogs when old Cobb passed away.

The next mention of these people came in a newspaper article I found slipped into one of her books. The article was old and yellowing, whereas the book was new—the copyright date only a year old. Mrs. Anwen Meier miraculously walked away from a collision on I-95 that totaled her automobile. Mrs. Meier was admittedly driving over the speed limit when she lost control of the vehicle. It left the road and crashed into the pillar of an overpass. Although suffering from mild shock, she was treated and later released from the hospital. In the margin of this article, Lily had written: "Anwen = 'very beautiful' in Welsh." So they were friends, old school pals? I thought the connection must be with Gregory. Why else would she look up the name of the other woman?

The third "piece" of the Meiers was another newspaper clipping, also yellowed. It appeared to be from the same paper, simply announced the couple were leaving Fowler and moving back to New Jersey, their home state. Gregory Meier is quoted as saying they had had a great four years here but felt it was time to go back home "to fulfill a lifelong dream for both of us, which is to raise pedigree dogs."

Lily had some other clippings and photographs but not many: a group shot of the gang at her restaurant, one of an older couple I assumed were her parents, a few of strangers (none fitting her description of Rick), but the Meiers won the contest with three items. Interesting.

I was embarrassed going to Mary again with my suspicions, so I asked around and found another good detective agency. As if sneaking into a porno movie, I hurried through their door and explained what I wanted to a sympathetic middle-aged man with fishing trophies on his wall: Anwen and Gregory Meier. Here's the address in New Jersey. Please find out everything you can about these people. It was a brief, comfortable conversation. But when it was over and I was driving to my next appointment, two things struck me. First, the detective, a Mr. Goff, hadn't once asked why I wanted to know about the Meiers. Who was I and where did I get off sniffing into their lives? What if I were someone bad, or dangerous, and compiling this information to use against them? Goff wasn't interested. Just the facts, bud. You want to know about their foibles and affairs, blemishes, hidden scars, what they eat for breakfast when they're alone together and feeling very in love? You pay and I'll find it.

I did not feel wrong doing this so much as stained. Sometimes it is right to look all around another's life; yet the act, however correct, lessens us. This notion led to the second thing that chilled me about the meeting with this detective: no matter what I discovered about Lily Aaron via the Meiers, I was breaking the trust between us by taking this course of action. Even if it turned out she was hiding something surprising, or dubious, I was the one to blame. Granted, I had already looked through our house for telltale signs, but that was only between us. We both lived there. Now I'd crossed the line—gone "out" to search, and that changed our world.

In the meantime Lincoln was home, energetic and apparently fit as a fiddle, despite a big ugly bump on his head. Lily allowed them to keep him in the hospital the necessary twenty-four hours, but was slipping the kid into his sneakers and jacket the moment he was cleared. We were told to keep close watch on his alertness, reflexes, and orientation. If anything was amiss, we were to get him the hell back fast. We kept him home from school three days, but by then he was so itchy to get back to his life, we let him, after telling his teachers to watch him too.

For the most part Lily returned to her old good self once she felt the crisis was past, although there were exceptions. For one, she didn't apologize, much less mention, her behavior at the hospital. Instead she acted as if nothing had happened. Even Lincoln's accident was like a years-old ink smudge on a white handkerchief: yes, if you looked hard you could see the faint shadow of a mark, but why look when its presence was all but invisible?

One Sunday the three of us drove down to Venice beach to people-watch and have dinner. The skateboarders, bag ladies, beach bunnies, Rastafarians on roller skates playing guitars, flat-out insanes, and other beings from the great beyond that congregate there were out in force and we walked among them as if they were the surreal topiary and great loony statues at Bomarzo or Disneyland.

In the past we'd spoken several times about having our palms or tarot cards read one day. Feeling this was as good a time as any, I suggested going to one of the many fortune tellers who'd set up card tables along Ocean Front Walk. Lily wasn't interested. I didn't push it, but Lincoln got excited and started in. She said no three times before permitting him, but insisted she choose the one, who turned out to be a hippie so stoned out and vacuous-looking that I was surprised he was even able to cut and lay down his cards without dropping them. A strange choice of soothsayers.

"Phew, kid, this is adamant stuff. The Ace of Wands is your card. I mean, there are *multiple* wands here." That comment and a few other forgettable earwigs cost five dollars.

There was a combined restaurant/bookstore nearby where we ate. After the meal, we went into the store to browse a while, each going in his own direction. About fifteen minutes later I looked up and by coincidence saw Lily outside talking with Lincoln's stoned fortune teller. Still sitting, he pointed to something on the table in front of him. I couldn't make out what but assumed it was one of his cards. Lily paid close attention and wrote hurriedly in a small notebook she often carried. He'd speak, tap the card, gesture, and she'd scribble scribble scribble. I watched until they finished. She took out money and gave it to him. They shook hands and she started back toward the store. I lowered my head to the book in hand. Don't ask me what the title was. I couldn't say. She came in and right over to me, smiling and friendly.

"What do you say, lover? About ready to go?"

"Give me another five minutes. I want to check one other thing."

She went to find Lincoln while I asked the woman at the counter for the section on tarot cards. There were two books. The first said, "Wands. This suit indicates animation and enterprise, energy and growth. The wands depicted in the cards are always in leaf, suggesting the constant renewal of life and growth. The associations are with the world of ideas, also with creation in all its forms." The second said, "It is the suit of beginnings, of formless fire energy. It requires clear goals and plans, it requires a firm foundation for the energy not to burn itself out. Notice that the knight rides through a desert, devoid of houses and people as well as trees and water. Without something to carry that energy to a purpose, the desert will not open up to life."

TOM ROBBINS

"Knowing like Pynchon, funny like Vonnegut,
winsome as Brautigan ... Tom Robbins
is one of our best."

—*The New York Times Book Review*